A Single Step

(Book 1 in *The Grayson Trilogy*)

GEORGIA ROSE

2nd Edition Published by Three Shires Publishing

ISBN: 978-0-9933318-0-0 (paperback)

ISBN: 978-0-9933318-1-7 (ebook)

www.georgiarosebooks.com

Cover design by the team at SilverWood Books
(www.silverwoodbooks.co.uk)

British Library Cataloguing in Publication Data

A CIP catalogue record for this book is available from the British Library.

This book is dedicated to Russell, my husband and
best friend, who fills my life with laughter.

Georgia Rose x

"Yet it would be your duty to bear it, if you could not avoid it: it is weak and silly to say you cannot bear what it is your fate to be required to bear."

Charlotte Brontë, *Jane Eyre*

Chapter 1

"Tell me about the kickboxing. How did you get into it?" A surprising first question that I'd neither expected nor prepared for. I met the cool blue of Cavendish's eyes, determined not to look away or show I'd been shaken, in an attempt to present good body language, just as the situation required.

"I took up kickboxing for exercise, mostly...but also to relieve stress a couple of years ago," I replied, a little bewildered.

"Stress?" He looked at me sharply as his brow furrowed, deepening the frown lines already forming between his eyes. Damn, I thought, my heart sinking, I've screwed up already – why did I mention that? He's not going to want someone working for him with stress problems. I was annoyed with myself for bringing it up, although it could have been worse I argued; I could have launched right in and told him all about my anger issues as well. I tried to explain in an attempt to mitigate.

"I'd had a bad couple of years and found this type of exercise more than anything else provided an outlet. It always succeeded in making me calmer and more relaxed so I stuck with it."

"Hmm...I can see how that would work," he nodded thoughtfully as though understanding, which was encouraging. "So, do I take it you prefer solitary sports to team games?"

"Yes." I could feel my anxiety rising as I couldn't think of anything to add to this rather blunt response.

"Okay, your instructor has indicated you're pretty good and I believe you've competed on behalf of your club a few times?"

He's spoken to my instructor?

"Yes, that's correct," I replied, not at all sure where he was going with this.

"You've also learnt self-defence, I see. Do you enjoy that?"

"Yes I do, and although fortunately I haven't had to use it in a real-life situation, I think I'm quite proficient if the need ever did arise."

"Excellent. Your instructor used the words, er…" He opened the envelope file on his lap on which he'd rested the rather sketchy copy of my CV and flicked back and forth between the surprisingly large number of sheets it contained. I took a deep breath in an attempt to relax and looked towards the far end of the room where there were four floor-to-ceiling windows which afforded a view onto a well-manicured lawn and immaculately tended flowerbeds, though these were currently not very flowery.

I'd been nervous coming to attend an interview anyway and had already been thrown on my arrival by finding that I was going to be interviewed by Lord Henry Cavendish himself, instead of Mr Trent, who was the estate manager. I'd then been further surprised when shown to the office by the butler, Forster, to find Cavendish – for that was how he introduced himself to me – was considerably younger than I was expecting. The title, I guessed, had mentally added at least twenty years but he was only in his mid-thirties; tall and attractive with a friendly, open face and dark hair, short at the sides and slightly longer on top, combed forward.

We sat in his large office on a couple of settees, of which there were several in the room, and I wondered when so much seating would ever be needed. Ours were set at right angles to each other around a large coffee table and in front of an unlit fireplace. The mantelpiece was stone, limestone I thought, creamy yellowy-brown, the same as the Manor and the wall that enclosed the estate. A tray of refreshments had been delivered by a young woman while I was waiting for Cavendish to find my file amongst the mountain of paperwork on his desk. She was slim and wore smart black trousers, a white fitted shirt and flat shoes. Her brown hair was tied in a high ponytail which swung as she walked. As she'd come across the room she'd given me a friendly smile which I'd tried to reciprocate, though mine had felt weak in response, betraying my anxiety. Carrying a large tray, she'd deposited it on the coffee table in front of me, whispered for me to help myself then quickly left the room. Looking at the cup of coffee in front of me now I could see a skin starting to form on the top as it cooled.

I started as Cavendish suddenly came upon what he had been looking for. "Ah yes, here it is – he used the words 'committed' and 'quite brutal' about your self-defence techniques." Cavendish looked back up at me, appearing to be highly delighted with this.

I could feel myself blushing. "Ah, yes...I caught him with a lucky punch one day, and he took some time to get over it."

"Oh, that's very good. Okay, I think that's all I wanted to ask you. Do you have any questions?" What? I thought with some alarm. Is that it?

"Well..." I replied, nonplussed, "I'm a little surprised by the direction this interview has taken. I was expecting some questions about my experience with horses, that sort of thing."

He looked at me in surprise, and then went on to explain: "Oh! I'm sorry, I'm not used to doing this. Trent usually handles all employee issues for me. I should maybe have explained at the outset that we've already carried out a fully comprehensive background search,

3

including references on you, your experience, etcetera, so there's nothing else I really need to ask. I've got it all here in my file." He shuffled through the pile of papers on his lap before pulling out a sheet which he then scanned down. "I've got details here of each riding school, livery yard or farm you worked at after school and during weekends and holidays in each of the places you lived, I believe swapping your work for lessons and riding experience?" As he looked up I confirmed my agreement with this. "And you then settled in Crowbridge and worked at the local riding school in your free time," and then hesitating, he finished quietly, "...until four years ago." He stopped as I tensed, exposing my unease as to what he might say next, and meeting his eyes I could see his discomfort. Realising my arms had unconsciously wrapped themselves around my body I looked away, reluctantly releasing them and forcibly placing my hands back in my lap. He didn't acknowledge my behaviour in any way, for which I was grateful, but cleared his throat before carrying on steadily, "We've taken references from all these places and they all say the same things. You're conscientious and knowledgeable and while you haven't had your own horses to look after you've often had sole responsibility for other people's horses.

"We're not looking for an instructor, Mrs Grayson, the children can already ride, although they will be spending time at the stables during their holidays which you would have to be prepared for and manage. Would you be all right with that?"

He was looking at me keenly and I nodded, partly with relief that the awkward moment had passed, but also as it seemed to be the right thing to do, although in all honesty I didn't know how all right I would be with that. However, I did know I wanted this job and having been surprised to have got as far as an interview I really didn't want to mess it up now.

The advert for the position had originally arrived through my letterbox on my birthday in January, anonymously, delivered as if it were a gift – it was my only one. It was quite short, torn from a magazine, advertising for a stable manager/groom to look after the family horses for the Melton Manor estate which, being some way away, I was not familiar with. A cottage came with the position and pets were allowed – I wouldn't have considered applying otherwise.

My interest had been immediately piqued and although I now doubted I'd have enough recent experience to be successful in getting the job, horses had once been my passion. They had provided the stability I'd craved during the unsettled years I'd faced growing up and were the recipients of the love I had to give in lieu of anyone else; I'd ridden and worked with them obsessively, as is common with many girls. But then unlike most, who tended to move on once boys came on the scene, I'd continued working at a local yard in my free time, always intending one day to have a horse of my own. That, however, was not to be.

I'd thought about the advert for quite a while considering the position. The fact that it had even raised my interest told me something and I came to the conclusion that as horses had provided the balm I'd needed to soothe my soul during turbulent years before, perhaps they could provide that relief for me again.

I'd also mulled over who had put it through my letterbox in the first place, dismissing most of the names I came up with and leaving me with one suspect. My still viciously raw feelings towards her and the thought that her motivation for doing this was to get me to move away almost made me tear it up. In the end, however, so as not to spite myself, I'd written a CV, attached it to an email as requested, and sent it together with a covering letter. And now here I was.

Cavendish continued, "Everything we've heard about you leads us to believe you're the person we're looking for and that's why my wife and I would like to offer you the job, if you want it?

"This interview was more so you could ask me anything you wanted to and for us to organise all the other things – what date you can start, signing the contract and the NDA, that sort of thing."

"So you're not interviewing anyone else?" I questioned with some surprise.

"No, although Trent won't be happy as he preferred another candidate, and I've rather taken advantage of his absence to offer the job to you." He smiled to himself as he said this, as if it gave him some satisfaction to be riling this Trent, which I found intriguing. He paused for a moment before meeting my eyes and said carefully, "We like to take care of our staff here, Mrs Grayson, and we like to think of everyone on the estate as one big family and we think you could do with having a family around you."

Now, I wasn't particularly interested in having a family around me but I thought that information was probably best kept to myself for the moment. However, he'd spoken these last words so softly and kindly I could feel tears starting to prick at my eyes and as I blinked these away I found myself accepting the position.

"Excellent. Now, down to business. There are a few things to be sorted out," he continued. "You'll have been sent a copy of our employee contract, which I hope is satisfactory, as well as our non-disclosure agreement. I insist there has to be absolute discretion by all members of my staff at all times about everything that happens on this estate. Do you have any problem with that?"

"The contract seems fine and no, I have no problem with the discretion part. I'd never dream of discussing anyone's business with anyone else, it's just that…" I hesitated, uneasy as to how my concern would be received.

"What is it, Mrs Grayson? You seem a little unsure about something," he probed.

"It's…I feel slightly uncomfortable asking this but I think I should just so I know what I'm getting myself into," I replied, feeling a little foolish.

"Absolutely…Go on, I shall brace myself," Cavendish said, smiling encouragingly at me, as making good on his word he adjusted his position, squaring his shoulders a little in readiness.

"It seems a little strange to sign an NDA for this type of job and I thought I ought to check that you're not up to anything…" I paused, searching for the right word, "…anything of a nefarious nature here?" I could feel myself blushing even as I said this.

To give him credit, Cavendish didn't actually burst out laughing but his face lit up, making it clear he found this highly entertaining. "Nefarious?" he repeated with some amusement.

"Yes, I wouldn't want to get involved in something I shouldn't, something that could get me into trouble," I explained in all seriousness.

"Quite right too!" he exclaimed, before continuing, I think to indulge me: "You're a wise woman, Mrs Grayson, and quite right to be cautious. However, I can assure you nothing that takes place on this estate is of a nefarious nature. This is essentially a family home and mostly the business carried out here is agricultural as you will find out, if you join us. However, some of us here, me included, do also have some work away from the estate which is perfectly legal, in fact it is fully sanctioned by those in authority, but it is confidential and therefore it's necessary to have the NDA in place for everyone who works here. There is the possibility you may see or hear things which shouldn't be repeated, discussed or passed on.

"I do hope this explanation will assuage your concerns and that you are satisfied enough to sign the agreement, because the more I get to know you, Mrs Grayson, the more keen I am to have you join us." He paused, looking at me expectantly.

"That seems reasonable enough," I said thoughtfully, pondering on the point that if he was up to no good he would hardly have been likely to tell me anyway. However, I'd felt his explanation to be plausible, and hesitating for only a moment longer I came to my decision. "Okay, I'm happy to sign." This response was based purely on my gut instinct; however, I'd taken an instant liking to Cavendish. He seemed to me to be someone in whom you could put your trust and I signed all the paperwork he put in front of me.

"Okay, next is the question of how you would like to be addressed?" As he saw my eyebrows rise he continued, "I apologise, but due to my public school and military upbringing I insist everyone is called by their surname while on the estate. The alternatives before you are that you could be Mrs Grayson, Ms Grayson or just Grayson."

"Grayson will be fine," I replied, then as I thought on this for a moment I felt compelled to continue. "Although can I ask, if it's not too impertinent, how should I address Lady Cavendish? Calling her by her surname seems a little…weird."

He smiled broadly and affectionately before sighing as he replied, "Ah yes…Well, Lady Cavendish is the exception as she will not indulge me in this little foible of mine, and is called Grace by everyone. In turn, she uses everyone's first name. I should also add that the children, being children, are called Sophia and Reuben.

"Right, Grayson it is. I'll be organising for you to have a credit card on your arrival for any purchases you need to make, as well as being added to the store credit system we have with the local country store and saddlery which you will be using. The horses will not be arriving until approximately the third week of May but you will have to get the yard and stables ready for them so there will be a lot to organise and buy. Are you happy with all of that?"

"I have no problem with any of that; it'll be great to set up the yard from scratch. I just wondered if there is a limit on the credit card or at the store."

"It's thoughtful of you to ask. I have to say you're the only person ever to have done so but no, there are no limits. I trust you to be reasonable on purchases. I also expect you to buy all your own clothing and equipment that you need for the job using the credit card and not your own money, okay?"

"More than okay actually – this is sounding like a dream job." I smiled briefly at him, feeling myself relax slightly for the first time.

Cavendish grinned back at me and then looked at what I assumed was his checklist and frowned. "Okay, I think the only other thing to ask is for a list of any relatives or close friends. It says in your background search here there is no one but I find that hard to believe."

"No, that's true. I was orphaned when I was five and had no relatives to take me in so I was brought up by foster parents. I'm divorced and there's no one who I would consider to be a close friend." I was more than embarrassed now at having to admit to having no friends. Cavendish scribbled my response on his notes and as he did so, he asked if there was anything else I wanted to know. Out of curiosity I jumped right in.

"I was wondering why you had such an interest in my martial arts abilities."

He looked up at me, grinning. "Let's just say that I like my staff to have additional skills other than the ones that I employ them for." Mystified, I was not sure what to make of that and although I knew my face betrayed my feelings as I met his open gaze, no further elaboration to this response was forthcoming.

"So unless there's anything else, when can you start?" Cavendish carried on enthusiastically.

We agreed on the first week of May and I was to let Ms Sharpe, his personal assistant, know the exact date so everything could be put in place for my arrival. As Cavendish showed me out he explained there would be plenty of time for everything else to be sorted out once I'd moved onto the estate.

I travelled back through the parkland considerably more appreciative now of the breezy but dry day. Weak sunshine kept finding its way through the endless stream of light clouds that passed swiftly across it, every now and then highlighting the soft rolling countryside only for it to be blotted out again moments later. But it was only when I was driving through the gates, through which I'd entered with such trepidation only a short time before, that I realised it might have been sensible for me to have asked if I could go and see my new home and possibly the stables. I hadn't even thought of that at the time. What I had thought was that this job, being somewhat isolated on a large estate, might just suit my desire to live as solitary a life as possible, perfectly.

Chapter 2

As I drove home I thought through the interview, drawn to the moment when I'd felt Cavendish had come uncomfortably close to following up on why I had no recent experience with horses. He must have known of course, because of the background check, but he'd stopped short of asking anything further, no doubt heeding the warning expressed in my defensive body language. Although I didn't see it as defensive, to me it was protective; the physical act of wrapping my arms around my body was an attempt to hold myself together when the hole that had been punched through my chest threatened to consume me.

Four years had passed, and yet some days it felt as if it were only yesterday; four years since I'd lost Eva, my beautiful daughter, who on her arrival had filled a part of me that had unknowingly been empty, and made me complete.

Alex and I had met at school and, having fallen hard for each other, made the ridiculous decision to get married at eighteen. This had sparked a great deal of gossip at the time, not that we could have cared less, but the gossips were proven to be wrong when Eva did not arrive in our lives until two years later, a much longed-for and loved baby.

When she was six, Eva became ill. She'd had the normal childhood illnesses as she'd grown up but was otherwise a robustly healthy child. So, when she was running a bit of a temperature I didn't think too much of it. I kept her at home, dosed her up on medicine, which is usually so effective, and expected she would bounce back

11

to her effervescent self within a few hours. However, the next day she was worse and had been sick a couple of times so I took her to the doctor. I was assured by him that it was a virus, told that there was a lot of it going around and fobbed off with the fact I should keep on doing what I was doing and try to get some liquids into her. I kept telling myself that children get these things and shrug them off again quickly, but I was not reassured and my unease niggled at me.

By the following day Eva was listless and unable to keep anything down so I drove her straight to the hospital. I'd called Alex at work beforehand to tell him what I was doing, and got the distinct impression he thought I was overreacting. The doctors examined her, but while I tried to tell them of my concerns they barely listened, putting her condition down to the fact she'd not eaten or taken on sufficient liquids for the past forty-eight hours. I felt ignored, then as I pleaded her case harder, pressing for tests to be done, I felt I was an inconvenience. Eventually I realised with humiliation that they were treating me as though I were an unduly overanxious mother, my views clearly not worthy of consideration, and as though my knowledge of my own child bore no weight at all in the decisions being made. They admitted her to a ward, set her up on a drip to rehydrate her and all I could do was cuddle and comfort her, watching and waiting for an improvement. My concern grew, gnawing at me as time passed.

Alex arrived at the hospital after work, having stopped off at home for some things I'd asked him for. I changed Eva into a clean pair of pyjamas and as I did so, I noticed a couple of small dark-red spots on her legs. As I looked at them I saw another appear. For a moment my heart stood still and then everything happened at once. I was yelling for help, doctors and nurses came running and Eva was moved rapidly into a side room where there was more space.

After being practically ignored, suddenly Eva was the centre of everyone's attention; intravenous antibiotics were started immediately, numerous tests carried out. But I already knew what the results would show – meningitis. The spots were multiplying alarmingly, merging to become a rash, spreading up her legs, breaking out on her arms and across her body. Nothing appeared capable of stopping the septicaemia. Alex and I kept out of everyone's way, frozen with fear at the scene developing in front of us and silently pleading with her to fight. Rooted to the end of the bed while the doctors worked on her we were then at her bedside when they could do no more, when it was just waiting.

By now our beautiful daughter was being kept alive through the tubes inserted into her and was hooked up to several monitoring machines. We watched over her, holding her hands, talking to her, but there was no response; praying, but there was no response.

The doctor eventually took us to one side, gently telling us she would not survive; she was in a coma, her body shutting down, and all we could do for her now was to be with her when she died. In that moment, as the window I faced opened onto an unchanged outside world, I felt ours shattering around us, and I clasped Alex's hands in desperation as we held on to each other in our disbelief. I remember turning from the doctor, cutting off anything further, a roaring silence filling my head, deafening me. My body, my arms, my legs were suddenly leaden as if the doctor's words had exerted a physical as well as mental toll, dragging me down as, shaking with emotion, I climbed into bed with my beautiful girl, curling her up into my arms, Alex sitting by our side. I held her close for a long time, all the while knowing it was never going to be long enough. Shutting out everything else I stroked her long dark hair, soothing her, hoping for a miracle, hoping she would prove the doctors wrong. As we lay together I gazed into the face I knew better than my own, one that I could never get enough of, absorbing every detail, her full lips relaxed and making her look merely asleep. Her soft peachy cheeks, paler now, providing the resting place for the thick eyelashes which swept across them and which I willed to open, to give me one more chance to gaze into the beautiful eyes beneath that I'd been lost in since the first time they'd opened on me at her birth, when I'd silently promised her in that precious moment that I would protect her until the end of my days...And yet, here we were and I'd failed her.

Her eyes didn't open and as I felt life leave her Alex gripped my hand tightly, as tightly as he had on her birth, trying to absorb some of the pain from the anguished cries that started to tear me apart. As we held each other, our baby cradled between us, I could feel Alex's body shaking with the release of his tears and we clung in anguish to each other in the initial despair of our loss. We were given time to say goodbye, time to prepare ourselves, but when they came to take her away I couldn't let her go. No amount of time could ever prepare me for that. My arms closed around her instinctively as I hugged her body to mine, and all I could hear were Alex's sobs, his pleas, his pain, as he tried to reason with me, as he tried to gently peel my arms away to release her; and as he did, I felt part of my heart break away as acutely as if someone had reached into my chest and ripped it apart.

Alex tried to fill my now-empty arms, holding me tightly, holding me back from her, my hands clawing at him as he sank to the floor with me, rocking as he tried to soothe me, the room filling with distressing noises that could only have come from a wounded animal, that I didn't recognise as coming from me, struggling as I tried to cut myself off from the brutal reality, the crushing pain closing in, as mentally I started unravelling.

Over the next few days I heard the murmur of voices: of Alex talking on the phone, of people coming and going. As immobilised as I was in my grief, I lay in bed in the hope death would claim me too. The doctor had sedated me into a state where I was beyond feeling anything, but which had allowed me to go home. Our doctor came with more pills and I took whatever was offered, unquestioning, keeping myself numb and holding off what I knew was waiting for me.

Amy, my friend, came round every day, trying to make me eat and sitting with me in silence. I didn't cry, being too paralysed from the drugs to have that much emotion. Alex kept asking me questions about funeral arrangements; I think I replied but I had no idea what the questions were or what answers I gave. I assumed he eventually sorted it all out with Amy.

The day I dreaded arrived and I dragged myself from my bed to get ready. Alex had informed everyone attending they should wear the clothes Eva would most recognise them in rather than black, but as that would have been jeans and a tee shirt in my case I chose a navy and cream dress Eva had given the seal of approval. I stood, unmoving, staring out of the sitting room window onto the road. Waiting.

The hearse pulled up and the man in the passenger seat climbed out, making his way to our front door. Alex had already wrapped his arm around my waist in support and, taking my hand, encouraged me to move as we answered the door together. As soon as it opened I could see her – her coffin, so small; I felt myself gasp then struggle to recover my breath. Alex's arm tightened as we walked down the path towards our daughter. Beautiful flowers filled the space around her in every shade of blue, mauve or violet, set against white. She would have liked the variations of blue, always being a tomboy; pink had been banned from every aspect of her life.

We started away slowly. Walking, we followed the hearse and while I never took my eyes off Eva I became aware of others joining us. Amy reached out to take my hand in support as we walked together, the villagers, our friends, our neighbours coming out of their houses, joining our sad procession as we wound our way to the church. When we arrived the crowd made its way into the church and the vicar came to greet us. He was kind, I was aware of that, and of him taking my cold hand between his two warm ones as he talked through what was going to happen, trying to engage with me. But I felt distanced, as if I were underwater when you know someone is speaking to you but it's too muffled to understand what's being said. Distracted, I couldn't stop watching as they took Eva's little coffin out of the hearse. Once ready we followed her into the church.

Classical music played, beautiful, sweet and heartbreaking as we walked in. I knew Alex would have arranged it – music was one of his passions. I heard the sobs start around me on her arrival and I gripped tightly to Alex and Amy in my battle to control myself. The service started: wonderful words were spoken of Eva, words of kindness were offered to us and the church swelled with the sound of the hymns sung, but throughout I kept my eyes fixed on her coffin as Alex and I held each other's hand tightly. All I could hear around us were the cries of distress, the muffled sobs of those unable to comprehend the loss of one so young; the pain of those other parents, the parents of Eva's peers, on having to come face-to-face with the worst fear of any parent. I was glad the pills had deadened me to this – it was the only way I could have coped with the almost palpable grief that surrounded us, coating us so thickly it was as if a blanket had been wrapped around us, weighing us down.

We took Eva back into the sunshine and for one fleeting moment I closed my eyes and could see her as I had so many times, running ahead of me through the churchyard, laughing and giggling with a friend as I walked them to school, this brief glimpse momentarily giving me respite from facing the grim reality of the burial before us. That was for family only. Alex's parents, his sister and her husband were there – I was not close to any of them – together with Amy, the nearest thing I had by way of family. More words were spoken that I didn't hear, then the coffin was lowered and it was at this point that my breathing faltered, my breath sticking in my chest as I struggled, convulsing as I tried to control the panic rising in me. Alex held me to him, trying to calm me as the vicar spoke his final words.

Alex and I were left at the graveside, holding each other in our grief.

"How do you think anyone survives this?" I whispered.

"I have no idea," Alex sobbed, and having provided precious little support to him so far I held him now as his body wracked with tears.

Within days I'd decided I needed to stop taking the pills. I thought I'd got through the worst and would be able to face what was to come, but as they wore off I was overwhelmed with a physically excruciating pain that felt like my heart was breaking – the tears that had been held back for so long came, unbidden, my eyes constantly overflowing from an unstoppable supply. I woke screaming, sobbing from the unbearable nightmare that haunted me, Alex holding me, soothing me back to sleep. Each morning I woke exhausted, my pillow soaked, and it was as though the torment would never end.

Eventually though, the tears did stop, the time between the broken nights gradually becoming longer, but the pain and guilt remained, and I knew that somehow I would have to live with that.

Alex and Amy did everything to support me during those first few weeks. I knew Alex must have been in the same pain as me but he was stronger. His grief quickly turned to anger, and his anger turned itself on the hospital. He felt he had to do something to make sense of her death; he wanted answers, he wanted retribution, and he wanted someone to blame but he didn't see that that person was right in front of him. He wouldn't listen to me, wouldn't believe me when I told him, and we were torn in our opposing views. He wanted me to support him in the legal action he started against the hospital but I couldn't do that, knowing him to be in the wrong, and I distanced myself from having anything to do with it.

Amy was incredibly supportive to us and I valued her friendship – we both did. She cooked us meals, did housework and helped Alex sort out all the other household tasks that used to occupy me. She was the only person I could bear to have around me, the main reason for this being the fact that she was childless. I didn't make friends, close friends, easily but we'd got on well ever since finding ourselves sat next to each other at school.

I'd always found school an inconvenience, but one that had to be endured, never being there a moment longer than required. As I grew up I learnt to keep my head down, to do the minimum necessary to make myself invisible, thereby keeping people off my back. At the various schools I attended this was how I coped with what I deemed to be the pettiness of the institutionally enforced discipline.

When I was fifteen I was simultaneously struggling against the rules set by my new foster parents as well as those at what would turn out to be my last school. Mine and Amy's relationship grew through our mutual disdain for the boundaries set that we felt were an imposition, bonding as we both strained against the limitations put upon us, then finding relief at finally gaining a little more freedom once we made sixth form. This freedom was the only reason I managed to stay on at all. We'd remained firm friends since leaving school which meant a lot to me, particularly now, when I'd cut myself off from everyone else. They'd all come round initially, supportively, all the people I chatted to at the school gates, at school functions, who had children that Eva used to play with. They were kind, and I could feel them wanting to help, but the common ground we'd shared was gone and we had nothing outside of that. It was far too painful to be constantly reminded of their children and of the happier times we'd had together, as well as it being desperately uncomfortable for them to have to spend any time with me.

Life, I was told, had to move on and Alex went back to work and his usual activities as soon as he felt confident I wouldn't slit my wrists the moment his back was turned. While I was hurt by the apparent ease with which he got over our loss so quickly I found it a blessed relief not to have him hovering around me, watching me anxiously all the time. However, apart from eventually having to go back to work, I couldn't move on, couldn't resume anything from my previous life; even my passion for horses died as I found my life grinding to a halt.

I realised mine and Alex's relationship was struggling terribly, and at the point when we'd needed it most we'd lost our ability to communicate. That which had once come so naturally to us felt awkward and stilted. Alex tried to resume some semblance of normality in our life together but I didn't see how he could. I'd lost all interest in him and as I pushed him away he became more and more wary of me. I had difficulty in even looking at him. When I did he reminded me of Eva – I could see her in the movements he made, in his mannerisms, his expressions, and those subtle similarities between them that had once enchanted me now hit me each time with another lance of pain, irritating my raw wounds as acutely as if I'd worked salt into them.

As I now drove back into Crowbridge and approached my house I realised how much had changed in the intervening four years. The painful reminders Alex had provided had gone, along with the debilitating phase of my grief, which eventually passed, as all things do given enough time, but I'd been left feeling as if all that remained of me was a shell: a hollow, fragile version of my former self, although enough of that person remained that made me not want to show this frailty to the world.

Chapter 3

I woke, opening my eyes to the comforting familiarity of my bedroom for the last time as I remembered with a pang of anxiety that the day had finally come when I would be leaving. It was still early but I knew even after the restless night I'd had there'd be no going back to sleep. Getting up I pulled on my dressing gown, pushed my feet into my slippers and went downstairs. Susie was waiting to greet me, her tail wagging, although not with its usual exuberance – it appeared to be too early for her too. I opened the back door to let her out, breathing in the fresh, early morning air.

Turning back to the kitchen I made Susie's breakfast, which she tucked into with enthusiasm while I took tea and toast outside. It was a beautifully quiet morning in early May, holding the promise of a glorious day.

Although presently muted in the early morning light the garden was a riot of colour, the fencing covered in a jungle of climbing roses, honeysuckle and clematis. The wide border below was crowded with plants that vied for attention and were seemingly held together by a sea of forget-me-not blue. Here and there rose a taller spike of promised beauty in the form of a delphinium or foxglove, the full glory of which I realised, a little sadly, I wouldn't be there to see revealed.

I couldn't take the credit for the beauty of this garden; that was all down to the foundation laid by Alex, the work he'd put into it years ago. But now as I looked round I could see it was all overgrown – some plants had disappeared, choked out of existence by their stronger, greedier neighbours, and that was down to me, to my neglect.

Susie wandered out of the house having finished eating and came to join me, flopping down to lie under the table. She was such a huge part of my life and had brought me so far it was hard to believe she'd only been with me for two years. I could remember the day she'd arrived vividly. That morning I'd received a letter from my solicitor enclosing the Decree Absolute. That was it, my marriage was over, my sense of loss and sadness compounded and my depression deepened.

In the afternoon Alex had appeared on my doorstep, the first time he'd done so for a while. He carefully placed a large box on the ground beside him and looked up at me with concern as I opened the door – I knew I'd lost weight and was pale from lack of sleep and lack of interest in myself.

"Did you get the Decree Absolute this morning?"

In response I nodded, then asked quietly, "How long do I have before I have to move out?"

His brow creased in confusion as he said gently, "You really haven't been paying attention, have you? I've signed the house over to you; you don't have to go anywhere."

I felt an unexpected but palpable sense of relief at these words which must have shown on my face. He shrugged, adding, "It was your inheritance that allowed us to buy the house in the first place, so it's only fair." He indicated to the box with a gesture of his head. "I've brought you a present."

I lifted one hand up to cover my mouth in mock horror. "Oh, Alex, I'm so sorry, I didn't realise that giving gifts was the correct etiquette for this day, what must you think of me? I didn't get you anything."

He gazed at me, raising one eyebrow to show irritation at my sarcasm though with half a smile on his lips, before saying dryly, "Good to see you haven't completely lost

22

your sense of humour. Actually, this is something you always wanted when we were together but I didn't. Now that I no longer apply I was hoping she would help."

She? I knelt down to open the box and looking up at me from inside with the largest, brownest eyes imaginable was a scruffy ball of dog. Susie had entered my life and by becoming the focus of it, she saved me.

As she lay at my feet now, I thought back to those first few days with her. Alex had bought out the pet store and carried everything into the house. I was cuddling Susie when he turned to leave, leaning in to kiss me goodbye, but I shied away. Forgiveness was not in my nature at all, let alone that easily.

"I hope she helps, Em…Please start to look after yourself," he'd sounded apologetic, guilty even, being only too aware of what he'd done to me. Then he was gone.

Susie obviously wasn't Susie when she arrived but that was the name that sprang to mind when I first saw her and it stuck. She was eight weeks old, a cross-bred terrier and when I'd first lifted her out of the box she'd been warm and soft and had snuffled her nose into my hands. At that time she'd easily fitted into my two hands and while she had obviously got bigger as she matured, she was a small dog, even now. Her coat was a patchwork of colours: underlying white with smudges of black, brown and tan merging into each other over the top. She was short-coated but there was a kink to the hair and I could already see longer hairs starting to tuft out around her face and suspected that she would eventually become a rough-coated dog. I had been proved right and she had matured into what could politely be described as an untidy dog and we suited each other perfectly.

Susie and I had spent the next few weeks getting to know each other. Making her sleep on her own in the kitchen, without her crying for her mother, was the most

23

challenging test for us, and painful to listen to for a few nights, but she eventually settled down. Her pleasure at seeing me again each morning was uncontained in its exuberance and I felt my heart lift each day at her apparent joy just at being with me. For the first time since Eva there was some meaning back in my life, something to get up for. I now had a friend and I started to get stronger, with Susie pulling me slowly back out of the dark.

Her influence made me want to work on building myself up, mentally as well as physically, wanting to be comfortable with being completely independent again – something I'd prided myself on as I'd grown up. When I looked back I realised I must have been a real headache for my foster parents: determined to do my own thing, and always challenging, which was perhaps why none of them had put up with me for too long. But the years with Alex had softened me, and had got me used to having someone around to rely on. As it was, all my marriage had taught me was that you couldn't depend on anyone, and as I toughened up I became hardened in my resolve that I'd never let anyone near enough to hurt me this badly again. Susie was all I needed. I knew she would never let me down and I had no intention of ever letting anyone else into my life again that could.

The sun's rays were starting to find their way into the garden and as I'd finished breakfast I went back in to clear up the kitchen. Then having a shower I washed my hair which was thick and dark brown; left to grow it would curl in soft waves. As it was, it had recently been cut into a sort of pixie cut, although still with a bit of a fringe sweeping across my forehead. I wasn't really sure if I liked it or not. Time would tell on that one, I thought, but at least it was practical. I was too pale – even my eyes were washed out from their once-vibrant blue. As I glanced in the mirror they also looked tired, I noted, and I put on a bit of mascara to liven them up. That was about as far as my make-up routine ever went anyway.

I dressed in my habitual jeans and tee shirt, pulled on my plimsolls and took Susie for a quick walk through the village, ending up at the church. I passed through the gates and went to sit on the bench next to Eva's grave. I couldn't leave the village without saying goodbye and although I carried the memory of her within, I'd always found great comfort being in the churchyard where she lay. I hadn't been so far from this place before and didn't want her to feel abandoned; I wanted to let her know I would be back.

Susie and I returned to the house to finish packing. My employer, Barney, had been kind when I'd handed in my notice though I suspected he was secretly relieved I was going as he'd be able to employ someone who would be a little more focused on his business. I'd finished work a couple of weeks before which had given me enough time to have already cleared the house of most of my things, putting them in storage. I'd cried myself into a state of exhaustion as I'd dismantled Eva's room, untouched since she died, putting aside a box of her things to take with me. Her favourite cuddly rabbit had been buried with her so I chose a teddy she'd slept with, her favourite bedtime stories, some pictures she'd drawn for me, and a few other bits and pieces.

There was not much left to take besides Eva's box, only my clothes, photos, books, a few other personal items, Susie's things and a box of provisions from the kitchen. I'd arranged to rent the house out and needed to drop the key into the letting agent on my way. I loaded everything into my ancient car, which while rusting in places and a rather unpleasant brown colour, I adored nonetheless, and then went to take one last look round the house. As I headed back towards the front door I stopped, opening the door to the cupboard under the stairs. Memories flooded back as I looked at the markings on the back of it and tears pricked my eyes. There were several pen marks on the lower half of the door ending about halfway up and next to the top one was written 'Eva, age 6'. As I looked up there was another one with 'Mum' written next to it and about two inches above that was the last one for 'Dad'. I fixed a piece of paper to the door using Blu-tack on which I'd written 'Please do not paint over this' and closed it quietly.

I was pleased I'd decided to rent the house out rather than sell it as I knew if things didn't work out I'd have somewhere to run to. This home had been my refuge but I knew it was time to leave and as I walked out the front door, pulling it closed behind me, I took my first step down a path I'd travelled along a thousand times before, only this time for it to be leading me in a different direction.

Chapter 4

My apprehension had grown on the journey though I tried to reassure myself with reminders of how welcoming I'd found the estate when I was interviewed. After announcing myself on the intercom, a disembodied voice, which I thought was Forster's, welcomed me.

"Good afternoon, Grayson, please proceed." The imposing wrought-iron gates were already opening and I drove forward. Whereas before to reach the Manor I'd gone straight on, my instructions to reach the stables were to turn left as I entered the estate. The road followed the wall for a short way, then gradually veered away from it and I found, as I travelled along, each side of the road became more and more densely populated with trees until I was driving through quite thick woodland. I'd left the bright sunlight behind me and now the light was subdued and dappled down through the tree canopy. I drove further, the road undulating and twisting with the natural curves in the ground until eventually the trees thinned a little to the right-hand side and I spotted a small stone cottage.

I liked what I saw. Set a little way back from the road behind a small strip of grass, the thinning of the trees afforded the cottage enough light to enable roses to grow up the front, and this area was bordered by a black metal railing fence, broken by a gate which led to a dark green front door, although I'd been told to enter the property through the back.

There was a window to each side of the door and above these two more which were unusually shaped as half circles and were buried into the roof line. The tiles were an array of colours provided by the mosses and lichens that grew there and were topped off by a chimney. The overall impression was comforting and I proceeded past the cottage and turned into the drive, passing through a pair of five-barred wooden gates that stood open. Continuing round to the back of the cottage, I found the area I'd driven into was a large flat expanse of compacted ground. There was a black pickup parked there but I couldn't see anyone else. Letting Susie out, knowing she wouldn't wander far from me, I looked around.

Across the yard I could see there were six brick-built stables in an L shape. In front of them was a large area of concrete and this was all enclosed with a post-and-rail fence. The roof overhung the front of the stables giving them some protection from the weather. The whole stable block area looked shabby: paint peeling, weeds growing anywhere they could get a hold. Plenty to keep me busy for a while. At the end of the row of stables were three more doors, which for the moment would have to await further investigation, as I turned my attention back to the cottage.

The rear was similar to the front, except that at the gated entrance end of it I could see what appeared to be the double doors of a garage. I picked up the first of my boxes from the car and made my way up the path through the garden, which was neat and tidy with what looked like an apple tree growing up out of the middle of the lawn. On the other side of the path were a small table and a couple of chairs and newly planted hanging baskets hung each side of the back door.

This, painted in the same green as the one at the front, was of a stable door design and had a cat flap fitted. The key, one of a small bunch, was in the lock of the door as I had been told it would be, and I freed a hand to reach up and open it.

I walked into a cream-painted area that I would call the boot room, purely because that was where I'd be putting

28

mine, which was functionally equipped for all laundry needs. There were quarry tiles on the floor which flowed through to the kitchen where I put the box I was carrying down on the corner of the old pine table in the centre of the room. This had piles of things on it already which I ignored in favour of exploring the rest of the cottage first.

The kitchen had a comfortably cosy feel to it and appeared to have everything a kitchen should, even extending to a range which was inset under an alcove; the areas of wall not covered by anything else were painted a warm, rich red. The cupboard doors were cream and black ceramic worktops ran round three of the walls with cream tiling above them. The fourth wall, through which a staircase exited, bordered the passageway from the boot room to the sitting room, which I went into next to find a wood-burning stove buried in a fireplace with two large, squashy, dark-red settees settled around it. A door led off to the left and through this was a smaller room set up to use as an office, a laptop and printer on a wooden desk which was pushed up against the opposite wall.

Going back through to the kitchen I ran up the stairs. Directly ahead of me at the top was a doorway leading to the main bedroom containing a beautiful black ironwork bed made up with a thick white duvet and plump pillows. To each side was a bedside cabinet in dark wood and on each of these sat a dark-red side lamp. An armchair that matched the settees downstairs was in the corner and the only other piece of furniture in the room was a set of drawers. A door in the corner led to a built-in cupboard giving some wardrobe space. Another opened onto a shower room. Other doors off the landing revealed a second smaller bedroom and a bathroom.

The floors were laid throughout with dark-green carpets and each window dressed with curtains complemented the cream-painted rooms. The whole cottage was simple and beautiful and someone had obviously worked hard to make it so. From the lingering smell of fresh paint in the air it looked to have been freshly decorated, and as it appeared as if everything in it was new, it seemed to me that the cottage had not just been spruced up after its last occupants – I didn't believe anyone had lived here for a long time and in fact a full refurbishment had been carried out because of my arrival. That made sense when I thought about it – the stables hadn't been in use for some time, years probably, so there likely hadn't been any use for the cottage until now.

Having explored, I went back to the kitchen and thought I'd better have a look through the things that had been left on the table. I moved the box I'd brought in to one side and sat down. There was a printed-out sheet addressed to me which I read through.

Dear Grayson

Welcome to the stables. I trust you will find everything to your liking, but please let me know if you have any questions or need any help with anything. I have organised a few things to help you settle in and get you started in your new role, as follows:–

1. There's a black pickup in the yard. This is for your use and you will find the keys on the table. Your car can be stored for safekeeping in the garage. All costs for the running of the pickup are covered and you can fill it with diesel at the farm. Turn right out of the yard and keep following the road round the estate. You will reach one fork in the road – keep to the left-hand road to get to the farm, the right-hand road takes you to the Manor.

2. You will see a small box with two buttons on it next to the keys. This will open and close the front gates and should be kept in the pickup.

3. For your information, your cottage will be cleaned every Wednesday morning. The cleaners have their own keys so you do not need to leave the door open.

4. The gardeners will call to cut the grass periodically and will generally maintain the gardens within their usual schedule.

5. There is also, on the table, a new phone for your use. This has already been loaded with everyone on the estate's contact details should you need them. I have also taken the liberty of adding all the local suppliers that we use, as well as the vets and farriers. Feel free to use this as your personal phone and add any numbers you wish to. Note there is one app already downloaded. This is an emergency call button. Please carry this phone with you – and keep it charged. If you ever get into difficulty, use it and we will come and find you.

6. While on the subject of safety, there is a panic button in the kitchen of the cottage by the back door in case there is any sort of situation at the yard that needs our assistance.

7. You will need to use the local country store and saddlery and, as agreed with Cavendish, there is a card here for you to use to spend there on credit. There is also another general credit card for other purchases.

8. I have attached directions to get you to each of the local suppliers, including those mentioned above.

9. There is a gym (next to the kitchen at the Manor) which you are encouraged to take full advantage of whenever you would like to.

10. Mrs F has left some supplies which I hope will make your first evening comfortable. She has also invited you to tea in the kitchen between 3 and 4, if you arrive early enough today. If you drive to the Manor and then follow the road round to the rear of the house and into the courtyard you will see the kitchen door at the top of a short flight of steps.

I apologise for not meeting you today but will call this evening to sort out arrangements for tomorrow. I hope you settle in well and look forward to meeting you soon.

Kind regards

Trent

I finished reading and sat for a moment, taking it all in, almost having to pinch myself to believe it was real. Clearly keen on my safety and security they really knew how to look after people here. This was much more than I'd ever imagined and it made me feel…wanted, which was unusual.

I went to see what supplies Mrs F had provided. In the fridge there was a steak with new potatoes and a green salad, as well as some eggs, bacon, milk and cheese and a bottle of white wine chilling. A bottle of red was on the side together with a tin of biscuits and a loaf of bread, both of which appeared to be home-made. In one of the cupboards there was a supply of jam and marmalade, again home-made, and tea and coffee. I warmed to Mrs F immediately and felt I should definitely join her for tea; it would appear rude not to thank her properly.

With that thought in mind I got on with emptying my car of the rest of my belongings, which for the moment I brought into the house and dumped in the kitchen. I set up Susie's bed and water bowl in the boot room and put the rest of her supplies in the cupboards. I took my clothes upstairs to my room with the intention of putting them away later. The only thing I did unpack was my framed photo of Eva, which stopped me in my tracks as I sat on the bed to look at her, taking a moment to imagine how she would have loved to have come exploring with me.

"Don't dwell," I told myself firmly as I got up, placing her photo on the bedside cabinet before leaping back down the stairs, unloading the provisions I'd brought with me into the fridge, freezer and cupboards as appropriate, keeping busy in an attempt to distract myself from my thoughts. I walked back outside and opened the garage doors before reversing my beloved car into her new home. Closing the doors I headed over to the stables, closely followed by Susie.

Opening the gate in the post-and-rail fence I had a look over each door. There were four large and two smaller pony stables. Each had a brick floor, an inbuilt corner manger and a window next to the door to give more light, fitted with shatterproof glass and protected by a wire mesh covering. The main structure looked sound, but the stables had clearly not been used for a long time and needed to be completely cleaned out, though it seemed a bit of general maintenance and painting should be all that was required to make them ready for the horses' arrival. I made a mental list of what I needed to get at the hardware store later, in readiness for my start the next day.

I'd noticed that there were padlocks on the three remaining doors, and bringing out the bunch of keys from my pocket found there was a key on the ring which fitted all three. The first door opened to a room that looked like it had been used as a feed room in the past, as there were large rodent-proof metal bins along one side. The second and third rooms were currently empty and I decided I would set one up as a tack room and the other for storing items such as the wheelbarrows, forks and yard brushes.

Behind the stables was a large brick barn which on examination was empty. There were two paddocks behind the barn, and as I looked across these I saw that the ground dropped away a little, and further downhill I could see the Manor in the distance, which from first sight I'd found to be attractive and welcoming. Trees were scattered across the parkland and whilst stark and wintery when I'd come before now they were verdant. From here I could see the Manor was huge, spreading out a long way behind its façade with various other buildings behind it.

Next to the paddocks was a large all-weather schooling arena, which looked like a recent addition, and both this and the paddocks were surrounded by post-and-rail fences.

I checked my watch and seeing it was three o'clock already went back to the house to get the keys for the pickup and the gate control box, slipping the credit card into my back pocket. Susie was in her bed when I left, telling her I'd be back later.

I started the pickup, which felt huge compared to my little car, and set off out of the yard, turning right and driving through woodland again before coming to a fork in the road. I took the right-hand option and a little further on emerged from the trees, finding myself then only a short distance from the Manor. I followed the road round to the back of the main house, pulled into the courtyard, parked and got out.

I went up the steps Trent had referred to in his instructions and knocked timidly on the kitchen door, suddenly feeling a bit nervous at the thought of meeting someone new. As I knocked the door moved, so I pushed it open a little, calling "Hello" as I did so. Hearing a responding, "Hi, come on in," I opened the door fully and was met with a view of the most astonishingly large kitchen I'd ever seen. It was beautifully old-fashioned with dressers and wooden cupboards and shelving, all packed with equipment and ingredients, as well as a couple of huge range cookers. A variety of gleaming copper pots and pans lined the walls on high shelves which ran round the expanse of the room. The most noticeable feature though was the long, scrubbed wooden table that stretched from nearly one end of the room to the other, and it was at the end of this that a group of women sat looking at me. I hadn't anticipated there being anyone else here other than Mrs F, and hoped I didn't look as surprised as I felt.

One of these women stood as I entered. She was a little shorter than me with neat auburn hair feathered around a smiling face.

"You must be Grayson – we've been looking forward to meeting you. I'm Annie Forster. Please come and sit down and have a cup of tea and we can do the introductions." She was welcoming and saying a general hello to the group I sat between her and an older woman who wore her grey hair in a smart bob.

"How do you like it?" Mrs F asked, pouring me a cup.

"Milk, no sugar please."

She pushed the cup towards me and indicated to a plate of biscuits. "Help yourself."

"Thanks," I said, taking one, only then remembering I'd not had any lunch and was now famished.

"Okay, so…introductions. I'm the cook. Elsie Bray, sitting the other side of you, is the housekeeper. Then we have all the girls who work wherever needed on the estate – Chloe West, Clare Greene, Lizzie Young and Kay Burton." With each name Mrs F indicated who it belonged to and we exchanged smiles and nods as I tried to link names with faces.

"I'm Emma Grayson. I wasn't sure if I was to use my first name or not."

"We tend to use full names for introductions, surnames only from then on when on the estate, and first names when off, in our own time. Although, we get so used to it being surnames only it's quite often easier to stick to that off the estate as well," Mrs F explained. She then added, "Though I'm Mrs F and Elsie prefers Mrs Bray."

I frowned, a little confused. "Can I ask why you're Mrs F?"

"Yes, sorry, should've explained that. I married Forster, who I know you've already met and it seemed easiest so there's no confusion between us."

"Ah, I see," nodding at this clarification. Now the introductions were over everyone relaxed and the girls went back to finishing whatever they were talking about before I'd entered the room.

"Have you got everything you need at the stables?" Mrs Bray asked.

"Absolutely," I replied. "I can't believe how lovely everything is there." And turning a little to Mrs F, I continued, "Thank you for all the wonderful supplies you've left. That was a real treat to arrive to and completely unexpected."

"No problem at all. You'll find as produce becomes available on this estate it tends to get shared out among us all, so don't be surprised if you find other things turning up on your doorstep."

I noticed then that the four girls had turned their attention and conversation in my direction, and suddenly I was at the centre of an inquisition, the like of which can only be experienced when faced with four such bubbly girls who were intent on extracting information from you.

I thought probably Greene was closest in age to me; she had long blond hair which was tied in a single plait falling forward over one shoulder. The other three were in their early to mid-twenties and I'd recognised West as she'd brought in the refreshments when I came for my interview. Burton stood out among the group, having the most striking combination of fiery ginger hair and vibrant green eyes.

They started asking all about where I'd moved from and where I'd worked before but I felt the questioning only really started getting interesting for them when they got onto my relationship status. I fended off the questions as best I could, eventually explaining that I was divorced before starting to turn the questions back onto them which they seemed to be equally happy with. Young was perhaps the quietest and studied me carefully, only dipping into the conversation now and then as her fingers played with one of the many rings her ear was adorned with.

It was a strangely enjoyable, if rather draining experience for me, having not been involved in as stimulating a conversation for a long time. At four o'clock I made my move to go, thanking them all for the tea and company. Mrs F told me I was always welcome in the kitchen, but they had a pot of coffee on at around eleven and tea between three and four if I was ever able to get away and join them. I didn't want to hurt any feelings so I said I would, though qualified this by explaining that once the horses arrived there'd be less chance of being able to do so, keeping to myself my reluctance to commit to any socialising due to my desire for solitude.

"You'd better try and come as often as possible in the next couple of weeks then," Mrs F said with an encouraging grin.

I left the kitchen and set off in the pickup to go and get supplies for the morning. Managing to negotiate the main gate using the magic button I headed off towards the hardware store using Trent's directions. It was only a few miles away and I found it easily enough. I wandered the aisles, filling my trolley as I went with a variety of cleaning products, including a couple of yard brushes, disinfectant, buckets, pots of white paint, paintbrushes, a few tools and a pair of one-size-fits-all overalls.

When I got back to the yard I unloaded everything into the feed room before locking that for the night, then carrying the overalls I went back to the cottage to be greeted by Susie who leapt out of the cat flap before running towards me. On investigation I was pleased to find the cat flap could be locked closed, deciding I'd lock it each night and anytime I needed Susie to stay in, for her own safety. I didn't want her wandering about in the dark or when I was not around.

I gave her a cuddle then finished unpacking before cooking dinner. Putting the potatoes on to boil and the green salad onto a plate I poured myself a glass of red. As I waited for the potatoes I had a look at my new phone. Trent had indicated I could use it for personal calls so I entered the only number I needed from my old life, being the one for the letting agent. I decided to cancel my old number, severing my last link with Alex. Well...other than the one with which we would always be bound: Eva. Since he'd left me he'd irritatingly dropped round occasionally to see me. To bring this to an end I hadn't told him I was moving and now he wouldn't be able to call me either. That suited me – I'd thought he'd only kept contacting me to ease his conscience anyway and I didn't want the reminder.

I cooked the steak in a pan and decided to go and eat in the garden, it still being warm enough. The sun was low in the pink-tinged sky, casting long shadows across the yard from the buildings, and it was incredibly peaceful as I sat eating and contemplating the plans I had for the stables. This place was idyllic, I thought. I enjoyed the isolation – this was what I'd wanted, this was what I'd hoped for, and I felt myself relax, at last.

After clearing up the kitchen I went through to the office to sort out my paperwork. I'd only just sat down when my phone rang. Feeling inexplicably nervous again when I saw who was calling I answered rather apprehensively: "Hello, Trent."

"Good evening, Grayson. Apologies again for not being there to welcome you. I trust you've found everything to your liking?" His voice was smooth and deep, his words formal.

"I have, thank you for organising everything for me, it's all been much more than I expected."

"You're welcome. Now tomorrow I'll be sending four men over to start about nine o'clock." This took me by surprise and my reply was quick and to the point.

"That's not necessary, I don't need any help. I'm more than capable of getting the stables ready on my own." There was silence on the phone as I waited for his agreement but when the response came the voice unexpectedly sounded more authoritative.

"I can't allow that. I insist my men come to help you. You're not expected to get all the work done on your own." I can't allow that? I could feel my hackles rise at this unwanted interference in my plans.

"I can assure you I am perfectly able to get it all done." There was definitely an edge to my voice now.

When he responded it was with an air of finality. "I'm not prepared to argue with you on this. The men will be there at nine o'clock – I suggest you organise a list of jobs they can get done. I'll see you late morning. Goodnight, Grayson." Before I had a chance to respond I realised he'd ended the call.

What a cheek, he'd hung up on me! I could feel myself bristling over the conversation. Damn it, he'd made me annoyed; I hated people controlling me – not that it had happened for a while. I'd got the impression from Cavendish that I had autonomy over the stables but it appeared that was not to be the case. So much for my isolation, for my peace and quiet; that was about to be shattered by men I didn't even want here and Trent clearly thought I was incapable. What a great start. I thought back to the interview when Cavendish had indicated I was not the person Trent would have chosen for this job and started to worry that he was going to make my life here difficult.

I tried to gather my thoughts and they came down to the fact that Trent was in charge on the estate and, while I hadn't anticipated this interference, I was clearly going to have to put up with it, at least until the stables were done. Hopefully I could then get rid of everyone. I prepared a list of the jobs so that at least I had a plan for the morning and by the time that was done and I'd finished my wine, I'd calmed down a little and decided to go to bed. I let Susie out and locked up, turning out the lights before heading upstairs. I got ready for bed and, after setting the alarm, snuggled up under the duvet. It was incredibly comfortable and as I lay there I thought that apart from the irritation caused by the call from Trent, which I was trying to put out of my mind, I was feeling okay and looking forward to getting stuck into some physical work.

Chapter 5

I'd set my alarm for seven but was awake well before it went off. The upstairs rooms of the cottage were built into the roof with the windows set low down to the floor, and as I lay there, staring out of the window down the lane, I saw a man in sweats running past. He looked deep in thought, running to the beat in his head from the earphones he was plugged into. Someone else's activity spurred me into action as I leapt out of bed, grabbing my dressing gown before going downstairs and opening the back door for Susie. I quickly fed her then myself before jumping in the shower, and as I dressed I thought through my plan of work for the day. I'd decided I was just going to have to accept the help these men were bringing as graciously as I could. It wasn't their fault they'd been told to come and help me, so I should at least try and play nicely. It meant the stables would be ready quicker anyway and then they could go and leave me alone and as these were other employees on the estate I was going to have to learn to get on. Be a team player, I thought, though that had never been my thing.

Once I was ready I opened up the overalls and pulled them on over my jeans and tee shirt and it was at that point that I realised the one-size-fits-all was only applicable if you happened to be the size of a really big man. They were huge on me and I looked ridiculous. I rolled up the arms so I could see my hands again; then, once these were free I bent down to roll up the legs so they weren't dragging on the floor and pulled my old boots on. Standing up again I peered at my reflection in the window, these alterations had not made much difference to the overall picture. The crotch of the overalls hung down somewhere towards my knees and the body of them was so baggy two of me could have fitted in there. Still, I tried to rationalise, it's not like I needed to impress anyone – I was only doing my job so I'd have to make do.

I made a cup of coffee and took it over to the stables to get started. Susie came with me, taking up a position in the sun which was already feeling quite warm. The sky was a cloudless blue and there was a stillness in the air that indicated a settled day ahead. All the stables needed to be swept out first, including the removal of all cobwebs, before being disinfected, so I made a start on that.

A little while later I heard a vehicle as it drove into the yard. Susie gave a low growl of warning, and glancing at my watch I saw it had just turned nine. Here we go, I thought, time to meet my working party. I walked out of the stable to be greeted by the sight of a red pickup similar to mine drawing up, and as it came to a halt two men leapt out of the back of it. Two others got out of the cab and they all walked towards me, each one greeting Susie as they did so and looking friendly enough. The one who'd been driving came right up to me; I fancied he saw himself as the self-proclaimed leader of the group, although that may have been because he looked to be the oldest, while the others hung back a little. He had short, dark hair, blue eyes and was very attractive, giving off an air of confidence that made me think he knew it. He was grinning at me and I noticed his grin widen as he looked me up and down.

"Hi, I'm Will Carlton." He extended his hand to shake mine, holding it for a fraction too long. He indicated towards my overalls, adding, "Did you buy a pair you could grow into?" and he chuckled, the others following suit.

"No, I've just discovered that one size does not, in fact, fit all," I replied tightly, then forcing myself to at least try to appear relaxed, smiled briefly back at him. He turned and indicating to the others, said, "Here we have Scott Wade, Ben Hayes and Josh Turner, at your service." I raised my hand to them in greeting.

"So what do you want us to get started with?" Carlton asked. I led them over to the stables and explained what I'd started and therefore what they could continue with. I was a little concerned that I wouldn't have enough equipment for them all to use but they'd brought some of their own anyway so they all got going. Carlton and I continued with the stable I'd already begun, and Wade and Hayes started in the next stable while Turner began diluting the disinfectant ready to use on the first stable as soon as we'd finished. Turner was the youngest, probably only in his late teens while the others were early to mid-twenties. He still had the gangly build of youth, yet to fill out like the others who all had the muscled frames of young men who worked at it. The gym must be a popular place here, I thought. I found Carlton easy to work with; we chatted quite comfortably, there being no awkwardness in the silences either.

Mid-morning I made coffee for everyone and later on, Susie, happy that it was safe for me to be left for a while, wandered off exploring. We'd completely finished three of the stables. Carlton was just starting on the fifth box, being the first of the pony-sized ones, and I was about to join him when I looked up to see a man coming across the yard towards me. As it was by then late morning, I guessed this must be Trent, recognising him as my early-morning runner. He was dressed casually in jeans and a red checked shirt, his collar open, his sleeves rolled up. I was surprised as he looked considerably more casual than his manner on the phone last night had indicated he might be. I was also expecting someone older, but he could only have been in his mid-thirties. The most striking thing about him though was his hair, which was dark and unruly, cut in a medium-short style with wavy curls contrasting sharply against the very short hair sported by all the other boys in the yard. I walked through the gate in the yard fence to meet him and as he approached I could see him look down at my overalls, a small smile coming over his previously serious face. I was already feeling quite tatty by then and was pretty sure I had cobwebs in my hair so I probably wasn't in the best shape to be meeting someone for the first time. He held out his hand as he approached and I shook it firmly.

"Good to meet you, Grayson, I'm Trent," and I could see a twinkle come to his eyes as he added, "Nice overalls."

"Thank you, Trent, they're very, er…practical," I replied a little indignantly, for some reason feeling the need to defend my overalls.

"How are my boys working out then?"

"Very well thanks, we're making good progress," and I gave him a short update on what we'd achieved so far.

"Sounds good. Everything else okay with the cottage?"

"Yes, it's all fine, thanks again for organising everything."

"No problem. Now, thinking about the work for the rest of the week – the boys, or at least some of them, should be able to come over most days to get all of this sorted out for you."

I could feel myself start to tense. "There's really no need, Trent, I'm sure they have other duties to do, and I wouldn't want to keep them from that. I'm more than capable of doing this alone you know," speaking as if trying to convince him.

"Hmm…You let me worry about their other duties. While you may well be capable of doing this work alone, they're available at the moment to help. They will be here each day, until the yard is ready," he answered firmly, his tone stern, eliciting no response from me as I bit back the one I wanted to give in my frustration at him appearing to exert his control over what I already saw as my domain. I'd been a little intimidated under his intense gaze as he'd spoken, but I met the steel of his blue eyes with my own challenge, determined not to be the one to look away.

I felt Carlton bounce up beside me, breaking the moment. He wrapped his arm around my shoulders and much to my surprise, hugged me towards him, nearly lifting me off my feet.

"Hi, Trent, isn't she adorable?" he said enthusiastically, and I saw what looked like alarm flicker across Trent's eyes as his gaze passed fleetingly from one of us to the other.

"You certainly seem to be finding her so," he murmured thoughtfully, his smile not reaching his eyes this time. Carlton met his gaze calmly for a few moments before letting me go, excusing himself by muttering he'd better get on and turning back to the stables.

"Right, I'm going to be off now, let me know if you need anything," Trent said, looking at his watch, and at that moment Susie appeared from round the back of the stables running towards him, barking at the latest stranger who'd appeared in her new territory. Trent, taken by surprise, warned, "If that dog starts wandering the estate I'll have to chain it up."

That sealed it. He was too controlling, and while it was one thing him trying that on with me it was quite another bringing Susie into it and my natural instinct to defend her was behind my firm response: "If you want to touch a hair on my dog, you're going to have to come through me first and you don't want to make the mistake of thinking that will be easy." I was glaring at him, Susie softly growling at my side, and he stared back at me, his eyebrows raised in astonishment. His eyes sparked with some emotion I couldn't fathom, followed by the briefest twitch of his mouth as if he found this amusing, me amusing, and I narrowed my eyes at him, just daring him to smile. He hesitated for a moment before closing his eyes briefly as he raised his hands in defence.

"Okay, okay, I won't touch your dog," he said, in an attempt to placate me.

"Her name is Susie."

"Of course…Susie…" Giving me a small smile he turned to leave. "It was good to meet you Grayson…Have a good day."

I stared after him, unmoving, though softly told Susie to quieten as I watched him cross the yard. When he'd gone I turned back to the stables and the boys, who'd all witnessed this exchange, and who now returned quickly back to their respective jobs. I went to join Carlton in silence, Susie now close by my side.

"That went well," he joked sarcastically.

"Too much?" I asked, hearing the anxiety in my voice.

"Little bit…possibly. I've never seen anyone speak to their boss like that before, and on their first meeting too, and I'm fairly certain Trent has never experienced anything like it." He grinned as he said this.

"Oh God," I moaned, "I'm not going to last a week here am I?"

Carlton chuckled, infuriating me even more.

We worked on in silence, giving me more than enough time to think through what I thought Trent would perceive as an irrational reaction brought on by my need to defend Susie. I knew some would say she was only a dog but to me she was a lot more than that, she was all I had. I tried to rationalise my outburst by putting it down to the fact he'd already wound me up. I wasn't used to having someone telling me what to do, and in fact generally kept away from people who wanted to. It certainly wasn't something I'd ever accepted well. I remembered only too vividly the running arguments I'd had at my last foster home with my foster father, Brian. It had been unfortunate that I'd been placed with him and his wife, Sheila, when I was fifteen and in the most belligerent phase of my teenage years. He'd tried to control everything I did, said or wore; he tried to stop me working at the stables because he didn't like horses, and I'd rebelled against his constant interference in my life, arguing furiously and defying him at every turn.

Life had been miserable during that time but settled down once Alex and I got together. He was easy-going, and actively encouraged my independent streak, helped no doubt by the fact we'd met young, growing and developing together as we'd moulded ourselves comfortably around each other's lives. Though, as it turned out, he had not appreciated how special our relationship was as much as I had.

We stopped for lunch – the boys had brought their own and they came over to the cottage to eat, sitting in the garden. I brought out mugs of tea, and after finishing their food they ate their way through my tin of biscuits. There was good camaraderie between the boys as they joshed with each other, although I started to get the feeling they were playing it up a little in front of me as if vying for my attention.

We got back to work and by the end of the afternoon had all six stables fully cleaned and disinfected. Turner had also gone round each of the windows making sure all the grills were secure with no protruding nails.

They were about to leave, the other three having already gone to the truck, as I locked up the feed room and noticed Carlton hanging back a little. I looked at him enquiringly and without hesitation he asked me to go out for a drink with him. I was a little taken aback at his directness, although his naturally flirtatious manner had not gone entirely unnoticed all afternoon.

"Thanks for asking, Carlton, it's flattering, but I have to say no, I don't date."

"What, not at all?" he queried, frowning as he said this.

"No, not at all." I looked at him apologetically. Momentarily crestfallen he picked himself up remarkably quickly.

"We'll have to see what we can do about changing your mind then, shan't we," he said, winking at me as he sauntered off to the pickup before driving off. I felt uneasy at his response as I'd hoped he'd just accept my refusal; however, that didn't seem to be likely. I'd been determined in my resolution on coming here and I wasn't about to renege on that. I had no intention of getting involved with anyone, no intention of putting myself in the position of being able to get hurt again, but already that resolve seemed to be slipping away from me as more was being asked of me than I was willing to give and my quest for solitude felt further away than ever.

The next day progressed in a similar fashion to the first. It was the turn of the feed, tack and store rooms to get the scrub down. After lunch we tackled the barn, cleaning it down and sweeping it out thoroughly. We were going to get finished a little earlier than the previous day but there was no point in starting anything else and I was putting away the brushes when Wade appeared in the doorway of the store room. Leaning against the doorjamb he crossed his arms, showing off the tribal tattoos that ringed his biceps; he gave me one of his stunning smiles, flashing a set of perfect teeth. Judging by the way the boys had all behaved with me during the day I suspected I knew what was about to follow and when he started to say, "I was wondering if you..." I stopped him by raising my hand firmly.

"Whoa. Are you about to ask me out?"

Looking a little dumbstruck at my abruptness, he nodded, then squeaked a reluctant, "Yes."

"Right, come on, and round up your mates. We need to have a talk." Leading him out into the yard I headed purposefully in the direction of my cottage, indicating that they should all follow me, which they did straight into the kitchen where I sat them down at the table.

"Now, we need to get something straight," I said, still standing. "I've enjoyed the last couple of days working with you but for me that's where it has to end. I may be being presumptuous here, but I need to head this off now. I don't date and I don't want to be constantly having to watch my back wondering who's going to pounce next. I've never been used to this sort of attention and I don't know if it's because I'm some sort of fresh meat on the estate or something but it's got to stop..."

"But why wouldn't you want to go out with one of us?" Turner interrupted.

"Firstly because I'm quite a bit older than all of you...and particularly you," I said, as I looked pointedly at him. "And secondly..." I paused, not quite sure how best to get my point across. "Secondly, I have a whole load of shit going on that believe me none of you would want to get involved with, not least of which is that I've recently come through a divorce from which I'm only just starting to recover. The most I'm looking for is friendship – I can't do the whole one-on-one thing." I paused again, looking hesitantly round at them before finishing cautiously, questioning, "What do you think, could you work with just being friends?"

There was silence for a moment, then Carlton piped up. "I guess we can give the 'being friends' thing a go," and he grinned up at me. The others relaxed and the tension in the room dissipated.

"Okay," I said, smiling back at them with relief. "Now who wants a beer?" Going to the fridge I took out the bottles I'd brought with me, handing them out. As we drank we chatted. I'd found it reassuring that the boys had clearly not been aware of anything about my past. I'd been concerned on coming here that because of the background search carried out maybe everyone here already knew things about me I'd rather they didn't, but that was obviously not the case. It was likely then that the only people who did know were Cavendish, Grace and Trent and they appeared to show discretion when it came to someone else's business, for which I was grateful.

"What you've just told us does at least explain why you're so solemn. It hadn't gone unnoticed over the last couple of days," Hayes said, as he stretched back in his seat.

"I've not had much to laugh about for an awfully long time," I replied by way of explanation.

"Well, we shall see it as our mission to get you laughing again then, because even though I say it myself…we're fucking hilarious," he responded, grinning at me, his deep brown eyes, as richly dark as his skin, shining at me with humour as I smiled back and the others laughed.

"We'll be going to The Red Calf in Melton on Friday, it's our local. Would you like to come with us?" Wade asked.

"I'm not sure, I'm not really planning on doing any socialising," I replied carefully, still not wanting to involve myself more than I had to. They then badgered me incessantly, wearing me down until I accepted the invitation, then, thinking they were helping, reassured me it wouldn't only be them there, I'd have the chance to meet others from the estate too. Great, I thought as they left, just what I wanted, more people to meet.

As I went to shower I thought about the word Hayes had used to describe me. Solemn. It was a good adjective to express how I felt most of the time. There hadn't been much to lift my spirits over the last few years. The devastation I'd experienced at losing Eva had been compounded, cemented into place by the betrayal that followed until it'd felt like an impossible load constantly weighing me down.

I'd been at work one day, a few months after Eva had died, and had been asked by Barney to attend a meeting with one of our suppliers. I'd seen it in my diary a few days before but it had slipped my mind when I'd left for work that morning, and as I'd gone to work in a plain skirt and shirt, and as I was passing our house on the way to the meeting, I'd decided to call in to pick up a jacket in an attempt to look a little more professional.

I'd gone upstairs quickly, heading straight to my wardrobe. There was a full-length mirror on the front of the door and as I reached in the door swung fractionally and a small movement in the mirror caught my eye. I'd turned round slowly to see Alex and Amy looking at me in horror from our bed. The initial shock had hit me with a force that sucked the air right out of me; my mind struggled to fully comprehend, to fully believe, but when it did the realisation released a raging storm in me, which almost forcibly threw me into the next part of the grieving process – anger.

"You've got to be fucking kidding me!" I'd screamed at them. My pent-up emotion built up over so many weeks and months spewed out in a torrent of furious verbal abuse that I'd hurled at them. Alongside the vicious words, I'd thrown anything I could lay my hands on – they'd looked ridiculous as they dodged the shoes and books that came their way, both naked, both trying to grab clothes, fighting over the duvet to cover up what little dignity they had. My fury threw them out of the house and I was left shaking, my body reeling, retching as I vomited up my disgust.

I'd sat for a while on the bathroom floor, trying to get a grip on my emotions, but the anger had continued to rage through my body as I'd then arranged to have the locks changed, putting everything that Alex owned outside in a pile of boxes and bags.

I'd woken the next morning, after a bad night, and realised the true meaning of being alone. I'd always thought of myself as alone ever since my parents had died but now realised that even the differing levels of company provided by my various foster parents had been better than this.

When I was five years old I was placed with my first foster parents where I learnt a hard lesson. Unsurprisingly I'd been frightened and lost and latched onto them in my grief but was left hurt and bewildered when I was passed on after only two years to another couple. My perception then was that I was only being looked after because they were being paid to do so, not because they'd cared. From then on I'd seen each set of them as providers of a roof over my head and food on the table and I hadn't expected anything else. Suspicious of any sign of affection that might draw me closer to them, I rejected any love that came my way knowing it would only be taken from me again anyway.

Alex had been different, he'd worked hard to get close to me, he'd made me believe he loved me and that I could love in return, he'd made me believe I was everything to him. But after this how could I ever trust anyone again?

I'd known there wasn't anyone who would come to help me. Alex's family wouldn't. They'd never liked me anyway, seeing me as too strong-willed, too single-minded. Not the sort of girl they'd wanted for their son. I'd had the impression his father in particular had wanted someone for Alex who could be kept in line, controlled; someone like his mother, someone who I'd viewed as weak. I'd known they'd be only too delighted he'd left me.

Alex had come round every evening trying to talk, wanting to explain apparently, although it'd seemed quite self-explanatory to me. I couldn't see him, I was too furious with him. Amy had tried to contact me too but I never wanted to see or hear from her again; I never even wanted to hear her name. What sort of woman did that to another woman? What sort of woman did that to her best friend? What sort of people could do this to someone who was at the lowest point in their life? He was meant to have been the one person above all others who should've been on my side, who was meant to protect me, and instead he'd chosen this betrayal. Deep down though, I'd known my behaviour was the cause of what had happened and I'd have to shoulder that burden. I'd pushed him away in my grief and he'd turned to someone else for solace and although I couldn't begin to make sense of what they'd done I'd blamed her more than him – she could have said no, couldn't she? She knew he was married, yet she chose to destroy us and I hated and despised her for it.

I'd had to face Alex eventually, I'd known that, but felt I might not be able to control my anger at him. So several weeks had passed before that happened, and by then I had my façade in place. I'd been cold, detached and told him unemotionally that I didn't care who he was shagging – they deserved each other. I'd heard the spite and bitterness in my controlled voice but managed to keep myself calm as I told him impassively I wanted a divorce. He took one look at me and didn't bother trying to reason with me at all, knowing me well enough to know he would've been wasting his breath. He knew how I'd despised Sheila, my foster mother, who I'd seen as pathetically weak and feeble for taking Brian back when he'd been caught cheating on her, time and time again. There was no way I'd ever be treated like that. Alex had dealt with all the paperwork; I'd signed everything that was sent through without reading it, uncaring as to what happened to me.

Unfortunately, I wasn't as emotionally detached as I'd made him and everyone else believe. I was hurting badly, very badly. I'd lost everyone in my life, again, and this time I was without the support of foster parents. I'd hated the fact that people pitied me as the woman who couldn't manage to keep her child alive, or her husband faithful and I'd been desperately lonely and isolated with no idea of how to go about recovering or even if I wanted to.

The boys were back in the morning and after clearing the yard of weeds we spent the day painting the doors of the stables white and staining all the woodwork a dark brown. By the end of the day everything was looking smarter. Before they left we made a plan to sort out the paddocks the next day.

Just as they were driving out of the gate, and I was heading back to the cottage, a smart four-wheel drive vehicle entered the yard and I realised it was Cavendish behind the wheel. He stopped, got out and after raising his hand in greeting went round to the other side of the car to open the door for his passenger. I was already walking back towards them and Susie ran ahead of me, softly growling. As I approached he called out.

"Hi, Grayson, hope you've settled in all right? We've come back from a couple of days away and thought we'd call in, Grace was anxious to meet you." He bent to stroke Susie and I looked now at his passenger who turned to greet me. She was everything I wasn't: elegant, delicate and stunningly beautiful. Her long blond hair curled in waves down her back, tendrils delicately framing her face out of which she looked towards me with calm brown eyes that were lit up with the smile she shone at me. I liked her immediately, and she, too, bent to make a fuss of Susie.

"Hello, Emma, I'm so pleased to meet you. I know you're going to fit in here wonderfully."

Suddenly I felt conscious of how extremely dirty and awkward I was next to this vision of ethereal loveliness, although if she noticed she didn't show it, and I managed to smile back, assuring her everything was going well so far.

"At least this is my last day wearing these," I explained, indicating towards my overalls.

"Ah yes, we've heard all about those." Cavendish smiled as he said this, and I wondered, from whom? "The plan is to get the horses here in a week or so. Do you think everything will be ready by then?"

"Yes it will. We're sorting out the paddocks tomorrow, then after the weekend we have some deliveries lined up. I'll equip the yard and we'll be good to go."

"Excellent, it's all looking very smart already, so well done. We'll leave you to your evening then and I'll be back in touch towards the end of next week to liaise over dates for delivering the horses. Although I do have this for you." He reached back into the car to retrieve an envelope which he handed to me. "This gives you some information on the horses coming and their current feed details so you'll know what to buy."

"Okay, thanks, that's helpful. I'll order that in for next week, and look forward to hearing from you further then as well. It was lovely to meet you, Grace." I smiled warmly at her as they got back into their car, watching them leave the yard before turning back towards the cottage, Susie at my heels.

I knew it would only take a couple of hours the next day for the refurbishment of the yard to be finished. It had been a good week's work and while I reluctantly had to admit it had been much quicker with the boys' input I still couldn't help but look forward to the time when they would no longer be needed.

Chapter 6

Friday evening I showered and dressed ready to go out. I pulled on a pair of my smarter black jeans which I teamed with a white fitted shirt and my black ankle boots that had a bit of a heel. A short while later when I saw the red pickup draw up at the back of the cottage I went out to meet it, saying goodbye to Susie and making sure the cat flap was locked on the way out. The boys shouted out greetings to which I responded, smiling back at them. Wade got out of the cab and jumped into the back, allowing me to sit in his place. Carlton was driving and he smiled across at me as I got in.

"You look good, nice to see you without those hideous overalls on."

"Thanks," I replied as we drove off.

Leaving the estate we drove into Melton village, pulling up outside The Red Calf. As we went in I said the first round was on me for all their help but they refused, explaining that everyone from the estate who turned up put into a kitty so no one got stung with a huge round, which seemed reasonable and I was happy to go along with whatever system was in place. The main bar had several booths running down one wall with one noticeably larger circular booth at the back of the room, and it was to this one we headed. Carlton went up to the bar to get in the first round and when the drinks arrived and Carlton had slid along the bench to sit next to me I raised my glass, thanking them for all their help.

We'd barely got settled when the door opened and West, Greene, Young and Burton walked in and I started sifting through my mind trying to remember first names.

Walking over to join us, smiling and exchanging friendly greetings, they paid into the kitty then went to get their drinks before coming and sitting down. I noticed that Young made a point of sliding into the booth first to sit next to Hayes and suddenly had the unpleasant feeling that I was going to be sat there as some sort of horrible gooseberry because all the others were paired up – or trying to get paired up. Fortunately, as things settled down it became obvious this wasn't the case and we all chatted amiably.

Only four others came in from the estate that evening: Oliver Stanton, one of the gardeners, with Hannah Lawson, from the farm, who I learned were engaged to be married. Then later a couple of the other farmhands. I sat quietly, taking it all in and finding myself acknowledging halfway through the evening that this was in fact not too bad. I even felt quite relaxed which I found surprising, though realised, of course, that it was because no one here knew anything about me. I didn't have to endure the sympathy and pity that had surrounded me in Crowbridge. This really was a new start and I found that refreshing. As the evening wore on, and I guess as the others got to know me better, I came in for a lot of light-hearted teasing, both about the overalls and my run-in with Trent, which everyone appeared to have already heard about.

The pub gradually filled up with locals chatting and laughing in groups, but I noticed one man drinking alone in the corner of the bar all evening who spent most of his time watching our table, which I found a little disconcerting, though no one else seemed bothered by it. Later I had to leave our booth to visit the ladies, which meant having to squeeze past Will, who enjoyed it rather too much, and when I came back I offered to get in the next round.

I was standing at the bar waiting for the drinks when I realised the man I'd noticed earlier had moved round the bar and was now standing next to me – and far too close for comfort. He was taller than me, overweight, and I could see from the sheen on his face and his florid complexion he was uncomfortably hot, but despite this he wore a thick, shabby jumper over a checked shirt, the collar of which was worn. I shifted away a little and he noticed.

"Don't move away. I wanted to introduce myself. I'm Gary – are you new to the estate? Could I buy you a drink?" He appeared to have already drunk quite a bit from the glaze in his eyes and was close enough for me to smell the beer on his breath as well as the stale smell of cigarette smoke he was infused with as he stood before me, holding a half-full pint glass in his hand.

"I am, and no thank you. Excuse me please, I need to get these back to the others." Picking up the tray of drinks, I carried it back to the booth.

"I'll be seeing you again," he said to my back. Not if I see you first, I thought. Then I felt slightly guilty at brushing him off so abruptly. I realised I hadn't given him a chance; perhaps he was a real charmer, I thought, though somehow I doubted it. First impression: he gave me the creeps. I put the tray on the table and sat back down. Will looked at me, a little concerned, asking if I was all right; I told him that I was.

"I was about to come to your rescue but you got rid of him quite easily."

"He wasn't that insistent, so no problem," I answered, pausing for a moment before continuing, "But for the record, I don't need you coming to my rescue, I can look after myself." I smiled at him as I said this, softening my words and not wanting to hurt his feelings. Chloe leaned across then, telling me he was always trying it on with the girls, especially with anyone new, but other than being drunk and lecherous most of the time he appeared to be harmless. Good to know, I thought.

The boys dropped me back at the cottage at about midnight, Carlton insisting on delivering me right round to my back door, and they waited until I was inside before driving off. Susie was delighted to see me and we had a cuddle before I headed off to bed.

The next morning I'd left my alarm off so I could have a lie in. I'd decided to make the most of doing that while I could as I wasn't going to get the chance once the horses arrived. I was planning on spending the day food shopping and stocking up on some clothes. So, when I got up and was ready I drove off the estate and towards the nearest town.

I parked up, heading for the centre first to look for clothes. The range I owned was fairly limited, so I bought some lightweight cut-off trousers, shorts and assorted summery tops which I'd noticed were similar to those the girls had been wearing in the pub, and knowing nothing about fashion, ended up picking things that were not too hideous or uncomfortable-looking.

I then went to the supermarket, filling my trolley with the items I had on my list, plus all the other bits and pieces I found I suddenly needed when my memory was jogged by seeing them on the shelves. I was perusing the wine selection when I became aware I was under scrutiny and looking up was met by the still gaze of Trent.

"Hi," he said, holding a half-full shopping basket in one hand, a bottle of wine in the other.

"Hello," I replied, feeling a little flustered and blushing as I recalled our last meeting.

"The stables are looking good."

"Thanks, nearly all done now I think."

He nodded. "Did you enjoy yourself at the pub last night?"

"Yes thanks, it was good to meet a few more people. Didn't see you there though?"

"No, I couldn't make it last night; I'll probably see you down there some other time. I hope the boys behaved themselves and got you home safely."

"They did, thanks," I smiled.

"I'd better get going," he said, and as he did he held out the bottle of wine he was holding towards me. "Try this, I think you'll like it." After I took the bottle from him he turned and walked off. The whole conversation had been stilted and awkward which was perhaps not that surprising given our last interaction. I looked at the bottle in my hand: it was a Pinotage, a grape variety I was unfamiliar with, and my immediate reaction was to put it back on the shelf. I felt affronted that Trent appeared to be exerting control over my wine choices now as well as my work, but taking a moment, I made myself think more realistically – I was overreacting, he was only being friendly and I should give it a try. I wasn't sure why I reacted to him as I did but as I drove home I thought that not only did I not like being told what to do, I also knew he didn't want me there and both those facts were making me anxious and defensive.

The next morning it was raining, so making the most of the opportunity I snuggled in bed for a little longer before eventually getting up. After breakfast I'd decided to do a little exploring round the estate, so dressing for the weather and calling Susie to me, I set off out of the yard.

When previously driving round the estate, I'd noticed many paths leading off from the road into the woodland, so I took the first one of these I came across. The countryside here was soft and lusciously green. The woodland was open and in this part of the estate it was of a mixed deciduous type. There was a leafy canopy above us which let enough light through to the woodland floor to allow for the growth of other small trees, bushes and ground-covering foliage. Susie spent her time running between the trees, sniffing, exploring and generally rummaging around.

It was incredibly peaceful walking through the woods, giving me plenty of time to think. Perhaps dwelling on the thoughts that filled my head was not good for me, thoughts that constantly turned to memories of Eva and Alex and inevitably to their loss, memories that gnawed at me so that if I wasn't in a sombre mood already I'd be in one before too long. I'd have to work on that, I thought, try to think more positively. At least I'd not cut myself off from everyone as I'd initially thought I would, which was a surprise. I had instead started to make some friends, which seemed like a good place to begin. Maybe, I thought, I could get the balance right between the reclusiveness I sought and the socialisation it was probably more healthy for me to have.

As I walked and took in the scenery around me I realised I couldn't wait to be riding through these woods. With that thought in mind I decided I needed to visit the gym during the coming week to start getting in shape for that. I'd never really gained the weight I'd lost during the last few years so was still quite slim, probably too slim. I could do with building up and improving my muscle tone and flexibility, as well as increasing my stamina, particularly because of the hard physical work I had ahead of me so decided it would be my aim for the week ahead to go to the gym and set up a workout programme.

We were out for a couple of hours and I thought we probably hadn't covered even a tenth of the estate. When we got back to the cottage I made lunch and, having put off the gym visit in my mind until the following week, spent a lazy afternoon watching a couple of films. Trent called early evening to let me know there'd be deliveries of hay and straw coming the next day. Adam Porter, the farm manager, was going to call us to confirm the delivery time, and Trent would send over whoever was available to help unload. Before I had a chance to say anything, Trent surprised me by continuing firmly:

"Don't even think about objecting to the help offered, Grayson, there are three hundred bales to unload and you can't do that on your own, however much you may want to." Though a little taken aback at him being so direct I found this interesting – he'd pre-empted me, and read me well. I had been about to object but he had a point: three hundred bales was a lot, and it had always been my least favourite job.

"Much as I'd like to object to the offer of help, a trait of mine that you seem to have accepted, on this occasion it will be welcome, thanks."

"I haven't accepted it, and I intend on challenging it whenever possible," he responded shortly, sounding tired, I thought, and more than a little grumpy. "However, thank you for not arguing. I didn't need any aggravation from you this evening. Goodnight, Grayson."

"Goodnight, Trent," I replied. His formality made me smile a little, though as the call ended I frowned, thinking it was tiresome he felt the need to challenge me at all. I hoped he wasn't doing it because he thought he needed to test me, because he considered that I wasn't up to doing the job, and these thoughts left me feeling unsettled. I knew he was the estate manager but I wouldn't be able to accept him exerting his power over me with any graciousness. I hadn't accepted the authority of my foster father and the spirit I'd had then had made me fight back, made me stand up for myself. I wasn't sure I had the strength to display the same resistance now. While I'd tried my best to heal myself I knew I was a shadow of the woman I'd once been and I'd hoped life was going to be easier here, not made up of more challenges.

When I received the call from Porter I wandered out to the yard to open the gates for the delivery, being surprised when Carlton and Trent then drove into the yard. Susie was at my side, and as they climbed out of the pickup she growled, and although her tail wagged when Carlton greeted her, she made a wide circle around Trent, still growling before huffing a couple of times, showing her disgruntlement as she headed back to me. I quietly told her to hush, a little embarrassed by her behaviour.

"Bit short on numbers so you've got the boss rolling up his sleeves today," Carlton explained light-heartedly while Trent smiled briefly, his serious countenance momentarily lifted, before going to the barn to open the doors. Porter drove in shortly after, turning the lorry in the yard and reversing up to the entrance of the barn. He leapt out, introducing himself and another of the farm hands, who had come to help. I knew from the discussions in the pub that Porter was married with children and lived in Melton. He was broad-shouldered with floppy blond hair and had the sort of tan that comes from working outdoors all the time. He let down the back ramp of the lorry and pulled down the first few bales to make some room, then he climbed up and started throwing them down the ramp. The rest of us picking them up and stacking them in the corner of the barn. We had the straw bales on this load, the hay was coming later.

I'd forgotten how hard this was on the hands and could feel mine becoming sore. Years in an office had done this to me; no doubt a few months in this job would harden me up again but right now I was feeling it. When the lorry was about half-unloaded we had a short break and Trent disappeared, presumably to the pickup, coming back carrying a pair of gloves, reinforced across the palm and fingers, which he handed to me.

"Here, put these on."

"I'm fine really, thanks, you can use them," I replied, trying to give them back to him.

"Just do it," he said, more forcibly as he glared at me. Then he turned and went back to the lorry to carry on, as did Carlton, but not until he'd given me a big smile and a wink behind Trent's back. I shook my head, pulled on the gloves and went to join them. When we'd finished the lorry left and was due to return shortly with the hay, so I invited Trent and Carlton over to the cottage for a drink, pouring them glasses of juice which disappeared rapidly and which I refilled.

"I have a feed delivery coming tomorrow and wondered if I needed to arrange anything with regard to them being able to get on the estate," I asked Trent.

"The feed company knows to arrive through the farm so there should be no problem there, and they know where to deliver to. I've informed them they need to offload the feed for you into the barn so it should all be sorted."

"Oh…okay, thanks," I replied, a little surprised he'd even known I'd already put in an order, and I couldn't help wondering if there was anything that he wasn't on top of already.

Trent then announced that Carlton would be my backup in the yard whenever I had any time off. I'd not really thought long-term on this issue, and hadn't considered there might be times when I'd need a day off. I'd spent so long just working on my day-to-day survival, I'd forgotten the need to plan for resilience and this was now brought home to me.

Carlton apparently had the most experience around horses and also rode, so if necessary could take over the exercising. I didn't want that level of involvement from him so I retaliated, stating that while it wouldn't be required I'd set up the yard to work smoothly just in case, making it clear it would only be as a last resort. Carlton grinned at me throughout my exchange with Trent over this, which didn't help as I sensed Trent's tension increasing the more Carlton appeared to enjoy the situation. Fortunately, we soon heard the lorry return so headed out to unload the hay, which came as a welcome relief to the atmosphere that had been building in my kitchen.

I had a few things I needed to get done before the horses arrived, so after the feed lorry had delivered the next day I grabbed my keys and wallet to set off on a shopping spree. As I left the cottage I found Stanton cutting the grass in my back garden. He introduced me to Oscar Peters who was hard at work tidying up the front. I had managed to keep watering the hanging baskets, so felt reasonably proud that my efforts had kept them alive.

I set off, calling in at a stationery store first to buy various essential bits and pieces for organising the yard so it could continue to run efficiently should I ever be absent.

I then went to the country store and saddlery which was where the serious shopping occurred. Going round the country store section first, and bearing in mind I may occasionally have assistance in the yard, I bought two of everything, from wheelbarrows to forks and brushes. I also added a couple of fire extinguishers which were an essential in any yard. Turning my attention to the saddlery section I bought four different coloured grooming kits, head collars, lead ropes, an assortment of buckets, as well as racks and hooks for the tack and everything that would be needed to clean that. I'd have to see what the horses arrived with by way of rugs and then replace or replenish those as necessary.

Lastly, I went through to the clothing section and bought everything needed to kit myself out for riding, whatever the weather. By the end of this spending frenzy I was confident I had everything I needed to get me started and hoped Cavendish wouldn't be too shocked by my profligacy.

On my way back I passed the main gate, carrying on round the estate. Eventually I came to another entrance which led into the farm yard and, unlike the main entrance with its imposing wrought-iron gates, this one had metal five-barred gates which stood open, pinned back to the surrounding buildings, looking like they spent most of their time like that. I drove in to see if I could fill up with fuel and saw Porter, who waved and changed direction to start walking towards me. He showed me where to fill up and while I was doing that he called out to see who was around. An athletic-looking woman came out of a nearby barn and he introduced her as Georgina Summers. We had a quick chat while I filled the pickup and I ascertained she worked with the chickens, pigs and sheep mainly, but also helped out with the arable when needed. I'd learned from Porter that the farm was mixed and while it was mostly arable it also ran a productive beef herd and a flock of sheep as well as a small number of pigs and chickens to serve the estate. There was also a herd of deer, which I was still yet to see, kept on the parkland. Letting Porter and Summers get back to work I drove straight through the farm and headed to the stables. I'd brought a toolkit with me and taking this over to the yard I drilled holes into the walls of the tack room in order to fix the saddle racks and bridle hooks in place. Making sure everything else was in its rightful place I locked up. The yard was now as ready as it could be for its new arrivals.

That evening I opened the bottle of Pinotage Trent had chosen for me. He was right, much as I hated to admit it, I did like it.

Now the yard was ready I went to investigate the gym facilities. I'd hoped that by going early afternoon the rest of the staff would be gainfully employed elsewhere, and that proved to be the case, the gym being deserted when I entered. It was set up in one huge room; the walls and ceiling were painted white and the floor was covered in a laminated wood – it looked like any commercial gym. There were three or four sets of each type of equipment, which gave me an indication as to how busy it must be at times.

I picked out the machines I wanted to use, knowing that between them they'd give me a whole body workout, then put together a routine I knew I could stick to. When I came to think about it while I was exercising, it was obvious that everyone on the estate was encouraged to use the gym, and that all were apparently keen to make the most of the opportunity. It had not gone unnoticed how fit and athletic everyone was here and I decided I was going to have to put in some hours to get myself to the same level of fitness.

I'd noticed a punch bag hanging in the corner of the gym so I wandered over to that, thinking I might finish off with a few kicks. The bag, which looked like new, hung down on a chain from the ceiling then was pinned to the floor by another chain. On the ground in the corner was a box with some gloves in it, so I pulled a pair on and started warming up with a few punches. It was good to be back doing this; with all the activity in the last few weeks before I moved here I hadn't been going to my kickboxing classes. After a few minutes I slipped off my trainers and socks and started to practise a few kicks. However, after all the exercise I'd already done it was not long before my legs were burning with the build-up of lactic acid. At that point, deciding I'd probably done enough for that session I put the gloves back, pulled my socks and trainers on, and left.

As I was walking back Cavendish called to let me know the horses would be arriving early the following week, which lifted my spirits even further from the serotonin-induced high they were already on from the exercise. As the call ended and I looked up from my phone

I realised Trent had pulled up beside me; his window was open and his face was serious. When wasn't it?

"I see you've been wielding a drill," he opened, accusingly.

"Yes…why shouldn't I?" I questioned, wondering what could possibly be wrong with that.

"You could've asked one of us to do it. Why do you have to do everything?" He sounded irritated.

"Because I'm more than capable and I really don't need to keep getting someone else in to do these things for me. I don't know why you have to be so cross with me all the time," I retaliated, pausing for a moment then deciding I might as well air my concern; at least then I'd know if it was justified. "I know that you didn't want me to have this job, but I'm here now so you're just going to have to get used to it."

"Who told you that?" Trent questioned sternly, his eyes narrowing as he frowned.

"Cavendish, when I came for the interview."

Trent's frown deepened as he then spoke quietly: "Did he now…That was a little indiscreet. He was correct though, I'd have preferred to have employed a man in this position. I really do not need another woman to look after."

I retorted indignantly, "You don't have to look after me. I'm more than capable of looking after myself."

He looked at me steadily, his eyes widening slightly in their challenge, before saying dryly, "Then you'll be the first woman I've come across that is."

I gasped in disbelief, my eyebrows rising in astonishment as my mouth started to open but I'd been left speechless and nothing came out. Being unable to come up with a response I stared at him, seeing a darkening in his eyes at my reaction, his lips parting as if he was about to follow this up with some other ludicrous statement, but he must have thought better of it as with his final words left hanging in the air he was gone, his truck disappearing up the lane. I was left glaring at the back of it as it disappeared into the distance. I actually felt like I wanted to stamp my foot but refrained from doing so as not only was it childish, but I had the horrible feeling he might see me in the rear-view mirror and realise he'd got to me.

I couldn't believe he could have come out with something so sexist – it was almost as if he was trying to wind me up. As I completed my journey I fumed at what I perceived as his misogyny, annoyed that my previous high spirits had been swept away and replaced by anger.

Chapter 7

I woke early the next morning, early enough to see Trent run past and I idly wondered if he did that every morning. He was such an uptight control freak I suspected he had his routine and stuck to it, rigidly.

Today was the day I was finally going to meet the horses so I leapt out of bed, went to feed and let Susie out, had a shower, dressed in my jodhpurs and grabbed some breakfast. Susie came with me as I made up beds in three of the stables, filled water buckets and hay nets, and with nothing else left to do, returned to the cottage to make myself a coffee. As I drank this in the garden, I heard the lorry approaching and practically skipped across the yard to meet it. Cavendish beamed at me as he brought the lorry to a halt, turning off the engine.

Greeting me with his usual enthusiasm, my anticipation heightened as we went round to the back of the lorry to let down the ramp. I climbed up and ducked under the partition, undoing the lead rope to the head collar of the first pony, Benjy. Cavendish unbolted the partition and opened it up as I turned Benjy and led him down the ramp. Tying him to a ring on the fence I went back to the lorry and undid the second partition so Cavendish could lead out the next pony, Zodiac. We went through the same pattern for me to lead Grace's horse, Monty, down the ramp and finally Cavendish brought out Regan, smiling when he saw the look on my face when I first looked up at him.

"Magnificent, isn't he?" he said with pride.

"He certainly is...I can't wait to ride him," I exclaimed. Regan was dark bay and big, standing well over seventeen hands; he was a handsome horse with great presence and I fell for him immediately.

Cavendish went to tie him up, then we unloaded the tack, rugs and other paraphernalia from the lorry, closed it up, and Cavendish took it round the back of the barn where it would be permanently parked. As he walked back round I saw Trent drive into the yard, raising my hand in silent greeting, which he acknowledged by nodding his head. I hoped he wasn't going to be getting out of the truck as I did not want another run-in with him to spoil my mood. Fortunately he made no move to open the door. Cavendish came towards me to ask if I'd be all right as Trent had come to pick him up. I assured him I'd be fine and off they went.

I took off Regan's travel boots, checked him over to make sure there'd been no injury, then led him out to the paddock, taking off his head collar to let him loose. I wasn't going to get to ride him for a while as he was having a holiday after hunting for the season. I watched him for a minute or two to check he wasn't going to do anything stupid but he seemed quite calm, so returning to the yard, I took off each of the other horses' boots.

I was planning on riding Monty out but didn't think it wise to immediately lead out one of the ponies so they were going to go out into the paddock a little later, when I'd be able to keep an eye on them. I was too big to ride either of them so would be relying on leading them out or lunging them in the arena each day to keep them fit.

So putting each pony in its stable I turned my attention to Monty. He was a good-looking thoroughbred horse, medium height, light bay and finely built and I imagined his elegance suited Grace well. Tacking him up I grabbed my gloves, hat and stick, mounted him and we set off, out of the gate and along the lane. I'd decided I'd only ride him along the estate roads today to get him used to his new surroundings. He was alert, responsive to my touch and we set off enthusiastically. I realised after the first couple of hundred yards Susie was following us – I'd forgotten to close the cat flap. Initially worried by this as I didn't want her to get lost, after a while I relaxed as she stuck with us and got her exercise for the day as well. We were out for about an hour, returning to the stables unscathed, and as I put Monty in his stable I saw Susie disappearing into the cottage and smiled to myself – no doubt she was going back to bed.

I turned both the ponies out with Regan for a couple of hours, then after having a quick lunch I spent the afternoon organising all the equipment that had arrived before starting on evening stables. I groomed Monty, and then, getting Zodiac and Benjy in, groomed them too.

Once evening stables had been completed I stood for a moment, leaning on the post-and-rail fence, breathing it all in. The atmosphere had already changed in the yard; the evening air was warm and it now carried on it the deliciously sweet smell of horse and hay that was so comforting to me, that evoked so many memories of my past, of growing up alone but never lonely. It felt good to have the yard to myself at last, to work in silence uninterrupted by anyone else's demands.

I went to change and set off for a workout. I was already feeling calmer than normal, caused no doubt by the arrival of the horses plus the physically active day which the workout would add to. Since Eva's death, exercise had not only provided an outlet for relieving my stress but had been what I'd used as a natural way to try and lift my depression, being unwilling to take pills to combat it. That was why I'd become so focused on the kickboxing, needing to keep feeling the release of endorphins, training every day just to get that lift.

The next day I certainly knew I'd been riding – muscles I didn't know existed complained as soon as I got up, but I knew I was going to have to do the same that day, and every day after and my body was going to have to get used to it.

Gradually our days fell into a routine which filled the next few weeks. I enjoyed getting to know the horses and was soon greeted by their welcoming nickers in the morning. They were all good-natured and affectionate, loving the attention I gave them, with Benjy being the cheekiest of them all. He'd clearly been spoilt in the past as I frequently felt his nose nuzzling in my pockets to see if I had any treats for him.

I went to the pub most Fridays, the pickup arriving to give me a lift already loaded up with whoever was ready to go. Generally the girls arrived later, taking longer to get ready than the boys had patience for.

On one evening towards the end of June we were occupying our usual booth, which was getting quite rowdy, when I got up to get in the next round of drinks. I went to the bar and, while I was waiting, gazed across the room to see Trent sitting there, at a table, alone. He was leaning on his elbows with his chin rested on one hand, the other wrapped around his glass which he was staring down into. He looked so sad, the expression on his face desolate, and an unexpected wave of tenderness washed across me, catching me by surprise. As I watched him his head lifted, his gaze coming up to meet mine. Heat came to my cheeks as I blushed having been caught staring at him, but I found I couldn't look away and he continued to look steadily back at me, raising his head briefly in greeting. A small smile came to his lips, but it wasn't strong enough to warm his bleakly dark eyes. I smiled in response and as I did so I saw his expression harden, concern flickering across his eyes. I realised the reason for the change in him as I became aware of Gary sidling up, his beery breath giving him away as it wafted over me. I sighed, irritated, and when I turned to him he was leering at me through his alcohol-dulled eyes.

I'd put up with him patiently and politely enough for weeks now, but this evening I was not in the mood for dealing with yet another clumsy attempt to chat me up. He didn't seem to be able to take no for an answer so before he had the chance to say anything I glared at him and warned, "Back off," through gritted teeth. Surprisingly he did just that, shrugging and muttering as he retreated to the other end of the bar, temporarily chastened by my reaction, but I didn't like the look that came across his face when he stared back at me. I turned again to the bar to pick up my tray of drinks, taking the opportunity to glance briefly across at Trent. He was smiling now, and looked pleased, but shook his head as if he didn't quite know what to make of me. I smiled back, a little embarrassed, and took the drinks over to the others.

Sliding back onto the bench next to Will I told him Trent was there.

"Why does he stay over there drinking alone, rather than joining us?" I asked.

"He will join us, if it's only us boys drinking, but as soon as it becomes mixed company he takes himself off on his own. Some of the girls tend to start getting all gooey around him and he doesn't like that for some reason." Will pulled a face at this incomprehensible thought. "Though I suspect it's because of his marriage break-up."

"Oh…I didn't realise he'd been married."

"He never talks about it, and I know nothing more, but I believe he had a pretty rough time of it."

I thought for a moment, deciding to voice my own theory. "Maybe it's that, or maybe it's that he doesn't like women?" I ventured.

Will frowned at this then turned towards Kay and Lizzie sat on the other side of him, bringing them into the conversation.

74

"What do you think? Do you agree with Emma?"

Both of them looked back at him, bewildered by his questions coming out of the blue at them, so I filled them in on my thoughts.

Lizzie spoke up first. "I've never actually seen him with anyone, but then he is very private so maybe he likes to socialise away from the estate, but I've never had any reason to think he doesn't like women," she answered, seeming bemused that I would have found him otherwise.

Kay was of the same opinion; apparently he'd never been anything other than polite and courteous to her. Must just be me then, I thought.

I enjoyed exercising Monty every day; he was lively and I definitely had to keep my wits about me while riding, and when handling him. Sometimes I schooled him in the arena but the rest of the time was spent exploring the estate – there were so many different paths and routes to take that there was no chance of getting bored, although every chance of getting lost, as I found out on more than one occasion.

One such time was when I found myself riding round the back of the Manor for the first time and was somewhat surprised to spot a helicopter parked there. It was matt-black and bulky, not sleek and shiny like the sort of helicopter I'd seen before, but definitely something more like the military would use. I supposed that was only to be expected with Cavendish's background; he obviously gravitated to all things military. I'd heard what I'd thought was a helicopter flying over on several occasions, but due to the tree cover I hadn't actually seen it before and certainly hadn't realised it came from the estate.

Regan was due to start back in work at the end of June which I'd been looking forward to, but when the time came I found some of my enjoyment diluted as my anxiety levels were rising. The children would shortly be home for the holidays and I wasn't sure how that was going to go.

I'd not had anything to do with children since Eva, and I was concerned how I was going to react to them. I was especially worried about seeing Sophia and what would happen if she reminded me of Eva. I'd wanted to talk to someone about them, find out what they were like, but I didn't feel there was anyone I could talk to without them thinking I was a bit odd for getting all worked up about a couple of children turning up occasionally to ride. I would only be able to explain my behaviour by telling them about Eva and I couldn't do that. I'd never actually had to do that and I couldn't imagine having to say those words out loud to anyone; they brought a lump to my throat even thinking them. I was so concerned about questions being asked I'd even taken to hiding her photo in the bottom of a drawer every Wednesday morning when my cottage was cleaned. Of those that already knew about her, I didn't think I could ask Cavendish or Grace about their own children; it felt inappropriate and they'd employed me on the assumption I could deal with them; I had told Cavendish as much. That left Trent, and as I already knew he didn't want me here I didn't want to give him more ammunition by drawing his attention to my insecurities. So I was left trying to plan a few activities that I thought might entertain them and I hoped I'd be able to get through our first meeting without having some kind of meltdown.

As it turned out Cavendish and Grace had to go to a charity function the first day they were due to arrive at the stables so it was Trent who drove them over to me. I was feeling nervous anyway and his truck arriving only made that worse. He jumped out and walked towards me. Susie growled at my side as he came closer and I quietened her. He looked concerned as he watched me carefully and I sensed he understood my apprehension as he asked quietly, "Are you going to be okay with this?" I nodded nervously, trying to reassure myself as much as him, as I gazed anxiously towards the truck. The door opened and Sophia jumped out first. I felt myself relax as I exhaled; she looked like a mini Grace, delicate with long blond hair, and thank goodness, held no resemblance to my dark-haired angel. I smiled briefly with relief at Trent, grateful for his support, and nodded again in reassurance that this was going to be all right, my main concern had passed. He smiled gently back.

Reuben, who was eight years old, had now joined his sister, who I knew to be ten. He was completely different from her in looks, having dark hair like his father, and when they moved closer, blue eyes as opposed to her brown. He had a cheeky smile and was immediately distracted by Susie, who greeted them both with enthusiasm, and I could see I was going to have my hands full. The children were both now making a fuss of Susie, giving me a moment to gather myself. I'd been surprised at the sensitivity in Trent's question; it showed an awareness of my grief, revealing a side of him I'd not seen before, as he'd managed to check I was okay without me putting my guard up, without it feeling as if he was probing. As soon as I'd relaxed he'd seemed satisfied and hadn't taken it any further, for which I was thankful, and we stood comfortably together watching the children and Susie; then when they'd paid her enough attention they stood there a little shyly looking at me. Trent introduced us, and then, leaving us to it, returned to his truck and drove off. I smiled at the children and indicated towards the stables.

"I bet you're looking forward to seeing your ponies again."

They both nodded. They were quite quiet and I thought it might take some time for them to relax with me, and in fact, me with them. We went to have a look over the stable doors at Zodiac and Benjy and the children stroked their noses.

"Okay, let's go riding," I said, and we headed to the tack room.

"Now," I announced, "I have three rules." I indicated towards the notice board and one of my laminated sheets. "One, if you come into this yard you must wear proper boots. Two, if you ride you must always wear a riding hat. Three, if you want to ride you have to do some of the work involved with that. I'm here to look after your ponies for you but I won't just have them ready for you in the yard to get on. I expect you to look after your own ponies while you're here as you'll enjoy it more. Do you agree with all of that?" I questioned. They did, though were a little wide-eyed, I thought, as to what might be expected of them.

I carried on with a little gentle questioning of what they could do and we set to work getting the ponies tacked up. Both of them managed well, and once their ponies were done I tacked Regan up but left him tied up in the stable as I wanted to see the children ride in the arena first to see how confident they were. They led their ponies out, mounted and headed for the arena. I warmed them up with a few exercises then watched them go through the paces. They'd been taught well and were correct in their postures and in control of their ponies so after a short while I was satisfied they were more than capable of coming out with me on a hack and they waited while I got Regan out. As I led them out of the yard we were joined by Susie, which delighted the children. I checked back on Monty, who I'd ridden earlier anticipating I wouldn't have time to later on, concerned he might feel abandoned, but he was tucking into his hay and was settled.

I'd chosen to ride down a path where we could ride three abreast, with the intention of being able to keep an eye on the children but also with the hope of getting them talking. As we rode it became obvious they were less confident and able than they'd been within the confines of the arena. Reuben initially struggled to keep Benjy's head up as he kept trying to eat the grass and Sophia was startled, squealing when Zodiac spooked at a pheasant that flew up close to her, which didn't help anyone's nerves, and as I asked them more about the riding they'd done they told me they'd only ever had lessons so this was all new.

Once they'd got the hang of managing the ponies better in this environment the children seemed more relaxed so I thought I'd try to get them to chat a little, but it had been so long I wasn't sure what to ask and found myself thinking back to Eva and what had made her open up. I fondly remembered picking her up at the school gates, prompting her with questions about her day as we walked slowly home, enjoying her enthusiasm as she became more animated, filling me in on the parts that were important to her, that had stuck in her mind, such as the time when the best thing that had happened that day, in fact that week, had been that she had been the one to find a frog in the school pond. I looked over at the children hoping the same topic might work.

"So, tell me what it's like at your school? I've never been to a boarding school."

"We're not at the same school," Sophia replied, correcting me.

"Oh, is that because you go to an all-girls school?"

"No, my school has boys as well..."

"And mine has girls," piped up Reuben, wanting in on the conversation.

"So why don't you go to the same school then?" I queried, puzzled as to the reason.

"Reuben's school does a lot of sport and I really don't like doing any more sport than I have to," she answered a little dramatically, making me smile.

"Ah, I see, and I'm guessing Reuben does like doing sport?"

"Yes, I love it," he answered emphatically. "It's much better than being stuck in a classroom all the time, which is just boring."

I couldn't have agreed with him more as I thought back to my own school days. Although, as when I'd talked with Eva, I was fascinated by the enthusiasm they showed as they chatted about their schools and I couldn't help but think I'd missed out on something in my education.

"What do you like about your school then, Sophia?"

"I get to do more art and music – I'm learning to play the violin." At which point Reuben mimed sticking his finger down his throat and pretending to gag. Sophia leant over, punching him on the shoulder to stop him; I was hoping playfully, as I didn't want this getting out of hand. Fortunately, Reuben stopped after snapping at Sophia for punching him and before they had a chance to further the bickering I suggested a trot.

We returned to the yard over an hour later, by which time we were all chatting away and I was pleased to see Monty still looked calm. We'd decided on the ride to turn Zodiac and Benjy out for a couple of hours so once the children had taken their saddles off I suggested they jump back on bareback to ride out to the paddock. They both appeared a bit surprised at this suggestion – it was something they'd never been allowed to do before, but I encouraged them, helping them to get back on, and we wandered out to the paddock. There they slid off and, taking the bridles off, let the ponies loose. We all watched as both immediately dropped to the ground to have a good roll, then got up and shook themselves violently before wandering off to start grazing.

The children had brought packed lunches with them so we went over to the cottage. Making the most of the good weather, I spread a blanket on the ground under the apple tree and Sophia and Reuben sat on this to eat their lunch. I went in to make up a jug of juice and took that, some plastic glasses and my lunch out to join them. When we'd finished we all lay on our backs for a while looking up through the branches of the tree to the sky beyond. As I lay there I thought that this was going better than I'd expected. The children seemed quite happy and I liked them. I'd had a small concern that they might be a bit spoilt, coming from such a privileged background, but there hadn't been any sign of that, which really shouldn't have surprised me when I considered how down to earth Cavendish and Grace appeared to be.

A little later we went back over to the stables and I taught the children how to clean their tack, showing them how to strip down the bridle; then using a sponge and water they set to work cleaning the dirt off, then worked saddle soap into the leather, making it soft and supple. I knew it wouldn't be too arduous a job as the tack was cleaned regularly and as we worked I was reminded of doing the same with Eva, although it hadn't gone quite as well. Her hands had been too small and she didn't have the strength to get the buckles undone which she found frustrating, and I remembered her scowling as she struggled one day, refusing to give in and hand it over for me to do. As Eva had grown up I'd often taken her to the stables and it had become clear early on that she'd shared my love of horses. She'd started riding a pony we borrowed at the yard when she was five and I'd been so proud as she'd been coming along so well...I faltered, the warm memory instantly replaced by cold reality, tears springing to my eyes which I blinked back quickly, not wanting the children to see, furious that I'd allowed myself to drift so far into my memories. Forcing myself back to the present I smiled encouragingly across at the children, distracting myself by helping them reassemble the bridles and finish off before we went to get the ponies' stables ready for the evening. I showed them how to muck out and get the beds ready with banked-up sides. We filled the hay nets and hung them up, then I made the children put their hats on and we went out to get the ponies back in. This time the children put the head collars on and when I suggested they ride the ponies back in they were happy to, already feeling more comfortable riding bareback.

We tied the ponies to the fence and I showed Sophia and Reuben how to groom them from head to tail. Zodiac was palomino, his summer coat a creamy butterscotch colour which contrasted against his flaxen mane, whereas Benjy was the colour of rich, dark toffee and both of them shone under the care of their owners, who were just finishing when Cavendish and Grace drove into the yard. The children proudly showed them the good job they'd done with the grooming, filling them in on the details of what was involved. To finish off they put the ponies in their stables for the night and thanking me, headed off with their parents. Grace smiled gratefully at me.

"They've obviously had a good day," she said. "They won't be able to come every day, unfortunately, but I'll give you a call so we can synchronise diaries and you'll know what's going on from day to day. Cavendish is hoping to get some time off too so we can all ride together some days. I would like them to come to you as often as possible actually, as Reuben is already driving me mad at home. He keeps disappearing for hours on end. He says he's only exploring but he worries me sick."

"I think that's probably just what boys do but I can imagine it doesn't stop you worrying," I replied sympathetically. "Just let me know when you want to come so I can make sure everything will be ready for you," I added, smiling. They headed off and I returned the waves coming from the car, feeling guilty at the envy that rose up in me at the sight of Grace getting to take her children home.

At the end of the week I was about to set off on Regan, while leading Zodiac, when Cavendish arrived, saying rather mysteriously that he was taking the lorry and would be back later. I had no idea what he was up to but by the time I returned from my second ride on Monty, leading Benjy, the lorry was back. When I led the ponies out to the field to graze I was surprised to see a set of jumps in the paddock. There was also a set of jumping blocks and poles that would be ideal to set up in the arena to teach the children, as I knew they'd not done any jumping before. I sent a quick thank you text to Cavendish.

The children were coming the following day so I started getting the blocks set up so they could start by jumping down one line first. When they arrived I was pleased to see them head straight for the stables and get to work grooming and tacking up quite confidently. I told them we were going to start in the arena, so as soon as they were ready we headed in that direction, and I saw their little faces light up when they saw the colourful blocks and poles, although Reuben looked a little apprehensive.

We warmed up and I explained that although they were going to learn to jump we'd start slowly by trotting over some poles on the ground, and then I put up a little cross pole fence which they popped over. They learnt quickly, soon getting the hang of leaning slightly forward as they jumped to stay in balance with their pony. Before long I'd put up a line of small jumps along the fence and they were quite happy turning their ponies in and popping through those. However, Benjy, who was a cheeky little bugger of a pony, was not averse to putting in a naughty little buck or two which was a bit unnerving for poor Reuben, although he sat up, stayed on and coped with it admirably. Other than this behaviour from Benjy, it was a confident start I thought, and they'd really enjoyed it, laughing and giggling at each other.

It was nearly lunchtime when we stopped, taking the ponies in to take the saddles off. Before I suggested it this time, both of them were trying to get to the mounting block to get on bareback and because Reuben got left behind his sister at this point, he chose to try to jump on Benjy and managed it successfully, much to his sister's dismay. She immediately slid off Zodiac and then vaulted back on from the ground just so he didn't outdo her. Giggling now, they raced each other to the paddock and looking at them bouncing and slipping about all over the place, I decided we definitely needed to do some work on improving their bareback riding.

We had lunch under the apple tree then spent the afternoon setting up a jumping course in the paddock, and by the time Sophia and Reuben had finished with it I'd have been highly delighted if I'd managed to get Regan round it, it was so huge – I loved their ambition. I'd forgotten how it was to look at the world through a child's eyes, how from their perspective anything was possible, and I enjoyed watching them as they built their course as they wanted it to be, living in the moment and not taking into consideration the limitations placed on them by their abilities or those of their ponies – only thinking of the possibilities.

We finished off by cleaning the tack, getting the evening stables done, and bringing the ponies in for the night. Grace turned up a short while later to take home two happy children, who were chatting away to her about all they'd done.

The next time they came over I'd decided we were going to have a lesson in the arena. They started complaining when I took their stirrups away, moaning that I didn't realise how hard it was for them, and that it wasn't fair I wasn't joining in, so I went to fetch Regan out of the stable. They soon got the hang of riding without having the stirrups to rely on, and a short while later I made them tie a knot in their reins so they were riding round with their arms spread out to the sides as well.

They made sure I did the same on Regan, and in an effort to show them what was possible, I turned Regan into the line of small jumps I'd put up for the children the last time they came. It was a little reckless, not only because I didn't have my stirrups or reins, but also because I hadn't jumped Regan before; the jumps were too close together for him and they were also so tiny there was every chance he'd fall over one of them through not taking them seriously. Fortunately though, he behaved himself and we came out of the line in one piece, my arms spread out to the sides and the children cheering me on. It was the first time my blood had pumped round that quickly in a long time...and it felt really good.

This encouraged them to have a go, though we decided to take it a little slower. They both went down the line of jumps, first without stirrups, and when they'd done that successfully they went down again, no reins either. We all went back to the yard exhilarated by our morning's successes. This time when they took the ponies out both the children vaulted on and set off as if they'd been doing it all their lives. I was enjoying watching them blossom, their confidence already growing as they started to realise the extent of their abilities and I looked forward to the rest of the summer and spending some time in getting to know them better.

Chapter 8

It was already August and I was just finishing mucking out the stables one warm, sunny morning when my phone rang. It was Trent.

"I was wondering if you could help me out this morning. No one else is available and I'm going to need some help setting something up. It should only take about an hour." Intrigued, I replied that I could. "I'll pick you up in about fifteen minutes, if that'd be okay? Also, do you have a spare head collar and lead rope for each of the horses you could bring, and some baler twine? Probably a good idea to bring hay nets for each of the horses to keep them occupied as well." Even more intriguing, I thought. I assured him I'd sort all that out and he ended the call by adding, "Oh...and wear shorts." I could almost feel his smile in these final words which increased the mystery as to what he was up to.

It was already quite hot; the sky was a cloudless blue as I changed into shorts and flip flops then found the spare head collars and filled some hay nets. I checked everything was locked up, including the cat flap, and then went out to the gate to wait for Trent, although I didn't have to wait long as his dark-grey truck was already in sight. As he drew up I threw the head collars and hay nets into the back, then went round to the other side and clambered in. Trent didn't have a normal pickup like mine; his was a huge, great big bulky thing. There were four doors to the cab with back seats for additional passengers, plus a pickup back to it, and it was so much higher and larger than mine.

"Sure you couldn't have got yourself a bigger vehicle," I commented as I climbed in and we set off.

He'd seemed relaxed on the phone and now grinned while responding with, "Not my choice I can assure you. It comes with the job."

"Oh, and what would be your choice then?"

"Ideally some sort of classic car, a Mark 2 Jaguar, or something similar. Beautiful, but obviously not exactly practical for my way of life at the moment. How about you, or should I be guided by your choice of car in the garage? That must be nearly a classic anyway."

"Rude!" I replied, feigning indignation. "Actually, she is ancient. But I'm more of a Morris Minor type of a girl than a Jaguar. So where are we going?" I finished, changing tack.

"We're going to the beach," he said, as he grinned across the cab. He was wearing navy cotton fitted shorts that finished just above his knees. His legs, like his arms, were tanned, the hair on them dark, and his feet were bare on the pedals. He wore a cotton tee shirt of cream and navy horizontal stripes and with his tousled hair he looked more carefree and relaxed than I'd ever seen him. I was surprised, and not only by our destination.

"I didn't know we were that close to a beach?"

"You've obviously not explored the estate fully then. We're going there to set up a treat for the family," he volunteered. I was obviously aware the family were taking the horses out, as it had been arranged, but I hadn't realised it was for something more elaborate than an everyday hack out. By this time we'd driven through the farm, crossed the road and were going down a track at the side of a wheat field bordered to one side by woodland. Trent explained that while a good part of the estate, including all the grassland, was enclosed within the boundary wall, most of the arable land was outside the wall and covered the area all the way to the sea where a couple of beaches were also part of the estate.

A little while later the track turned back into the trees, which I noticed were now all conifers. These woods were more sparsely populated than those around my home, the trunks thinner and uniformly straight, the branches not beginning until they were well out of reach of the ground, it being more open and sparse of vegetation. After going a little further we came to the edge of the trees, out onto a small ridge where Trent stopped the vehicle briefly before looking over at me, smiling at my reaction. I gasped, whispering, "Wow." This was most unexpected. Ahead of us was a small slope which led down onto a beautiful golden sandy beach that stretched for several hundred metres.

At our end there was a small jetty built out into the water with a wooden building at the end like a shed, presumably for housing a boat. Looking along the beach, the trees followed it closely round its edge, but the line of them gradually rose until at the far end the beach was enclosed by a high wall of cliffs that jutted a little out into the sea.

Trent started forward again and we drove along the beach to the cliff. There he stopped and got out, as did I. I didn't quite understand what we were going to do next as we seemed to have come to a dead end, but Trent went round to the back of the vehicle and lifted out a toolkit and a bucket of something that looked like cement. I picked up the head collars then stood there looking at him, mystified. Trent tilted his head to one side indicating where we were going and encouraged me to follow him, raising his eyebrows and smiling with amusement at my rather astonished expression as he led the way, wading into the water, following the line of rocks out a little way to sea. The water was cold on my skin as it rose up my legs but the beach only shelved very slightly as it went out, the bottom remaining sandy. We soon got to the point of the rocks, turned round it, then followed them back in, making our way into another sandy bay. This one was smaller than the first and more secluded. The high cliffs followed the line of the beach all the way around and when I looked up I could see they were topped by trees. We made it back to the shore and put everything we were carrying down on the beach.

"We've two more trips to make I'm afraid," Trent said apologetically.

"That's no problem, it's lovely here," I murmured, looking around me. When we got back to the truck I helped Trent lift out a couple of posts that already had a rail joining them across the top. It was not particularly heavy, but was a bit awkward to lift; however, between us we managed to carry this round to the other beach. Lastly, we returned for a large picnic hamper, a separate canvas bag and the hay nets.

Once everything had been brought round Trent led me further up the beach until I could see a large entrance to a cave carved out of the cliff face. There was a slight incline up to the cave entrance so when the tide came in it would remain dry. I saw there were two holes already in the cave floor to one side, which Trent told me he and Wade had dug the night before, and into these Trent put the ends of the two posts, asking me to hold them in place. He retrieved the bucket of cement and proceeded to tip this into each of the holes, bedding the posts in place. I stood holding the rail steady and watched him working. He looked up at me a couple of times through the long, dark eyelashes that framed his deep blue eyes to check I was okay and that the rail was level.

"I've been meaning to thank you for your wine suggestion," I said to break the silence between us. He looked up at me, frowning with confusion.

"That day, in the supermarket," I added to jog his memory.

"Ah, yes, did you enjoy it?"

"Very much – I hadn't realised you were some sort of wine expert."

"Oh, definitely not an expert, but I know what I like." His eyes lingered on mine for a moment before he turned back to the job in hand. Once he'd got everything as sturdy as possible he collected a few rocks and placed these round the bases of the posts to help hold everything in place while the cement went off, then stood back to admire his handiwork. The rail along the top already had metal rings attached to it and to each of these I tied a loop of baler twine so the horses could be secured safely. I left the hay nets ready to be tied up when needed, putting the head collars and lead ropes on the ground.

While I'd been holding the rail in place I'd had a chance to look round the cave. It was large and the ceiling was high. As Trent worked he'd explained that this whole coast was peppered with caves that in years gone by had supposedly been used by smugglers for storing their ill-gotten gains. It was also said that some of the caves led to passages that went up through the cliffs and ended up in the woodland somewhere and that the smugglers used these to get their loot up to the village. The cave did seem to go quite a long way back, so once I'd been relieved of having to hang onto the rail I ventured a little bit further into it. My adventurous spirit did not last long, however, as while I didn't actually come to a dead end, it had all begun to get a bit dark, damp and claustrophobic and, starting to feel panicky, I returned to the sunshine quickly.

When I got back to the railing Trent was bringing in the hamper and announced, "This is one of Mrs F's famous picnics – all chilled wine, smoked salmon nibbles and tasty little cakes." My mouth watered at the thought.

"Mmm, sounds delicious," I responded. "What's in the canvas bag?"

"That contains towels, swimming costumes for them all, things like that, put together by Cavendish."

We were all finished, so waded round to the truck and drove back across the beach.

"That was a very thoughtful thing for you to have done," I said as I looked across at him, thinking that I was seeing yet another side of this increasingly complex man.

"They're good friends of mine and need to spend some time together as a family. They do too little of that."

"Oh, I didn't realise you were friends, I thought you worked here, the same as the rest of us."

"Well I do, but Cavendish and I go way back, we were at school together. We became friends one day when he was getting beaten up and I stepped in to give him a hand. Although that is not the story he tells of how we got to know each other." He grinned as he said this.

"I hadn't realised you went to the same school."

"Cavendish was there because of all this," he waved his hand, generally indicating the estate, "and I was there because I won a scholarship. We had very different backgrounds."

We were soon at the stables and, thanking me for my help, he then took a moment looking across at me as he commented, "We've actually managed to spend some time together without any acrimony – that's a first."

"I'm quite happy to come and help you out, but I don't like having anyone's help or interference foisted upon me when it's unnecessary."

"You're just going to have to learn to accept assistance more graciously then aren't you," he said insistently but with a smile. "Have a good day, Grayson."

"You too," I replied, thinking I'd better get out while we were still on good terms, and he drove off. I'd never

91

known him to be so open and friendly and it made a refreshing change.

The next time I rode Regan out on his own I rode through the farm and saw that harvest was well underway. There was a field of stubble running alongside the road which looked so tempting. I thought back to a recent experience when I'd been jumping bareback in the arena with the children. I'd been sailing around the arena, my blood racing through my veins, and I remembered how good it had felt, so I took Regan into the field, moved swiftly into a trot then a canter, travelling alongside the hedge, a blissful feeling running through me as Regan opened up. It was one of those moments when I wished I didn't have to wear a riding hat, when I wanted the freedom of feeling the wind through my hair. A movement caught my eye and looking sideways I realised a pickup was travelling along the road beside me. Wade was driving, Carlton hanging out of the nearside window grinning at me as I looked over.

"Race you," he yelled, as I pushed Regan on into a gallop, not that he needed much encouragement. Adrenaline surged through me, an exhilaration I'd not felt in so long. Obviously we weren't going to beat the truck but the boys kept level with me, whooping me on. I could see the end of the field coming up so eventually had to sit up and try to slow Regan down enough to negotiate the gateway. I shot out of the field breathless and laughing into the lane. The sound of my laughter was strange to me after so long yet I felt it releasing a tension within like that experienced by the compressed spring of a jack-in-a-box as the lid opens.

"Told you we'd get you laughing again," cried Carlton delightedly as he and Wade joined in with me.

"Well, you've not managed to get me to laugh at your awful jokes yet! Next time I'm bringing Monty – he'll give you more of a challenge."

"You put up a good fight there, Grayson," Wade said, then he looked up and his smile faded.

Carlton muttered, "Uh oh," under his breath and I twisted in the saddle to see what had happened to change the atmosphere.

Trent was standing in the next gateway, leaning against his truck, his arms crossed and his face like thunder. He stood up, walked towards the pickup approaching the nearside window, and with a serious tone to his voice said, "Don't encourage her in this reckless behaviour. I can do without having to pick up the pieces."

"Yes, boss," they replied in unison, looking suitably chastised. They glanced guiltily at me then drove off. Trent stared after them for a moment then slowly turned back to look up at me. Both Regan and I had caught our breath now and I was glaring at him.

"What do you think you're doing?" he asked.

"I'm only letting off steam – I recommend it. It might just loosen you up a bit," I replied, trying to be light-hearted, but I knew I sounded annoyed, because it was like I was being told off – again – and actually because I was annoyed, damn him. I'd felt so good and all that positive feeling was being knocked right out of me by his attitude.

"You assured me you could look after yourself, but you keep taking these risks so I don't see you making enough effort to do that successfully," he scolded.

"I work with horses, Trent, and there are inherent dangers involved with that. But I'm not foolhardy – I take calculated risks such as this one, that for a moment…just for a brief moment lift me to a place that I haven't been in a long, long time." I paused, exhaling my tension away, then questioned, "Don't you ever want to do something that makes your heart beat just that little bit faster, Trent, so that it makes you feel alive?"

He frowned at me. "Is that what this is about? Some sort of thrill-seeking? I get quite enough of that in my life thanks, and certainly don't need to add to it by careering around the countryside on a horse." He continued to look at me steadily, thoughtfully, as if weighing me up before adding, "You really are most unexpected, Grayson...Please do your best to look after yourself. I think that's about as much as we can hope for."

I assured him, most seriously, that I would, though I wasn't sure he believed me as I saw him shaking his head in exasperation as he returned to his truck. I watched him drive off before returning home at a steady pace, so Regan would have a chance to cool off before we got back. I thought through the brief conversation and wondered what it was that Trent got up to that made his pulse race – I couldn't see there was much in the quiet life he had here that would achieve that.

The rest of the school holidays flew past. The children came several times a week and we did many different activities: plenty of bareback riding and having fun, learning to play gymkhana games, jumping round a full course; the whole family even went off one day to a local horse show, successfully coming back with a few rosettes. Reuben had fallen off whilst jumping and found that small boys bounce very well; I'd fallen off playing gymkhana games and found older women didn't!

Eventually though, our final day came, and we went to the beach to take the horses in the sea, galloping across the stubble on the way there, racing each other in a way I thought might have Trent bursting a blood vessel, although it would have been worth him catching us when I got to see the excitement on the children's faces. When we returned to the yard we had a picnic under the tree as always and finished off all the jobs before Cavendish and Grace arrived to pick them up. The children had come so far this summer, learning to love and cherish their ponies, learning the joy that could be had riding. As they said goodbye, both thanking me, Sophia surprised me by wrapping her arms round my waist, hugging me to her. I was taken aback and tears came to my eyes. It had been a long time since I'd received that kind of hug and I was unexpectedly filled with a pang of sadness and longing I'd not felt so powerfully for a while. I smiled happily but when I looked up at Grace and Cavendish I knew my eyes were shining, my emotional state not being lost on them.

Chapter 9

Life settled back into its steady routine once the children had gone and I missed having them around the yard. Autumn progressed through September and into October and I watched the changing colours of the season as it did. It became gradually cooler, though the weather kept mostly fine and made for good riding, and the views around the estate, accentuated by the vibrant colours of the trees, were spectacular.

Trent caught me on the stubble again. This time I was on Monty and going considerably faster. He was travelling along the road while I raced him on the other side of the hedge. He didn't stop this time, but as he drove off I could see him shaking his head as I grinned, hoping he was looking in his mirror.

Some days Grace came to ride and we would occasionally ride out together. I found her easy company to be with, and to talk to. We chatted about the latest news from the children, and although I could tell how much she missed having them with her from the way she spoke, she never mentioned it, thinking of me and of how thoughtless it would seem. The more I got to know her the more I realised that she was the heart of this estate, that she cared for everyone on it and spent a lot of time and effort trying to make everyone's life that little bit easier, that little bit more comfortable.

It had been agreed that Greene could ride out with me if she wanted to on her days off, so occasionally she joined me. I put her on Regan initially as he was an easier ride, but once I was confident she'd be able to handle him I let her ride Monty, as he was better suited to her size. I found out she was relatively new to the estate, like me, having only started work a couple of months before I arrived. We both agreed at the outset not to talk about our pasts. She already knew I was divorced, and she'd come out of a painful break-up with her long-term partner that, like me, she did not want to be reminded of. She appeared to know nothing of Eva and for the moment I chose to keep it that way. Eva was a subject I couldn't discuss with anyone.

Greene was trying to start again, and with this common ground we started to become closer friends. Although I'd initially been cautious and hesitant about encouraging that after my experiences with Amy, I tried to put my mistrust to one side and over time found I enjoyed it; it felt good having female companionship again.

The horses were going to be hunted occasionally over the winter so my main concern was in making sure they were fit and ready for that. Their winter coats started to come in and I clipped out Regan and Monty in a full hunter clip, which meant they had to be kept warmly rugged up and exercised every day as they wouldn't be going out in the paddock.

Zodiac and Benjy became paler in colour as their winter coats grew in, though I only clipped them under their belly and neck to help keep them clean, adding rugs as it got colder. The ponies still went out in the paddocks for a few hours each day, and I spent a lot of time and effort changing stable rugs for waterproof ones when they did. When it rained it was a challenge to get the field rugs dry again for the next day and I seemed to be constantly rotating wet rugs for dry ones and adjusting the horses' stable rugs so they didn't rub anywhere, adding more layers as the temperature dropped.

With all the exercise I got at work, as well as my almost daily trips to the gym, I was feeling fit and confident about my body, probably for the first time. I'd toned up, but more than that I was strong and flexible. As my confidence had grown I'd invested in new gym clothes, now working out in three-quarter-length sporty fitness trousers and fitted tee shirts which were lightweight and considerably more comfortable. I tended to pull tracksuit trousers on over the top, plus a sweatshirt, and then jog to the gym as a warm-up, using the walk back as a cool-down.

One evening in mid-October I was late finishing work because the farrier had delayed the evening stable routine. By the time I hit the gym a lot of the people I usually met had already gone. I greeted those that were there, being mostly from the farm, plus Hayes, Carlton and Trent. Stripping off my sweatshirt and tracksuit trousers I started on the programme I'd originally put together, which worked well for me, although as time had gone by I'd gradually increased the number of repetitions.

The guys from the farm left when I was about halfway through my workout, and the gym was then about the emptiest I'd known it since the first time I'd been in there. I'd ended up having to leave the cross trainer until last this evening, as they'd all been in use when I first arrived, so I was on this and nearly at the end of my workout when I looked up to find Trent standing in front of me, watching. I could tell he'd been working out hard from the sweat-darkened patches on his grey tee shirt and the curls of his hair which lay damp against his forehead. The look I gave him questioned why he was there without the need for words.

"I noticed you hadn't increased the number of repetitions you do recently and thought I might be able to offer some assistance in putting together a slightly more challenging workout for you if you liked?" he said.

I felt my eyebrows shoot up in surprise as I then frowned at him before answering, "Are you suggesting I'm not working out hard enough?"

At this point Carlton came past Trent, clapping him on the back and muttering, "Good luck with that," before grinning at me. I scowled back at him then turned my concentration firmly back to Trent, waiting for his response.

"No...I only thought you might want to push yourself a little harder, that's all." Even as he said this I could sense his discomfort as it occurred to him, far too late, that he might be on shaky ground, probably gauged from the look on my face.

"So you don't think I'm fit enough? Or that I work hard enough? Because I do have a physical job you know, riding three hours a day, managing four stables plus all the other yard duties," I countered, and at this he ran his hands through his hair in exasperation and, I imagined, was probably wishing he'd not started this conversation.

"You do look perfectly fit enough...I just thought I would offer my help," he ended weakly, clearly floundering and at a loss as to how to go about extricating himself from this situation. Astonishingly, I thought I would help him out.

"Oh...you want to offer your help," I clarified, feigning surprise, as if I'd only just then understood and that this explained his interference perfectly and made it acceptable, then I thought for a moment. "There is something you could help me with actually," I added sweetly.

"Excellent, what can I do?" he asked, clearly encouraged.

"You could come and hold the punch bag for me while I get in a bit of practice. It's more stable that way," I explained, leading the way to the corner, pulling on a pair of gloves and taking off my trainers and socks as he took up position on the farthest side of the bag. I started by warming up with a few punches, practising moving lightly on my feet before warning Trent I was going to move on to kicks. These were more powerful in comparison to my punches, which no doubt he'd thought were feeble.

I heard yelled goodbyes from Hayes and Carlton as they were leaving and raised my hand in reply. Trent acknowledged them then adjusted his position slightly to take hold of the bag more firmly. I started with some front kicks and then side kicks, changing between the two, practising keeping balanced. I moved onto a roundhouse kick, slamming the front of my foot into the bag as I swung round. I was starting to swing round to deliver another when I heard the gym door open and Carlton yelled at Trent, "I forgot to tell you that I can make nine in the morning after all."

Trent turned towards him, distracted for a moment, answering that was fine as my foot slammed into the bottom of his rib cage which was now where the punch bag had been moments earlier. Trent exhaled harshly, groaning as air was forcibly expelled from his lungs. Shit. Letting go of the bag he put his hands on his knees, gasping as he tried to drag air back in.

Realising Carlton had already gone after hearing Trent's response, the door swinging closed behind him, and that no one else was around, I stood, frozen for a moment; then tearing the gloves off, I moved towards Trent, not really sure what I should do. Where he'd bent over his tee shirt had risen up, exposing the area I'd kicked, and tentatively I reached out to put my hand there. I wasn't sure why I did that, but had some vague childhood recollection of injuries being rubbed to make them feel better. When my hand touched his skin, however, it was as if I'd been hit by an electric shock and I gasped, along with Trent, and rapidly pulled my hand away. I stared at him in alarm. The effect of my touch had made him stand up quickly and he looked down at me, meeting my eyes with a look of concern, his breathing

could feel coursing through me, a need which had been dormant for so long. I'd been caught unawares, shocked by the attraction that had been sparked. I didn't feel like that about him at all – at least I didn't think I did. Though it now sounded as if I was trying to convince myself of something I hadn't even been consciously aware of half an hour ago. There was no doubt of his superficial attractiveness but we struggled to spend any time together without becoming antagonistic towards each other, so how could I be drawn to that? Clearly he felt the same way judging by his final comment. That was fine with me, I decided, as I had no intention of going somewhere I didn't want to go; even the thought of opening myself up to the intimacy of a relationship that would bring with it all sorts of emotional anxieties I was incapable of dealing with, filled me with apprehension.

My mind settled on my course of action, my resolve strengthened. I made sure I kept well away from Trent wherever and whenever possible over the next few weeks. I got to the gym early, did my workout and left. When we had to talk about any estate business I kept it short and sweet, well, apart from the remonstrations against anything he tried to impose that I disagreed with.

As November progressed the mist at the beginning of the month thickened into fog which descended over the estate. Eventually this broke up and the weather became dank, drizzly and damp, with it seeming to rain during some part of every day. Morning and evening stables were done in the half-gloom as the days gradually became shorter and on some days it barely seemed to get light at all. My time, and energy, was spent trying to keep the horses, and all that went with them, clean and dry.

The family were due to go hunting one Saturday and although I'd decided to stay in on the Friday evening because of the early start, Carlton had insisted I come out as it was his birthday. I didn't take much persuading but said I'd drive so I wouldn't drink, and could go home early. On the way there I realised how far I'd come; I was actually looking forward to the evening, something I wouldn't have thought possible only a few months ago. I got to spend a lot of time on my own with the horses, which I needed, but I also enjoyed having my friends around me and was really feeling I had the best of both worlds. I was calmer generally, confident I could do the job and that I'd managed with the children over the summer. I was looking forward to seeing them the next day, and as they'd both taken to occasionally texting me or sending me photos from school it made me think the affection I had for them might not be only one-way.

The evening turned out to be fun, as it always was when Carlton was involved, and it was actually just what everyone needed to lift their spirits with the weather being so miserable and depressing. Carlton was a popular person on the estate so almost everyone had come out to share a birthday drink with him, including Cavendish and Grace who had popped in early on. It was also a rare occasion as Trent joined in with the gathering, presumably only because of the birthday boy, and I'd seen first-hand what Carlton had meant as several girls were only too obvious in lavishing their attention on him.

As I was not drinking I'd been up to the bar several times getting drinks for the others and had had to endure Gary's attentions, which I'd brushed off, as usual. I delivered another tray of drinks back to the table before announcing I was going to leave. Carlton tried to get me to stay but I insisted as I had an early morning to deal with the next day. I made a quick trip to the ladies and when I came out, said goodbye to all and left.

Walking round to the car park at the back of the pub I had just got the key in the door of my pickup when from the corner of my eye I spotted the glow of a cigarette and became aware of Gary, emerging from the shadows at the back of my vehicle and coming towards me. Uh oh, I thought, this could be trouble, the prickling sensation on the back of my neck alerting me to the danger. He came right up to me, too close, and this time it felt intimidating. I recoiled from his breath which, as always, stank. He dropped the butt of his cigarette on the ground, grinding it out with his foot and started speaking softly.

"I've been watching you tonight, Emma, as I do every night you're here. I wanted to catch you before you left 'cos I want you to be friendlier to me. I want us to be friends," he mumbled creepily, slurring his words slightly and, bringing his hand up, he made a clumsy attempt to touch my cheek but I moved my head away, warily. I answered calmly, keeping my voice steady.

"I don't want to be friends with you, Gary. I thought I'd made that perfectly clear."

"You don't know what you want," he said, anger creeping into his voice. "You keep pushing me away, ignoring me. I don't get a chance against all those boys on the estate, you girls are all the same. But now I've got you alone…and I want a kiss from you."

My hackles stood fully to attention now. Fear trickled uncomfortably down my back like a rivulet of water and there was an unmistakable edge to my voice this time.

"Don't tell me what I do or don't want. You're making a big mistake if you think I'm going to kiss you. Leave me alone, go back into the pub and we'll forget this ever happened."

"I don't think so," he slurred, his voice sounding more menacing. "See, I've got you on your own. None of the boys are around to protect you and I think you'll find you can be nice to me…"

"I'm warning you," I said more firmly this time, pushing back the fear I felt, having no time for that now as my anger rose, "if you come any closer to me, if you touch me, you are going to regret it."

"You think you're too good for me…but do you really think you can fight me off?" As he finished he grabbed me round the waist, slamming his body into mine as he pushed me hard up against the pickup, lunging in to try and kiss me. I'd twisted slightly to one side as he grabbed me, in readiness, and now brought the heel of my boot down hard on the top of his foot. Startled, he moved back fractionally and I brought my arm back, aiming a punch and catching him hard, high on his cheekbone. Pain jarred through my hand as he cried out, both hands coming up to protect his face, which gave me more room and I clasped my hands together before swinging them round and into his stomach. As he doubled over I landed a double-handed blow to the back of his neck, bringing my knee up into his stomach, driving out the remaining air in his lungs. He collapsed to the ground, rolling onto his side as he clutched his stomach, gasping for air and groaning.

At that moment I heard the pub door crash open. Trent and Carlton came running round the corner, stopping abruptly at the sight before them: of me standing over the curled-up and groaning body of Gary. My breathing heavy with the effort expended, I calmed and turned my head slowly to look at them, stony-faced. Trent looked furious and I wasn't sure if that was aimed at me or Gary, while Carlton's look was one of astonishment. I turned back to my pickup to unlock the door and got in, starting the engine and rolling down the window.

"See," I said when they reached me, "I can look after myself," and as I drove away I saw Trent in my rear-view mirror, standing watching me as Carlton helped Gary off the ground.

I went home, checked the horses and calmed myself down with a glass of wine, finding as the adrenaline wore off I was left shaking, the pain now throbbing through my hand. I went to bed in hopeful preparation for the early start but it took a long time for sleep to come.

No sooner had my eyes closed than they were open again with the alarm, and the first thing I noticed, beyond my exhaustion, was that my hand hurt – a lot.

I dragged myself out to the yard and went through the pre-hunting preparations which brought more pain for my hand, particularly with having four manes and tails to plait. I finished by painting all the hooves black with hoof oil, which has, for me, to be one of the most delicious smells in the world, filled as it is with the intoxicating scent of excitement and anticipation for the day to come. But today not even that could lift my spirits from the miserable place they were in.

I was pleased that when the family arrived Cavendish and Grace seemed unaware of what had happened the previous night. I wasn't sure how they would react to me getting into a fight outside the local pub. Not exactly the dignified behaviour they might expect from one of their employees.

Cavendish eventually drove the lorry out of the yard, much to my relief, as relaxing a little I started sorting out the yard. A short while later, looking up from the door of the stable I was mucking out, I saw Trent, walking across the yard towards me, holding a bag. Oh, what now, I thought. No doubt he'd come to have a go at me about last night. I had to shush Susie, who was offering her usual greeting, then muttered, "Hi," when he got nearer, stopping in front of me.

"How's your hand?" he asked with no preamble.

"Not too good," and when he asked to see it I held it out to him, a little reluctantly, the dark bruises across the fingers now spreading down the back of my hand. He took it gently with both of his and I tried to ignore how that made me feel. His initial touch made me want to withdraw

106

it, and while he'd appeared oblivious to the charge I could feel running between us he kept a firm hold, appearing to have anticipated me trying to escape, carefully feeling down each of the fingers, over the knuckles, following the bones across my hand as I winced with the pain he was causing.

"Come with me," and leading me back to the cottage he sat me down at the table, bringing out an ice pack from the bag he was carrying and wrapping it around my hand.

"I don't think anything is broken so it should feel a lot better in a few days," and taking out a second ice pack he put it in my freezer before reaching into his pocket and bringing out a box of ibuprofen.

"How did you know about the hand?" I asked.

"I guessed when I saw the state of Gary's face." Then he sat down opposite me and asked carefully, "You okay?"

"I'm fine," I answered briefly, not wanting to reveal that I was feeling stupid for getting myself into that situation, angry that it had happened at all, as well as fragile and vulnerable because I was not as brave and fearless as I made out. I didn't want to say all of that so I just said I was fine. I don't think he believed I was fine for one moment but, probably thinking it was best not to probe further, he moved on. Although what followed didn't make me feel any more comfortable.

"I feel like you've been avoiding me recently." It hadn't gone unnoticed then, I thought, and I really didn't want to have this conversation, not now. "I wondered if I'd done something to upset or offend you," he asked quietly, he was serious, and I could tell this had been on his mind.

"I just thought…you know…after what happened in the gym I should perhaps keep away from you," I explained, feeling awkward and ignoring the slightly puzzled expression on his face as I said this. I changed tack, "Are you here to tell me off about last night?"

"Not at all," he said, surprised. "Why would I do that? You were protecting yourself. I'm only sorry we didn't realise Gary had slipped out ahead of you until it was too late. We should've been paying better attention. You did brilliantly, flooring him like that. I wanted to see you to check on you last night but your lights were already off by the time I'd finished sorting Gary out, so after I'd checked you were home safely I thought I'd leave you in peace and catch up with you this morning."

"I'm not sure why Carlton felt the need to help Gary up."

"I told him to. Having not so long ago been on the receiving end of one of your less ferocious attacks I had some sympathy for him," he teased, as I blushed slightly at the memory. "I don't know why you didn't just knee him in the crotch though, that's what most women would have done."

"He was drunk and therefore not that equal an opponent. I thought I'd better go easy on him and only do the minimum necessary to stop him."

"Very thoughtful...although I'm not sure he would have gone that easy on you had he got the upper hand," he frowned. "Anyway, the good news is it doesn't look like he's going to press charges against you." This brought a smile to my face.

"Now there's a surprise. If there's one thing I do know about men it's that their ego is never going to let them go into a police station and admit to being beaten up by a girl."

He smiled and nodded in agreement. "You have a good point there. As it is he's been strongly advised not to drink at our local any more so that should be the last we see of him, which is great as all the girls were fed up of him." He looked at his watch, before continuing, "Now, I have to go. Take a couple of ibuprofen while you finish off the stables and then rest for the day, icing your hand every half an hour. Keep taking the ibuprofen and it should feel better fairly quickly. I would send Carlton over to help you out but he's sleeping off his overindulgence of last night," he finished, frowning as if in disapproval.

"He obviously had a good time then, and thanks for the ibuprofen. I'm impressed you have these and ice packs so readily to hand."

"I keep stocked up, having gotten used to having to patch myself up after similar incidents," he replied jovially.

"Really, you have a problem with drunks attacking you in pub car parks as well – who would've thought we had so much in common?" I laughed lightly at having the opportunity to tease him.

He arched his eyebrow at me quizzically and shaking his head, got up to leave. "It's delightful to hear you laugh, even if it is at my expense. Have a peaceful day, and no more scrapping," he ordered, starting towards the back door. Then he hesitated for a moment, turning back slowly to look at me, adding almost as an afterthought, "And...don't ever feel you need to avoid me, Grayson."

Silently, I watched him leave.

Chapter 10

A few days later Grace came to ride Monty and when she got back asked if I was doing anything for Christmas. For the last few years I'd tried to ignore the festive season, in an attempt to protect myself from the constant bombardment of images portraying happy families filled with excited children. I usually chose to spend the day under my duvet, slipping into a painfully sorry state as I tried unsuccessfully not to torment myself with memories of previous Christmases I'd spent with Alex and Eva, when in reality there was no hope of me ever thinking about anything else. I'd assumed I'd be doing much the same this year. When I told Grace I had no plans her face lit up as she invited me to the Manor. They were planning on having an open house for anyone on the estate who wasn't going elsewhere. I accepted the invitation and asked what I should do about getting presents for those going, at which point Grace brought a bag out of her pocket.

"We thought we'd do a Secret Santa, so I'll put your name in here when I get back, but you can draw one out now." As I went to put my hand in the bag Grace spotted the bruising.

"That looks painful. I didn't want to say anything in case you were feeling a bit weird about it but well done for sorting that man out. What a creep. Henry is very proud of you, but I told him not to embarrass you by making a big thing of it."

I was surprised at hearing Cavendish's Christian name used for the first time, then, pleased they'd taken the incident with Gary so well, I replied gratefully, "Thanks for that, it's feeling a bit better now anyway," and withdrawing my hand, I pulled out a folded-up piece of paper. "Would you like me to do anything on the day, help with the food perhaps?"

"No, nothing at all thanks. You'll still be busy with the horses anyway, so all you need to do is turn up."

"Okay, I'm looking forward to it." I smiled at her as she turned to leave. Unfolding the piece of paper the smile faded from my face as I read the one word on there: Trent. Great, I thought with some dismay – the one name I could have done without pulling out. I wondered what the odds were on me doing that; then, for the briefest moment, a suspicion came to me that I dismissed just as quickly. I looked up to return the wave from Grace as she drove out of the yard, feeling a little guilty that my mistrustful mind had suggested she would do anything as underhand as only having the one name in her bag.

I spent the next few days wracking my brains trying to come up with something, anything, that I could get Trent as a gift, but only got as far as socks, immediately dismissing that thought – I couldn't get him socks. I was planning on going shopping the following Monday but it wasn't until late on the Sunday evening that inspiration came to me. I did some research on the Internet and the next day set off with a spring in my step, hopeful that at last I'd come up with something suitable.

I spent a few hours shopping, having decided I'd better refresh my winter wardrobe, such as it was, plus I would definitely need something vaguely dressy if I was going to be socialising on Christmas Day. I bought Trent's gift, had it wrapped, and stopped off at the saddlery on the way home to buy a small present for each of the children which I'd decided I'd give them when they came to the yard.

The run-up to Christmas was uneventful; my daily routine remained the same and the weather was reasonably kind. Apart from the occasional wet day, it was mostly dry and quite still; weak sun kept trying to shine through the brief breaks in the clouds, making the days a little brighter.

On one of the wet days I went out exercising as usual, having seen Young and Greene turn up to clean my cottage, being the angels they were. By the time I'd returned from my second ride out they were long gone and I was looking forward to finishing the horses for the morning, getting back to the cottage to change into some dry clothes and having a bowl of soup to warm me up. As I approached the back door I saw they'd hung from it a beautiful Christmas wreath made of dark green foliage and decorated with dried fruits, cones and frosted berries in deep purples and crimsons matching the colours in the hanging baskets which had been replanted in the autumn with winter-flowering pansies.

I went in, greeting Susie who was curled up in her bed sleeping off her earlier walk. Levering my feet out of my boots, I shrugged out of my wet coat; then shuffling into the kitchen in my socks, I was distracted by a glow coming out of the dark sitting room on this gloomy day. Going to the door I peered in, and there to one side of the fireplace was a fully decorated Christmas tree twinkling with red and white lights. Already filling the room with the scent that is so synonymous with Christmas it was beautiful. I sent a thank you text to all those who would have been involved and it put quite a bounce back in my step as I went upstairs to change into some dry clothes before having lunch.

Fortunately for me this year Christmas Eve fell on a Monday, which being the nearest thing I got to a day off, would mean I'd be able to get away for a few hours without anyone noticing. That morning I finished my yard duties as quickly as possible, then opening up the garage door drove my car out. I picked up a small bouquet of white roses I'd bought a couple of days ago from the vase

I'd been soaking them in, and after wrapping their stems in a plastic bag I checked everything was locked up, including Susie, and took them out to the car, placing them on the passenger seat before setting off.

I was making my first trip back to Crowbridge to visit Eva's grave and as I drove, although I kept trying to focus on the positives of my new life, memories of Eva kept finding their way through. Firstly, those happier Christmases we'd shared, particularly as she'd got older; starting to understand what was going on, her excitement building in the run-up to the big day, the early start on Christmas morning when she couldn't wait any longer to open her stocking. Then, inevitably my thoughts became increasingly filled with the darker moments of my old life as they turned towards the last days, hours and minutes with her, my overwhelming grief and the guilt I carried with me. Not a day passed when I didn't think of her, some days not a moment passed that wasn't consumed by her. I'd known what this trip would do to me. Known it would bring out the blackest of my thoughts, but what else could I do?

I arrived at the churchyard late morning and, not allowing myself to sit, did some tidying up, getting rid of the dead flowers and filling the metal container with water before arranging my roses for her. Though when I looked at them I thought the white against the black headstone was too cold, too severe, too bleak. I should have got red instead.

I'd started talking to her as I was tidying the grave, finding it easier to do when I was busy at the same time, and I told her some things about my new life. Things I thought she would have been interested in: Zodiac and Benjy, Sophia and Reuben, the beach…and the cottage. Until, finally running out of anything further to do, I sat on the bench, feeling her loss more keenly with her being so close. My arms, lacking any other occupation, ached in their emptiness, and wrapping themselves around my body, they held me tight. Tears came hot and angry down my cheeks and I found myself rocking, back and forth, as my distress grew. Allowing my tears to flow, needing the release of my bottled-up emotions, I sat for as long as it took, the tears eventually subsiding, the rocking slowing.

I stayed a while longer with her, reluctant to leave, though when I did tears came again; this time more gently, filled with the sadness of having to leave her behind, and I had to keep wiping them away as I started the drive back home.

My plan was to keep the horses in their normal routine on Christmas Day as much as possible, so I was up early to a frosty start that became a bright and sunny, though cold, morning, and carried out the yard duties. I wrapped up warmly to exercise and took out firstly Regan and Benjy, dutifully accompanied by Susie, followed by Monty and Zodiac, finding over time these combinations worked best.

While riding I tried to keep my thoughts buoyant and positive, only allowing myself a brief moment of sadness to think of Eva and of having what would now be my fifth Christmas stretching before me without her. I wondered if Alex went to her grave. There hadn't been any sign that he did and I found that sad. He'd already left me by the Christmas after she'd died and for the first time I found myself wondering what our lives would be like now if he hadn't betrayed me, speculating as to whether we would have managed to stay together, managed to find our way back to each other.

I turned Zodiac and Benjy out in their waterproof rugs, leaving Regan and Monty with full hay nets. Then dashing to the cottage, I leapt in the shower to wash my hair before quickly drying it and dressing in a longish dark purple and black flowing skirt that swept down from my waist, flaring out a little at the bottom, and a fitted crossover purple top.

I'd even put on tights, practically unheard of in my life, and black court shoes. Taking a quick look at myself in the mirror I added mascara. That was all I had available to try to improve the image staring back at me. I pulled on a chunky knit, wrap-around cardigan for the walk up to the Manor and got ready to leave. Susie was settled in her bed for the day so telling her I'd be back later I headed out the door.

I'd already delivered Trent's present to the Manor the previous week, putting it under the magnificently decorated huge tree adorning the otherwise understated drawing room. The room was large with high white ceilings and elaborate cornicing and mouldings with an ornate chandelier as its centrepiece. The rest of the room was decorated in off-white with a hint of blue. The settees, of which there were several, with chairs scattered among them, were of a deep Mediterranean sky blue. The floor was covered by a huge, thick, luxurious rug, intricately woven with a decorative display of foliage and flowers, in pale colours so as to blend in with the elegance of the room. The tree was decorated with white lights, garlands of silver and blue and coordinated decorations.

Arriving around noon, I entered via the kitchen where I was greeted with a great deal of activity and excitement. Dinner looked well under control and my offers of help were brushed aside, although I did then get to carry a tray of glasses through to the drawing room where everyone was gathering. Cavendish took these off me and grinning, he kissed my cheek in welcome with a "How's my little tiger then?" This term of endearment I took to be a reference to my recent altercation with Gary. I smiled back tolerantly, shaking my head at him as Grace scolded him affectionately.

"I told you not to make a big thing of it, Henry, I knew it would embarrass her," she said, then looking at me apologetically she also kissed me. There were already quite a few people there and as Cavendish set to opening bottles of champagne and filling glasses, I helped hand them out. Sophia appeared, running over to give me a friendly hug and she then helped, handing out and topping up glasses. A short while later we all heard Reuben approaching, shrieking with a mixture of imagined fear and actual delight. He was clearly being chased along the passageway towards us, a moment later bursting into the room laughing and closely followed by Trent, who grabbed him and threw him over his shoulder, whirling him around.

"I told you what would happen if you kept knocking on my door and running away, young man," his growling tone sounding severe, but Reuben was now giggling so much it was obviously all in jest. Trent put him down and he scooted off, probably to get up to mischief elsewhere as Trent went over to Cavendish, shaking his hand in welcome, then kissing Grace on the cheek. Cavendish handed him a drink while Grace apologised for her son's behaviour, although it sounded like that might be something she was used to doing to Trent as he responded with, "If it isn't that, it'll only be something else, don't worry about it."

"It's because he idolises you. You know that. It's all we hear, Trent this and Trent that."

"That's as it should be between us so it's no problem," Trent replied, then raising his glass to them he said, "Cheers," before glancing round the room for the first time to see who was there. He nodded at me when our eyes met and I replied in the same manner.

We mingled for a while, catching up on each other's news, and Sophia and Reuben came round with plates of nibbles which were very welcome as the champagne was going down only too well.

Grace announced we were going to open the presents so our attention turned to the tree, and the children were

put in charge of handing them out. I sat on the arm of a
settee out of the way and Sophia soon bounced up to me
with one that was about the size of a large, thick book but
felt soft, with hard, oddly shaped lumps in it. I opened it,
intrigued, to find a make-up bag bulging with products
which were all rather daunting, but I knew immediately
who'd given it to me. I looked up smiling to find Greene
watching me, and as my eyes met hers she looked away
immediately, trying to look anywhere other than at me.
Greene had commented on my lack of using make-up on
more than one occasion, accusing me of not making the
most of myself – whatever that meant. So I knew it was
her and when I eventually managed to catch her eye I
mouthed thank you, although she continued to maintain
her innocence for a while. I wasn't sure it was a present I'd
get much use out of, and I'd also have to discuss with her
later the fact that I had no idea how to apply the stuff. I
was sure she'd love to have that as an excuse to take me in
hand, which I wasn't so sure I would find at all enjoyable.

There was a lot of chatter around me now as presents
were opened and their contents shown to neighbours and
admired. I was still sitting on the arm of the settee, quiet
among the mayhem, when I saw Reuben hand Trent his
gift on the other side of the room. Reuben was obviously
keenly interested in what Trent had been given so stayed
close to him, watching carefully. Trent crouched down on
his haunches to be at Reuben's level so he could show
him. He carefully pulled one end of the ribbon tied round
the present to release it and then tore off the paper
revealing a small box. Lifting one side of the lid a little
way, slowly opening and closing it a couple of times, he
teased Reuben, who was trying to peer inside first and
whose eyes then opened wide when it was eventually
opened fully and he saw what was in there. Trent lifted out
the solid silver key fob I'd bought him in the shape of a
Mark 2 Jaguar and as he looked at it a broad smile lit up

his face. He was quite dazzling when he smiled like that and as I watched him show it to Reuben, explaining what it was to him, he looked up, meeting my eyes across the room, holding them for a moment, until I suddenly remembered this was meant to be anonymous and hastily looked away, busying myself in admiring someone else's present.

A little while later Mrs F called to a few of us, me included, to come and help her finish off in the kitchen, so we all got to work bringing everything to a head then carried it all through to the dining room. Everyone else was already coming through from the drawing room, taking their seats round the fortuitously long and elegantly decorated table. There didn't seem to be any sort of table plan so once I'd deposited my dishes of food on the table I looked round for a place to sit. Trent stood opposite me and having just placed his hand on the back of the chair in front of him, started to indicate to me that the seats either side of him were still free, but before he could utter a word Burton appeared to his left and Summers to his right, claiming both their places and hopefully their man, I guessed was their plan. He glanced at me a little bemused and I stifled the smile that came to my lips as he chivalrously pulled out their chairs, taking his place between them.

My hand was then grabbed by Carlton a couple of places down from where I stood, who had quite by chance got a seat free next to him, so I filled that. Greene was on the other side of him, which I was pleased to see. The dinner was delicious, traditional roast turkey and beef with all the trimmings followed by Christmas pudding and mince pies both served with rich dollops of thick cream. The wine flowed, as did the conversation and laughter. It was hugely entertaining, particularly being sat next to Carlton who regaled the table with such hilarious stories several people had to wipe away tears from laughing so much, myself included. Carlton turned to me later, obvious delight in his face at his success in making me laugh to such an extent.

"I knew I'd break you eventually," he murmured, leaning closer to me, his arm stretched across the back of my chair.

"It was impossible to resist any longer," I joked back at him.

"Oh, if only that were true...yet you seem to be intent on doing so." His expression became serious as his eyes locked on mine and I realised we were no longer talking about the same thing. I looked down.

"Carlton...I..." and I didn't know what to say.

"It's all right...I know," he sighed, whispering so close to my ear I could feel his warm breath, and as he pulled back his lips brushed my cheek, leaving the briefest of kisses in their wake. He gazed at me, his smile back in place but with a trace of sadness in his eyes. He reassuringly winked at me in his familiar cheeky way before turning his attention to the rest of the table once more.

I was a little flustered and pleased to see that our exchange seemed to have gone unnoticed by the rest of the table – although of course it hadn't. As I looked across I caught the look on Trent's face, his jaw clenched, his eyes dark as he stared at me with such intensity I had to look away.

Dinner was eventually cleared and after helping with this I was shooed out of the kitchen. I knew I needed to be heading back to the stables anyway so went to the drawing room which was now quiet and peaceful to collect my cardigan and present. I glanced out of the window and saw a herd of deer on the parkland only a short distance away, so I stood watching them for a moment, enjoying the tranquillity after all the excitement. I felt, rather than saw, Trent appear by my side, relaxed and with his hands in his pockets, as he too stared out of the window. He leant closer to me, saying quietly, "You look lovely."

I looked round at him, smiling shyly. "Thank you, I'm not used to being so dressed up."

"You look great. I wanted to catch you before you left to thank you for my present."

"I don't know what you mean," I said innocently.

"I knew it was from you as soon as I saw it. No one else would've been that thoughtful."

"No problem, I'm glad you like it...you're a difficult man to buy for."

"So I gather. Usually I get socks...or a belt," and he smiled again. "Did you enjoy it today? It was good to hear you laughing."

"I did, very much, Carlton is so funny."

"Yes he is...and he seems very keen on you."

I got the distinct feeling Trent was fishing, so shrugging, I replied, "Maybe...but I'm not capable of giving him what he wants so I'm afraid I've disappointed him again with my insistence on not wanting to get involved with anyone..." And there it was, I'd made myself as clear as I could.

"Right...I see...well, I'm sure he'll get over it." The briefest of smiles came to his lips as he said this, and I was not sure if he was still talking about Carlton.

"I must be off, I need to get evening stables done, although I'll probably float through the routine this evening the amount of wine I've had." I smiled as I left the room, briefly glancing back to see he'd turned to look out of the window again. I went to find Cavendish and Grace to thank them for their hospitality and left soon after to walk back to the stables.

I was feeling warm and slightly heady after such a convivial day and Susie was delighted to see me back. I changed, got the stables done quickly and with everyone settled for the evening, curled up to watch a film. Though I heavy as he struggled to control it, confusion clouding his eyes.

"I...I'm sorry," I stammered. "I was already moving, and you turned...I'm so sorry. Are you okay?" He continued to stare at me for a few moments, his breathing starting to ease. I could feel the charge crackling between us and suddenly I was too close to him, much too close. Needing to get away I turned, bending down to grab my socks and trainers, flustered, and trying to get them on as quickly as possible. I could feel he was still watching me but I looked down, concentrating on what I was doing, not wanting to meet his eyes. Eventually he spoke.

"I'm fine...thanks, just winded," as pausing he then continued quietly, "I'd hate to think you did that on purpose though."

I looked up at him, alarmed that he thought I might have done that, but he had a look of amusement now across his face, clearly teasing me.

"If I'd meant it, you'd no longer be standing," I replied with a smile, managing to relax slightly.

"Always so challenging, Grayson," he said as he tenderly felt his ribs, wincing slightly.

"Do you need me to do anything before I go?" I asked, feeling awkward.

"I don't need you to touch me again, that's for certain," he muttered darkly as I blushed with embarrassment. He made a move to pick up his things so I didn't think I could just walk out, and we ended up leaving the gym together, albeit as quickly as possible, awkwardly mumbling our goodbyes.

He wandered off in the direction of wherever it was he lived and I set off home. On the walk, and feeling shaken, I tried to process my thoughts. What the hell had just happened? I was confused by what I'd felt when I touched Trent, by what I could only describe as an awakening...an awakening in my body to a primal need that even now I had difficulty concentrating on it – my thoughts kept returning to my conversation with Trent. There was no doubt my feelings towards him were getting confused and I didn't want that in my life. I'd been adamant when I'd come here that I wasn't going to let anyone close to me and reasoning with myself now I decided that just because I felt a physical attraction towards him that wasn't a good enough reason to risk the chance of being hurt again – my wounds were barely healed from last time.

Chapter 11

A few days later I rode out one frosty morning with Grace and the children. Sophia and Reuben were lagging behind and Grace and I were discussing the events of Christmas Day. I mentioned the banter between Trent and Reuben and how well they got on and Grace explained.

"He's good with both the children. He's their godfather and takes his responsibilities very seriously."

"I hadn't realised that, you're obviously very close to him then."

Grace turned to me, saying earnestly, as if trying to convince me of something, "Trent's a good man and our best friend. We owe him everything." I frowned, a little surprised by her candour.

"Do you mind if I ask what you mean by 'everything'?" I queried, and she looked a little flustered.

"I'm sorry, I've spoken out of turn, I'd better leave it there. He's also a very private man and wouldn't appreciate me telling you. It's his story after all and, if and when it's appropriate, no doubt he'll tell you of our history. I'm just so fond of him and want him to find happiness so much that I get a little carried away sometimes. Forgive me, I shouldn't have been so gossipy."

I smiled at her. "Not a problem, you're hardly a gossip. Actually I'm starting to get cold so we'd better get everyone moving a bit quicker." I called to the children to indicate that we were going to trot. I thought it was probably wise to move off the subject of Trent with Grace. I hoped she wasn't pinning her hopes on him finding happiness with me; for one horrible moment I'd thought she was going to ask me what I thought of him and I wouldn't have known what to say. It wasn't clear in my own mind what I thought of him anymore. My head was telling me one thing but the truth was that my heart was starting to tell me something very different.

When we got back to the stables and had put the horses away, I gave the children their presents. I'd bought them both an equestrian multi-tool, which was a hoof pick that folded in half so it was safe to carry when riding and there was also built into the handle a small, single blade that folded into it like a penknife, to be used presumably for cutting such things as baler twine. It was a useful tool to carry when out riding and they were both very pleased and even more delighted when they found they fitted into the small pockets in their jodhpurs.

The weather turned icily cold when the children had gone back to school which made everyday life that little bit more difficult to deal with, as all types of bad weather does when caring for animals. Although I didn't have to spend time trying to get the rugs dry every day, I did, however, have to go out to the paddock to smash through the ice in the water trough, spread salt round the yard and carry hay out to the field.

My birthday was due to fall on a Monday, although no one knew about it, and I had no plans to acknowledge it in any way. Alex had made the effort to contact me each year, which I hadn't exactly welcomed, and I wondered for the first time when, or even if, he'd found out I'd moved and what he would make of that.

I'd woken to another dark and frosty morning which always made it a bit difficult for me to get going. I carried out my routine jobs but unusually rode out twice as the family had been hunting on the Saturday, so the horses had had their rest day on the Sunday instead. It was still bitterly cold when I finished my morning's work, even though it was now quite bright, and I was looking forward to having soup for lunch to warm me up. I'd had to take some hay out for the ponies and break the ice on the trough again and now went back to the cottage, rubbing my hands together to try and warm them up.

Sighing with relief when I walked into my toasty, warm kitchen, I stopped with a start when I saw there was a bouquet of flowers next to a hamper on the table. Opening the basket there was a flask, which on examination contained hot tomato soup, and next to the flask a couple of still-warm rolls. There was a container of some sort of chicken casserole and at the bottom was a large box in which there was a Victoria sandwich cake with 'Happy Birthday' written in icing across the top. I looked at that for a moment, my eyes narrowing in thought.

A few minutes later, having put the flowers in a vase and placed that back on the table, I was sitting eating the soup and rolls, both delicious, when there was a knock at the door. Susie started her low growl and when I yelled, "Come in," Trent entered. He frowned at Susie, who I told to be quiet, and looked over at me.

"Happy birthday."

"Ah, it was you who tipped them off – my background search," as the pieces fell into place and I showed him what had magically arrived in my cottage.

"Excellent," he said, then corrected me. "And it was your CV actually. Here's a little something to add to your day." He handed me a small package wrapped in a matt-silver paper with a curly shiny pattern running through it.

"Oh!" I exclaimed, a little surprised as I felt myself blushing. "This is unexpected."

"I wasn't sure if you would have something to open today, so I thought after my lovely gift at Christmas…" and he held up his hand with the keys hanging off one finger showing me the key fob attached, "I should reciprocate."

I unwrapped the present, carefully lifting the lid on the box within to find a pretty set of necklace and earrings. There was a silver flower hanging from the necklace made up of five petals which had a slight sparkle to them and were curled realistically to resemble a real flower, and hanging below the flower were three warm, deep red gems. The flowers on the earrings were much smaller, being just large enough to cover an earlobe, and had one matching gem hanging from them.

"How beautiful, Trent, thank you."

"They are garnets, your birthstone," he explained.

"Oh, I didn't know I had such a thing."

"Ah, well you do, although I'm not sure they're quite the thing to wear with jeans and tee shirts but maybe someday it will be the right time and place for you to put them on."

"Mmm...." I murmured thoughtfully, then looking up at him I asked, "Would you like to join me for lunch? It's only soup but it is Mrs F's soup and there's a lot left."

"Sounds good, thanks," and with that I took another bowl out of the cupboard and poured some soup into it while he took a seat at the table.

"Help yourself to a roll."

We chatted as we ate about inconsequential things and I enjoyed having the company, which was an unexpected feeling. Leaving after lunch and taking a piece of cake with him, I had to admit he made for interesting company; he was a complex character I found difficult to read which, rather than irritating me, I was finding rather fascinating.

I knew practically nothing about him; however, I did know I was letting him get too close to me which made me anxious. He'd shown he could be kind and thoughtful, but that was the nature of this place, and I knew I shouldn't read anything into it – he probably treated everyone else here like that as well. I also knew he could be intimidating, controlling and frequently infuriating, but I couldn't deny there was something between us, some sort of pull that was confusing me.

Why I was even spending time thinking about this I didn't know. What I felt was irrelevant considering the fact that he'd not given me any indication he might feel the same. In fact quite the opposite, he seemed to be unaffected by my presence, continuing to project the same appearance of cool, calm self-assurance, unruffled by anything or anyone around him. Even when we'd clashed he was always in control, which had tended to make me become even more annoyed with him.

As it happened both he and Cavendish were then away for a few weeks, doing whatever it was that they did, so I chose to ignore how confused I was by my feelings, burying my head in my work in the hope it would all just go away.

At the end of February, Cavendish had been back for a week or so and the whole family had gone hunting. The day had started damp and miserable and as it wore on the chill came down and they were cold and tired when they got back. After unloading I herded them all off home while I sorted the horses out, and once they were all eating and settled, I went in to watch some television.

I went out later to do the watering, wrapping up warmly as the temperature had dropped considerably, and as soon as I looked over Monty's stable door I knew I had a problem. He'd broken out in a sweat and kept looking round at his abdomen; I could see he'd been pawing at the ground and had already rolled as his bed was a mess. I was sure he had colic and would need the vet. Quickly checking on the others to make sure they were all fine, I then grabbed a head collar, returned to Monty and slipped it on, speaking softly to him as I did, trying to reassure him. Leading him out of the box I started walking him round the yard to keep him moving and prevent him from rolling. With my free hand I called the vet's surgery and went through to the emergency cover, where speaking to the vet on call I explained the symptoms to him. I thought the colic had most likely been brought on by the excitement and exertion of hunting that day; the vet agreed that it was most likely to be the cause but he confirmed he'd come out immediately and, after making sure he knew his way through the farm, I hung up and concentrated on Monty.

The vet arrived within half an hour and quickly assessed Monty's condition. He diagnosed it as spasmodic colic and gave Monty a muscle relaxant, suggesting I walk him round a little longer and then, once he seemed easier, put him back in his stable and watch him to make sure he continued to improve. If he didn't I was to call him again. I said I'd stay in the stable with Monty for the night, so he agreed to call later and see how I was getting on, and with that he left.

Monty and I walked round for another half an hour by which time he was quite calm. After tying him to the fence I quickly straightened his bed, adding more straw to make sure it was thick, banking the sides up high. I put him back in his stable then went to get a change of rugs, and using handfuls of straw that I twisted then folded round to make into a pad, I gave him a quick rub down where he'd been sweating, before changing his rugs so he'd be warm, dry and as comfortable as possible. He was more settled already, but I watched him for a good half an hour more before quickly going over to the cottage to make myself a flask of strong coffee, then returning to the yard.

I'd pulled on every bit of warm clothing I had but it was a cold night and I was already feeling it. Getting Regan's spare extra-warm quilted rug from the tack room and turning out the light, I snuggled myself up inside it in the corner of Monty's box drinking my coffee, with Susie tucked in next to me.

It was, by this time, already past midnight. Fortunately the sky was clear and the moon bright which gave me all the light I needed to keep an eye on Monty. Unfortunately, because of the same conditions, a harsh frost came down so that by the morning it was bitingly cold. The vet had called around three and I'd reported that all was well. I'd been getting up every hour or so to check Monty hadn't broken out in a sweat again, continuing this until about six. By then he was happily pulling at the hay in his hay net and with his appetite restored I was reassured he would now be fine.

I left the stable, going to the cottage to put the kettle on, planning on making Monty a bran mash for his breakfast so as to be as gentle on his stomach as possible. Once the kettle was boiling I took it over to the yard, putting on the lights and checking the others. I was starting my routine earlier than normal which was brought home to me when I looked up to see Trent in his running sweats coming across the yard towards me.

"Morning, you're up early, is everything all right?" he said as he reached me, looking at me curiously as I suddenly realised I was probably dreadfully dishevelled. I tried to smooth my hair down but found I was having to remove bits of straw from it first.

"It's all fine now but I didn't actually make it to bed last night," and I explained what had happened to Monty, finishing with, "He's okay now though, so I thought I'd get started on morning stables and plough on from there." I glanced back at him, surprised to see that he looked furious.

"Why the hell didn't you call for help?" he exclaimed loudly, incredulously. "I can't believe you've been out here all night on your own, anything could've happened to you – it's a completely ridiculous thing to have done! Why are you so fiercely independent, Grayson? You are infuriating!" Running his hands through his hair he glared at me in exasperation.

I could feel my anger building, fury accelerating through my veins as these words were thrown at me. I'd done everything I needed to do and I'd done a good job. Why couldn't he see that I didn't need anyone else's help? As well as being furious I was also tired and emotional which was why I exploded back at him, "I'm fiercely independent, as you put it, because that's what I've had to learn to be – it's the only way I can protect myself. I don't need anything from anyone, and I don't want to let anyone get near enough to me to hurt me again."

Trent paused for a moment. I thought it was in shock at my outburst and he was looking at me in bewilderment as I stood there glaring at him, though feeling dangerously close to having angry tears cascading down my face at any moment.

"I'd love to get my hands on whoever it was that did this to you," he grumbled before becoming decisive. "Right, I'm calling Carlton, he can come and finish morning stables. You can finish the feeding, by which time he will be here. You are then to go, have breakfast, get cleaned up and get some sleep. I do not want any argument about it and I do not want to see you on this yard again until afternoon stables, do you understand?"

I paused for a long moment then muttered, "I understand," in sulky agreement. I put a quick call through to the vet to let them know Monty was fine before finishing off the feeding, watched silently by Trent. Then Carlton arrived.

"God, you look like hell. That's what happens, missy, if you will insist on staying up all night. If you'd spent the night with me instead, at least I'd have let you get some sleep, being the gentleman I am," he joked, admonishing me gently, and as Trent glared at him I rolled my eyes and laughed lightly; he really couldn't help himself and at least it eased the tension in the yard, although it seemed not between him and Trent.

Fortunately, there was no exercising to be done, so Carlton could manage. I gave him instructions for each horse to be led out and walked round the arena for half an hour apart from Monty who was to stay in his box. Regan needed to have his legs hosed as they were slightly filled and these needed to be dried before he was put away again. Once I was satisfied Carlton could deal with all these details I headed off for some breakfast before having a very welcome shower and collapsing, gratefully, into bed.

When I woke it was early afternoon, and on going downstairs I found lunch already made for me on the table, probably by the wonderful Mrs F, together with a bottle of champagne and a note from Cavendish and Grace thanking me for my previous night's efforts. Well, at least they appreciated me, I thought as I put the bottle in the fridge, and then turned my attention to lunch, realising I was famished.

I went out late afternoon to do the stables after texting Carlton to let him know I was up and to thank him for everything he'd done in the morning. I was in the middle of filling hay nets when Trent arrived.

"Did you manage to get some sleep?" he demanded.

"Yes thank you, I feel fine now," I replied a little mutinously.

"Good. Now I think it would be a good idea if we went out for a drink together sometime. Would that be all right with you?"

I was taken aback at his directness.

"Thanks for the invite, but I'm sorry I don't date."

"I wasn't asking you out on a date, Grayson," he replied bluntly, and feeling myself flush with embarrassment I felt foolish – of course he wasn't asking me out on a date, what was I thinking, how arrogant of me to think that he was.

I closed my eyes in disbelief that I'd made such an idiot of myself, and I knew I was blushing furiously as I stammered, "S…sorry, my mistake. I just assumed…" and I trailed off, not knowing how to continue. I couldn't even look up at him as I knew he'd be watching me steadily as always, coolly in control, and unaffected.

"Don't assume – not everyone wants to go out with you," he added, unnecessarily harshly I thought. I was hoping the ground would open up beneath me and put me out of my misery but unfortunately it stubbornly remained as solid as ever as he then continued in a gentler, more conciliatory tone: "Look, we clearly have some difficulties in working together and I thought if we maybe spent some time together in a social setting we might find a way of getting along at work better. What do you think?"

I mumbled my agreement with this, wanting the whole horrible incident to be over and as he was going to be away again for a while he said he'd call me when he knew he would be back to arrange the details.

It was actually nearly the middle of March before he called. I'd hoped he'd forgotten all about it but sadly not. He was due back that evening and said he'd call to collect me. As it was, I heard the helicopter flying over later than expected. When he arrived at my door a short while after that he was wearing a black suit, white shirt and black tie, and when I opened the door to him my mouth must have actually dropped open a little as he looked breathtakingly attractive. I quickly pulled myself together as he followed me in, apologising for being late and for not having had time to change, he then proceeded to take off his tie and undo the top button of his shirt, which had the combined effect of making him even more distracting and my kitchen suddenly far too small.

Fortunately, I'd decided against jeans and had put on a decent pair of trousers, heels and a lightweight top, so I didn't feel too underdressed next to him. We set off and rather than go to The Red Calf he drove us to the next village where we went into a cosy-looking pub. The bar was quiet and small with a low-beamed ceiling, the lighting subtle though enhanced with a log fire. As we entered Trent pointed to a table in the corner for me to sit at, asking, "What would you like to drink, Emma?" I was surprised at hearing him use my first name.

"A glass of red wine, medium-dry please."

When he came over with the drinks, his appearing to be a pint of water, I thanked him, then once he'd sat down said, "I think you have me at a disadvantage."

He frowned a little, looking at me through narrowed eyes as he took a long draught from his glass before responding dryly, "Somehow I think that is highly unlikely."

"You know my first name, but I don't know yours," I clarified.

"It's Trent," he replied steadily.

"Trent Trent…a little unimaginative of your parents, don't you think?" I teased and he sighed.

"No, just Trent, I use one name," he explained patiently.

I paused for a moment. "What…like Pink?" He arched one eyebrow at me. "Or…Prince?" I pushed a little harder.

"If you like…and you do seem to be finding it amusing," he said, as I grinned.

"See, we're getting on better already. You were right, this was a good idea."

"Teasing me was not quite what I had in mind," he said shortly, although he didn't seem to be too cross about it.

"Oh, so what did you have in mind then?"

"I wasn't going to launch into it straight away, thought I'd get you round the outside of a glass of wine first, try and get you to relax a bit. How've things been going in the yard? Is everything all right?"

I decided to play along with him for a while so we chatted about the yard, the horses and any news I had of what had been happening on the estate, which didn't seem to be much. A little later, when I was on my second glass, he said, "So, we don't seem to have any difficulty in getting on in this setting do we?" I had to agree that we didn't. "And you don't have any difficulty in giving help and assistance to anyone who asks for it on the estate, do you?" Again, I had to agree I didn't. "So why do you find it so difficult to ask for help, and when help is offered to you, do you so vehemently resist it?" I thought for a moment before replying.

"If we take the recent incident with Monty being ill, I couldn't see any point in disturbing anyone else, or for anyone else to lose a night's sleep over something that I was quite capable of dealing with on my own. Where would the sense have been in that?" It seemed a quite reasonable and straightforward explanation to me. He considered my response for a moment.

"The thing is, Emma, we try to have a team approach on the estate. We live in an isolated community and we aim to support each other where we can. Cavendish, Grace and I have worked hard in putting all of this together. We want everyone to be happy and integrated with everyone else so that we all know we can rely on each other, and have each other's backs when necessary. You, however, are only fitting in one way – you're all about the giving while not being able to accept the help and support on offer."

"I wasn't aware of the setup when I came here and, having learnt to rely on no one but myself, I'd come with the intention of shutting myself away and not having to interact with other people at all," I explained a little sulkily.

"What…like some sort of recluse?" Trent asked, looking a little puzzled. "Why would you want to shut yourself off from everyone?"

"I have my reasons," I muttered rather dismissively, immediately regretting having led the conversation down this path. I didn't want to have to start explaining my thought processes and now realised I needed to come up with something that would satisfy him. "As it turns out I've found that I've enjoyed having people around me, at least some of the time, and making new friends, and I've tried hard to be more accommodating."

At this Trent leaned forward, studying me in silence for a moment, his expression serious. I didn't think I'd managed to satisfy his curiosity adequately after all. I was tense, holding my breath, wondering what might come next, but then while continuing to look at me he seemed to come to a decision, "Try harder."

I let my held breath go as I relaxed, hesitating for a moment before responding. "You know what, Trent, the day you contact me and find me compliant is the day I'll really be in trouble." At least he had the good grace to smile at this and relaxed back in his chair again, although he continued to study me in a way which I found a little intrusive.

Looking for a distraction I made a point of changing the tack of our conversation by asking what sort of work he'd been up to while away but he avoided giving me any details, saying something about consultancy and that it was far too boring to be of any interest to me, and although somehow I didn't think it would have been, clearly he was going to give me nothing.

We'd finished our drinks by then so we left with him explaining he was going straight back to work, hence the water. I did think afterwards that I had been more at ease with him by the end of the evening and it would be interesting to see if this would have any effect on our next confrontation.

Chapter 12

The cyclical passing of time brought round many anniversaries, and since losing Eva some were more difficult to deal with than others. The cruellest of them for me had always been in early April when I struggled each year to live through the memories of a time when I'd been exquisitely happy, contented and fulfilled for the first time in my life. Knowing now how easy it was to have all my hopes and dreams destroyed, it was this time that I found the hardest to survive and my change of circumstances didn't seem to make any difference to what started to happen to me as we reached April. It had been the same every year but I'd hoped with the Easter holidays starting I'd be kept busy and buoyant by the children and this year would be different. Unfortunately, that was not to be the case as Grace told me she would be away with the children visiting relatives for most of the holiday. I'd therefore be very much alone.

As each day passed I felt more and more vulnerable, and closer to the edge of my fragility. After only suffering a few times over the last year suddenly successive nights were broken by my recurring nightmare. Susie stayed close to me, sensing my mood as it turned darker and darker.

I accepted the usual invitation to go out Friday evening, hoping it would prove to be a distraction. Nothing provided the relief I needed so foolishly I decided drinking would help ease my pain, feeling I might as well seek oblivion in the bottom of a glass and get a few hours' peace.

The pub was busy, with many of the estate staff there making it noisy, but as the evening wore on I became less and less aware of what was going on around me and more and more conscious of Carlton next to me. Late in the evening I went to get in another round. I'd already had more to drink than I should have but that was not about to stop me and as I stood at the bar trying not to look drunk I saw Trent look up at me from the other side. His initially friendly expression changed to one of disapproval as he registered my drunken state which, as it turned out, I was not managing to hide that successfully after all.

Ignoring him I took the drinks to the table and slid back along the bench. Carlton put his arm around me, drawing me closer, and for once I didn't move it away again – it felt good. We all spilled out of the pub a little later; Wade was driving and Carlton held my hand as we headed to the pickup, then pulled me up and onto his lap, wrapping his arms around me. I tried to say I'd get in the back but frankly not that insistently. It was much more comfortable where I was and although I generally aim to abide by the law I was clearly in the mood for throwing caution to the wind and risk getting stopped in the half-mile journey along country roads back to the estate. Okay, so perhaps I was not a great risk-taker, but it was not the only thing I was about to be reckless over.

We pulled up outside the stables and I climbed out, followed by Carlton, who announced he was going to help me with the late watering, which sparked considerable amusement among everyone else in the pickup. We could hear their hollering even as they disappeared down the lane. I set off across the yard, over to the stables, the cold air hitting me but my face feeling warm as I let go of Carlton's hand and we successfully topped up the water in each stable, though I seemed to be slopping more around than was really necessary. When we'd finished I reached into the feed room to turn off the lights, closing the padlock on the door.

I turned and saw Carlton leaning up against the post-and-rail fence, watching me hungrily as he stood, quickly closing the distance between us. Putting one hand round my waist he pulled me towards him, wrapping his arms round me until I was pressed up hard against his body. Running my hands up his strong arms and leaving one hand on his shoulder I brought the other across onto his chest, where I let it rest, feeling his heart beating rapidly. He looked down at me, his eyes full of desire, and I knew that a night being fucked senseless by Carlton was exactly what I needed. One of his hands was in my hair as he brought his lips down to mine but before they met a dark voice came out of the night, speaking softly but firmly.

"It's time for you to go now, Carlton."

He exhaled harshly as he pulled back from me.

"Oh, give me a break," he said roughly, turning, and as he did I caught sight of Trent standing a few feet behind him. Trent stared straight at me and without breaking eye contact he indicated with his head to Carlton that he should leave. Carlton paused for a moment, taking another look at me, then shaking his head in exasperation and muttering goodnight walked away across the yard towards the gate. I stared after him in disbelief – how could he leave me just like that? Trent continued to look at me and when I met his cool gaze again he shook his head a little, frowning, as if confused.

"This isn't like you, what's going on?" He paused, but as no answer was forthcoming he continued more angrily: "You've got to learn to look after yourself better, Grayson. You've had too much to drink and you can't protect yourself in that condition. Fortunately, at least you were with Carlton and he cares for you, even if he's more interested in getting into your pants at the moment than in looking after you, but you shouldn't have put yourself in that situation. Don't you have any respect for yourself?" He was lecturing me as if he had some sort of right to do so and my eyes welled up as I looked fixedly down at my hands.

"I'm a grown-up, Trent. Why is what I do any of your business?"

"Because you're not behaving in a responsible manner," he snapped back, and then carried on, a harsh edge to his voice now. "What is it, Grayson? No smart comeback from that clever mouth of yours? That's not like you." His mocking tone hurt me but I had no intention of telling him what was going on; my feelings were already threatening to overwhelm me and as I looked up at him I could see the shock on his face as he registered the pain across mine.

"I need to go to bed," I whispered, and walked unsteadily towards the cottage. I remembered going upstairs, lying across my bed, then nothing more, letting the darkness take me.

The nightmare came, always the same: Eva, happily in my arms, comfortingly so real that I could touch her warm skin, so alive I could breathe in her scent from her soft hair, then suddenly, brutally, being taken by something unseen − torn from me, dragged from my arms, then fading from view, pulled away through a swirling, ever-thickening fog. My desperation growing as I tried to claw myself back to her, to save her; frantically trying to run after her but only in slow motion, unable to move any faster, being held back and unable to break away from some invisible force; reaching for her little hands as she held them out to me but they were always just beyond my grasp, the distance between us increasing all the time; sobbing as my terror grew at losing her, screaming for her to come back to me...then tonight being woken, crying and gasping in panic…feeling strong arms around me, rocking me, soothing me. Alex? No, not Alex…

I woke the next morning feeling better than I probably deserved to, but with the overall feeling of depression swamping me. I could hear the kettle boiling downstairs and remembering Trent's sudden appearance last night realised he must still be here. I got up to find that my jeans had been removed and were folded across the back of the chair in the corner of my room. I didn't remember doing that. I put them on and went downstairs. Susie greeted me in her usual manner. Trent was sitting at the kitchen table and looked up with concern in his eyes as I appeared at the bottom of the stairs.

"Morning," he said cautiously.

"Did you take off my jeans?" I could hear the anxiety in my voice.

"Yes, I thought you might be more comfortable sleeping without them. How're you feeling?"

I ignored his question.

"Did we er…you know?" Acutely embarrassed, I stared down at my hands and could feel the blush spreading across my cheeks.

"No, Grayson," he replied. "Despite your best efforts to get laid last night, I managed to restrain myself from taking advantage of your obvious charms. I watched you until I was sure you were unlikely to choke on your own vomit and then I slept down here." I winced at his words as he indicated towards the sitting room. "I've made up Susie's food as due to your laminating fetish I had full instructions, but she's refused to eat anything."

"That's because she thinks you're going to poison her," I replied, and turning to Susie, who was watching me closely, wagging her tail, said, "Eat up, it's fine," and she trotted off to her bowl in the boot room.

Trent, who hadn't taken his eyes off me said, "You might want to have a word with Carlton. You know how he feels about you and you shouldn't have led him on like that when you don't really mean it." Oh God, I was so ashamed of myself, although I couldn't help but feel a little indignant – who was he to say what I did or did not mean? "Also, I want to apologise for the way I spoke to you last night, I was unnecessarily cruel," he continued in a more conciliatory tone, then added, "I've arranged for you to have the day off. We're going out, and before you interrupt," and he held his hand up towards me, "this is not a date; there is something you need to do today. I will be back to pick you up in an hour." I'd automatically wrapped my arms around myself, physically trying to hold myself together as he turned to leave. Mystified by his plans for me I was also slightly panicky and nauseous at the thought of not having any work to do today. I'd thought that was the only thing that would get me through the day and I didn't want to have the time to think.

He paused when he got to the door, and half-turning to look back at me he spoke gently: "I'd like to think, Em, if we had spent the night together you would remember me in the morning." And with that he left. I closed my eyes, inwardly groaning with the humiliation I was experiencing, and I put my head in my hands, truly mortified.

I showered, dressing in jeans and a tee shirt, adding a thick sweatshirt for warmth before pulling on my plimsolls. The darkness continued to envelop me as I got ready and I then realised, with a sigh, I'd have to face Carlton before I left. Wandering out to the yard where he was mucking out one of the boxes I arrived at the stable door and distracted him, "Hi." He glanced up, frowning a little when he saw me.

"Hi," he glumly responded.

"Can I have a word, Carlton? I wanted to apologise for my behaviour last night. I was out of order and behaved completely inappropriately and I'm really, really sorry. I know how you feel about me and it was unfair of me to lead you on like that..." Realising I was gushing I stopped abruptly, looking down at my hands and feeling uncomfortable. When I looked anxiously back up at him I was surprised to see a small smile on his face.

"That's so like you, taking all the responsibility on yourself. It should be me apologising to you, not the other way around. I'm a big boy, I knew what I was doing and the consequences of my actions and I was quite up for taking full advantage of the situation last night and should've behaved better with you, so I'm sorry too." I saw the relief I felt mirrored in his face.

"So we're okay then?" I asked. "Nothing has changed between us, so we can just carry on as before?"

"Yes, Grayson, as unfortunately nothing did happen last night, nothing has changed between us and we're all good," he replied, somewhat regretfully, hesitating before continuing, "Can I ask though, did Trent stay with you last night?"

"Yes he did," I replied. "To keep an eye on me, make sure I was okay."

Carlton nodded, then said wistfully as he turned back to his mucking out, "He's a better man than me." Then he added a little more cheerily, "You know what? We would've had a lot of fun last night if Trent hadn't showed up."

"Oh, I don't doubt that," I replied, forcing myself to smile weakly at him.

Trent returned within the hour and we set off in silence. We'd been travelling for a while when I asked in a quiet voice, "Where're we going, Trent?" Although I already suspected I knew the answer.

"As it should've been Eva's birthday today we're going to the churchyard so you have a chance to spend some time with her," he replied steadily, glancing over at me carefully.

"Oh." I could hear my voice cracking. "How did you know?"

"I was concerned about you last night so I went over the background search we did on you and there it was. I'm only sorry I hadn't picked up on it before."

We travelled from then on in silence. Wrapping my arms around myself I concentrated on holding myself together as I thought through the events of the previous evening and found it difficult to excuse my behaviour. I'd experienced an overwhelming desire to be in a man's arms and that was an unwelcome weakness to be showing. As I stared unseeing out of the window I had to reluctantly admit that it was because I missed the closeness I'd once shared with Alex. Telling myself firmly there was no point in dwelling on another loss I decided I'd have to ensure it didn't happen again.

Eventually we arrived at the churchyard. Trent got out, opening the door for me before reaching into the back and taking out a bunch of daffodils which he handed to me. I stared at them, frowning, before looking at him questioningly.

"Stole them from the Manor gardens," he smiled conspiratorially by way of explanation.

"Thank you," I whispered hoarsely.

"I'll be waiting for you."

I turned to enter the churchyard.

I sat beside Eva, briefly allowing myself to remember the exquisite joy I'd felt when she was born on the most perfect day of my life. As always the guilt was soon back, swamping those feelings out of existence as I wept silently. I cleared away the dead flowers from Christmas and arranged the daffodils in the vase, remembering the time when I'd told Eva that these most beautiful of flowers bloomed especially for her, for her birthday, every year without fail, and I remembered how special that had made her feel.

Trent was waiting by the car when I walked out of the gates having composed myself again.

"Rather than having lunch in a pub I've taken the liberty of packing one of Mrs F's picnics. I thought we'd find somewhere along the way to eat if that's all right with you?" Trent asked as we got in the car.

"That'll be fine thanks," I murmured, rather distractedly, as we drove for a while before entering a country park. Trent parked up and I climbed out feeling hollow and weary. He took a picnic hamper out of the back and we proceeded to walk out of the car park and up a hill until we reached the top where there was a large oak tree for us to sit under. The view was spectacular when we turned to arrange the rug and set down the picnic, and we sat for a moment taking it in.

I knew Trent was watching me warily and sensing his eyes on me I tried not to meet them.

"Talk to me," he said, his voice soft. I glanced over at him but unable to reply, just shook my head. "Please," he continued, "I understand you're grieving, although not the depth of it as I've never been a parent, but I feel there's something more, something beyond the grief that I can't put my finger on. You had a nightmare last night, Emma, and I can't bear you being in this much pain and not knowing what's going on." I hadn't remembered the nightmare and was embarrassed he'd seen me in that state but being reminded of it now, the memories of being held and comforted came back to me. I felt I owed him some sort of explanation as to my behaviour so I took a deep breath to steady myself.

"I'm sorry you were there to witness that. It seems to happen more frequently at times when I'm feeling particularly vulnerable…like today…because I'm consumed by guilt as I blame myself every day for her death." I looked for his reaction but he just continued to watch me steadily.

"Tell me," and something in his tone made me take the plunge, letting out everything I'd kept buried inside for so long.

"I'm the one who's responsible for her death – I was her mother and it was my job to protect her. I should've realised how ill she was, I should've taken her to the doctor earlier, insisted they refer her to the hospital instead of allowing them to send us home. I should've fought harder for her and I should've made them all see how ill she was, made them listen. I should've saved her, but I didn't…I failed her, I caused her suffering and pain which is the most unbearable part and I'm condemned to live with the guilt of that every day…But on some days, like today, the pain becomes so overwhelming that I don't see any way of managing to survive it." My voice, that had begun cracking, failed completely, ending in a hoarse whisper as the tears started to flow unbidden and unchecked as my body convulsed with the pain running through it. Trent was at my side immediately, pulling me into his arms, holding me gently and letting me cry myself out. Eventually my sobs subsided and I felt calmer from their release than I had for a long time. Trent loosened his hold on me without saying a word and I moved away from him, suddenly feeling uncomfortable that I'd overstepped some boundary.

"I'm sorry about telling you all of that, burdening you with it," I said, once I was composed enough to speak again.

"Is that the first time you've told anyone how you feel?" And as I nodded he exhaled softly. "I'm honoured that you chose me. I can't believe you've been living with that inside you – no wonder you're so unhappy all the time." I looked over at him smiling softly at that.

"I'm not the only one who's unhappy."

"No, indeed you're not," he said, and I saw a cloud cross his face. "We all have our issues to deal with, I guess."

"I've told you what I live with every day, how about you tell me what you live with?" I probed.

He gazed at me for a moment then shook his head. "I think not." He smiled uncertainly, avoiding meeting my eyes again, before trying to lift the mood by changing the subject. "I'm famished so I think we need to distract ourselves by focusing on the picnic."

Realising I was also hungry, having not managed to eat anything for breakfast, we tucked into platefuls of coronation chicken, salad and couscous, followed by rich, lemony cheesecake.

When we'd finished eating and had packed everything away we both sat for a while, content to stare at the view, the silence eventually broken by me asking, "Why are you doing this, Trent?" I'd been mulling this over while eating, feeling the need for some answers.

"Doing what?" I felt him turn to look at me.

"Involving yourself in my problems, feeling as if you have to protect me." I turned my head then to watch him, uneasily, looking for his reaction. I was giving him an opportunity, an opening, but I saw his look become guarded, as he took his time in coming up with a response. It was as though he was weighing which words he should choose as to the effect they would have on me.

"It's my job."

I nodded as if I understood, as if I believed him, saying softly, almost to myself, "Of course…it's your job."

"That's part of my role on the estate, Emma. That's what Cavendish wants, me managing the staff, making sure everyone's safe, happy, coping okay. We live in a quiet place and it's easy for people to feel isolated and to get down. I try to head that off when I can."

"So everyone else gets this sort of treatment from you then."

He shrugged, the action dismissive, before answering, "Not necessarily...it depends...not everyone has had as much to deal with as you." I smiled gently, feeling tired with all the emotion of the past few hours.

Trent checked on his watch then sighed, and seemed unwilling to say it was time to go.

On the journey home I said, "Thanks for listening today and just accepting what I said...without asking anything or trying to solve my problems."

"It really wouldn't be my place, Emma," he replied. "I can't imagine the pain you've been through. So I certainly wouldn't be able to tell you how to get over what you're feeling. I don't think anybody should do that.

"I believe people feel a certain way about things that have happened to them for a reason, and they have to be given the right amount of time to find a way to resolve the situation, or learn to live with it, and that's not something that can be forced. I hope it's made you feel a bit better to have told someone though, even if it is only me and not some sort of professional person who might actually be able to help you."

"I do feel a bit easier in my mind after unloading onto you actually. Sharing obviously does help. Though I was sent to a counsellor but it didn't go well, probably because I went unwillingly. After that I didn't have much faith in any sort of professional counselling."

"I'm with you on that," he agreed, and there it was, another vague hint to his past, that something had happened that he had needed some sort of help with. Although it sounded as if his experience of counsellors was not any better than mine.

Chapter 13

A week or so later Carlton came over to help me out with a feed delivery and afterwards we sat drinking coffee together in my kitchen. Now Eva's birthday had passed my mood had started to lighten from the dark place it had been and I was able to feel a little more positive again. Something had been puzzling me from the night before her birthday and I didn't quite know how to bring it up. Carlton, who was slouched in the kitchen chair with one arm hanging down stroking Susie's ear, eventually said, "You seem deep in thought, anything I can help with?"

"Actually I have something to ask you."

"I thought you might. Go on."

"I was wondering, that night, when we were about to...you know...before Trent interrupted us."

"Yes, I remember *that* night only too vividly," he muttered a little grumpily, which I ignored as I continued.

"You seemed quite intent on your purpose at the time and I wondered afterwards why you'd given up on me quite so easily when he turned up."

"I can assure you it was not at all easy..." and he paused for a moment, contemplating me and what he thought he should say to me next. "But it was because he's my boss."

I frowned as I thought about this response. Somehow it didn't ring true and my thoughts were obviously reflected in my face as he then said, "You're not buying that, are you?" And as I shook my head he sighed, as if resigned to the decision he'd made. "Trent's not only my boss but also my Commanding Officer."

148

"You're in the armed forces?" I questioned, my eyes open wide with surprise.

"All the boys are. I'm RAF, as are Trent and Cavendish. Hayes and Wade are Army and Turner Navy...So now you know...and before you start, I'm not telling you anything else." With that he finished his coffee and got up to go, leaving me with much to ponder and many unanswered questions.

The following Saturday morning I set off on Regan for his daily exercise and for once it was just him and me. I was not going to have to lead Zodiac or Benjy out for a while as they'd both had their flu jabs and were going to spend most of the next week out in the paddock. It was a lovely spring morning; the sun was out and although I'd managed to miss a shower I thought it was highly likely I'd get caught in another one at some point on the ride. I rode along the lane for a while then turned onto one of my favourite routes through the woods. Everything about the woodland was beautiful at this time of year with all the trees and plants pushing out new growth and the woods becoming greener by the day. Clumps of pale yellow primroses grew wildly along with the more lemony celandines; the leaves of bluebells were coming up to carpet the ground in what looked likely to become a spectacular display of blue over the next few weeks.

It was easier to work on Regan's fitness on these occasions when we were on our own and keeping him moving forward in a trot with plenty of impulsion was making him work harder than usual. It felt good covering the ground so quickly, him moving strongly beneath me, and as we sailed comfortably along my thoughts drifted on to other things.

Since the revelation made by Carlton a few days before I'd had much to think about. There was more to the estate than I'd first thought, although I wasn't sure how it all fitted together. My thoughts were jumbled, and trying to straighten them as I rode, I wondered why everyone was in the armed forces and in fact questioned if everyone indeed was. Surely some of the older people here wouldn't be? And what was Trent's role – and Cavendish's – was this also connected to whatever work was done off the estate? It seemed people here abided by the NDA even while on the estate as no one had given me any indication of this.

My busy mind moved on to thoughts of Trent as I was also concerned about his feelings towards me. I didn't have a great deal of experience of men, none actually, other than Alex, and although I thought Trent had an interest in me he hadn't pushed it, hadn't asked me out like the others, which would have been easy to rebuff, so maybe, I thought, it was only an interest, as he'd said, required by the remit of his job. I moved on to how I was feeling about him – unsure. I was definitely attracted to him, and was starting to think it was more than just a physical attraction, but after Alex I'd decided I'd sooner not expose those feelings, not wanting to risk the chance of experiencing that hurt again and I was still convinced that this was the right course of action. I certainly wasn't going to make the first move and there was no indication from Trent he was going to even though I'd given—

With no warning a woman leapt out from behind a tree. Making a loud wailing sound she rushed towards us, her arms up like the sails of a windmill waving above her head, and Regan, startled, shied violently away from her. Deep in my thoughts, I was completely taken by surprise and flew sideways with him; then, having no time to hang on when he corrected himself I carried on going at full speed, losing contact with him as my back, and then my head, smashed into the trunk of a large tree, stopping me mid-flight. It knocked the wind out of me, my head ricocheting back off the tree before I crashed to the ground with a sickening thud. Waves of nausea and dizziness washed over me as I lay trying to catch my breath, vaguely aware of Regan disappearing up the path, but nothing else as the blackness descended.

I could feel myself trying to wake up, my head thumping, my eyes closed as I tried to work out what had happened. Obviously I was in hospital – there was no mistaking that smell. I remembered falling. Nothing else. Trying to stir, my body resisted all attempts at movement.

Slowly, slowly, slowly I could feel sensation coming back to me. My head still pounded and as my eyes eventually opened they alighted on Trent, who was sitting in a chair in the corner of the room. His eyes were fixed on me and when he saw I was awake he got up, coming across the room.

"Welcome back," he said, sounding relieved. "How're you feeling?"

"Sore," I replied croakily, my voice sounding hoarse. And that was the truth of it: I had a dull aching pain radiating throughout my body, emanating from my back.

"Regan?" I whispered.

"He's fine, back in his stable. Carlton's in charge, before you ask."

I nodded, although that movement caused pain to shoot down my neck. "Argh…Good. What's the damage?"

"You've been lucky, although it might not feel like it at the moment. You have a head injury and concussion; your riding hat was smashed. You have extensive bruising across your back and the rest of you is going to be pretty sore for a few days where you hit the ground, but there are no broken bones and no internal injuries so, as I said, you've been lucky," he finished brightly.

I cleared my throat, taking a sip of water from a beaker he passed to me. "That's good," I said, speaking more clearly now. Suddenly I had a mental flash of the woman's flailing arms and I gasped at the memory.

"What is it?" he asked, concerned.

"Is she here?"

"Who?"

"The woman who leapt out, was she injured by Regan?"

Looking at him as I asked the question, Trent frowned, responding, "There was no one else there when we found you, Emma."

"Oh…but I was sure there was a woman. She leapt out, which was why Regan shied…" and I tailed off, confused. I frowned, finding even doing that hurt, but I was trying to concentrate on the memory, trying to piece it together. It had all happened so quickly. I remembered her leaping out…an overall impression of paleness, but dark hair, dark eyes…no other distinctive details of her appearance, the arms up in the air, the noise she made – that was it. Although, even as I thought about it I questioned whether I was remembering correctly as nothing about it seemed clear or reliable.

"What did she look like?"

"I can't remember, it all seems so vague now. If she wasn't there when you got there, she obviously wasn't hurt, which is the main thing I guess."

"If she even existed…Are you sure your mind isn't playing tricks on you? Maybe it was a dream you're remembering?" He had a point there – I was experiencing the same sort of feeling you get when you wake up and try to remember the dream you were just part of, one that had been so vivid moments before but which now floated away from you, breaking up and thinning before your eyes, the weakening strands of thought becoming as difficult to hang onto as smoke.

"Mmm…perhaps. Maybe it will come back to me," I finished thoughtfully before turning my attention fully back to Trent. "Can I go home?"

"The doctor is due to come round and see you again soon and then we'll see." I realised I was dressed in a hospital gown and when Trent saw me looking down at this he said, "Your clothes have been taken back home. Greene came in and brought some clean things for you to wear —when you're allowed to go that is."

"That was kind of her. Thanks for staying too, Trent, I'm sure you have other things you should be doing though, so if you need to go and get on with those I'll be fine."

"It's not a problem. Cavendish has told me to stay and I'm here to take you home, if they let you out."

"Oh, okay that's good of you, and thoughtful of Cavendish to let you stay. It'll save me getting a taxi."

"I'm not sure you would be up to going home in a taxi anyway. You're going to have to take things easy for a while you know?" He was watching me for my reaction to this and I could see he was a little concerned.

"We'll see. I'm sure I'll be fine once I get moving," I said, brushing off the seriousness of the injuries I'd sustained. "How did you find me anyway? I know I didn't get the chance to use the app on the phone."

"Regan alerted us initially. He was seen galloping through the farm by Porter who raised the alarm. Regan managed to evade capture until he got back to the yard, where Carlton eventually caught up with him. We triangulated the signal on your phone and came to get you." Well of course you did, I thought – who can't triangulate! Or more importantly, who has the ability to…?

At that moment the door opened and a doctor walked in accompanied by a nurse. He was pleased to see me conscious and started on a round of questions and tests, shining a light in my eyes, testing my reflexes and so on, seeming pleased with the results.

"Can I go home?" I asked.

"I think so, but you've suffered a concussion so there must be someone with you for the next forty-eight hours or so, in case of any deterioration in your condition," he explained.

"Oh, there isn't anyone who can do that, I live on my own," I replied, disappointed that I'd have to stay.

"I'll be staying with her for the next couple of days so that's not a problem," Trent said. What? Where did that come from? I could feel warning bells going off, accompanied by the alarming feeling that this could be a bit tricky. I looked up at him sharply in surprise, causing more pain down my neck, but he was quite determinedly not looking at me.

The doctor seemed happy with this solution, taking Trent aside for a few moments to discuss what he needed to do to care for me and what to look out for if my condition worsened. The doctor and nurse left soon after saying there'd be some paperwork to be completed at the desk together with a prescription for stronger painkillers for me.

"Thanks for offering to do that, Trent."

"Only following orders, it's not a problem." Oh, so not his idea then, I thought, making me feel a little more relaxed, and I wondered if Cavendish had made him volunteer.

"Okay, where are my clothes?" I asked as I struggled to sit up on the bed, making painful noises as I did so, every part of me hurting, and I realised getting dressed was not going to be as easy as I'd first thought.

Trent held up my tracksuit trousers, and stifling a smile, he raised his eyebrows at me. "Do you want some help?"

I scowled back at him, feeling thankful that at least I'd been left with my pants on. "I'm not sure you helping me dress is entirely appropriate. Isn't it possible for one of the girls to come and help instead?"

"I'm sorry but everyone is busy with the Ball coming up and as I'm the least useful person on the estate at the moment, I'm afraid you're stuck with me." I therefore had to relent and grudgingly agree that I might need some help.

"Just bring the clothes over and I'll manage," I muttered grumpily. It was excruciatingly painful to reach my feet, feeling the agony of every bruised muscle across my back and through my pelvis as I stretched down to put my trousers on, pulling them up to my knees. With his help I struggled off the bed and then slowly, managing to bend a little, pulled them up the rest of the way, my head aching and swimming sickeningly as I bent down. Trent then put on my socks and plimsolls before tying the laces.

"Now to the top half," and reaching for the sweatshirt he turned to me with a glint in his eye. Oh, he was enjoying every moment of this – me actually having to ask for his help. Fortunately, Greene hadn't packed a bra as she had clearly thought that would have been beyond me and how right she was.

"I can manage," I said to Trent grumpily as he started putting the sweatshirt on me but I found once I had it over my head I couldn't move my arms up enough to get them in the arm holes. So I was stuck with the sweatshirt all gathered up around my neck and I still had the hospital gown on.

"Right, turn around," Trent ordered, taking charge, and when I had, he undid the fastenings down the back of the gown. As he went to slip it off my shoulders I suddenly became shy, "Don't look at me."

"I can assure you I have my eyes tightly closed," he replied, his voice quiet, and once the gown was off he helped put each of my arms into the correct armhole and pulled the rest of the sweatshirt down so all was present and correct.

"There you go, all covered up. Let's go," he said, and collecting the rest of our belongings, which didn't amount to much, we headed off – slowly in my case, signing the paperwork and collecting my pills on the way out. His truck was parked a little way across the car park and when we got to it he helped me up into the passenger seat.

"Did I get to go in an ambulance?" I asked on the way home.

"Yes, we didn't move you once we found you, not knowing how bad your injuries might be, which was just as well, as when the paramedics got there they checked you out and put you on a spinal board until you'd been scanned at the hospital."

"I can't believe all that happened and I missed it."

A short while later we drove back through the farm entrance and I waved to Porter and Summers as we passed, then we were at the yard. It was by then late afternoon and I was hoping to catch Carlton during evening stables to check all was in order. Trent came round the truck after parking outside the back door and helped me out. Susie hurtled over from the yard and after throwing a growling bark at Trent leapt at me with undeniable joy. I crouched down to give her a cuddle then struggled to get back up but when I did I looked over at the yard. Carlton was standing watching me and raising my hand to him I started to walk over slowly.

"What're you doing?" Trent asked impatiently. "You're meant to be going in to rest."

"I need to see Regan first," I said over my shoulder to him. He caught up with me and gave me his arm to lean on, making the journey a little easier. "Hi, Carlton, thanks for stepping in, is Regan okay?"

"He's fine, a bit worked up when he got back here but I've cleaned him down and he's now calm and settled," he explained. "More importantly how're you?"

"I'm quite uncomfortable actually, but glad to be home." I'd reached Regan's stable and stroking his nose, I opened the door wide enough to get inside; then breathing him in, I ignored the pain as I wrapped my arms around his neck and shoulders, giving him a hug before letting him go. Then, stroking my hand down his nose again I made soothing noises to him. He brought his head up and, resting his chin on my shoulder, I brought my face round, kissing and nuzzling the softest part of his nose, the silky hollow above his nostril. We were both quite content to stay like this for a while but Trent coughed, interrupting.

"Sorry to break this up but you need to be getting inside." I gave Regan one last kiss then left the stable, closing and bolting the door behind me. Checking on each of the others, I asked Carlton if Monty had been out.

"Yes, I exercised him earlier so he's fine."

"Thanks. What about feeding, do you know what to do?"

"Well, fortunately some control freak has placed a whole row of laminated instructions covering every part of the running of this yard on the notice board, so I'm sure I'll manage," he replied sarcastically, grinning at me.

"Very funny. You may be laughing at me but as it turns out it's just as well I did do that. Let me know if you need anything else," I responded, smiling at him as I headed back across to the cottage, leaning on Trent again.

We let ourselves in and Trent said immediately, "Right, straight to bed."

"Not so fast, I don't want to go yet. I feel like I've been in bed all day. Can't I stay up for a bit, watch a film perhaps, have some supper and then have an early night?" I gazed pleadingly at him and after frowning a bit he relented, helping me instead through to the sitting room.

Taking my plimsolls off he got me comfortable on the settee, getting additional cushions and a fleecy blanket to wrap around my feet and legs. Susie came in at that point and after huffing a couple of times on finding Trent there, she flopped down on the floor right in front of me.

"I'll go and see what's in the kitchen for dinner," he said before disappearing. Hearing him open the fridge, he then shouted through to me, "Mrs F's been busy. There's a chicken, ham and pasta dish here with a creamy sort of sauce, would that do you?"

"Sounds delicious," I replied.

"Okay, I'll stick it in the oven to warm through while I sort out a film for you." I heard the clank of the oven door closing, then he appeared back in the doorway again. "Right, what film do you want to watch?"

"As you're my guest, even though you're the one who's waiting on me hand and foot, you can choose from my collection." I pointed to the shelf where they were all lined up and he browsed along the titles.

"That's what I like to see, all dark thrillers, violent action and adventure and not a romcom in sight." He chose the first part of an action trilogy and set it up to play.

"Actually, before you do that shouldn't you go and get anything you need for your stay here?" I questioned.

"Already done. Bray came over earlier with Mrs F, after picking up some things I asked her to get from my place. They've made up the spare room for me so we're all set." Trent spread himself out along the other settee and we settled down to watch the film. Pausing it after half an hour to get our dinner together, he brought it in to eat in front of the television. The pasta dish was delicious and I felt full and contented, only just making it to the end of the film without dozing off.

As the credits appeared Trent jumped up saying he was going to run me a bath – doctor's orders apparently. I was feeling too tired to argue that I usually had showers so I left him to get on with it. He came back down, unwrapped me from the blanket, and helped me up as my muscles had stiffened and it took a lot of effort to get me upstairs and into the bathroom.

"I've put some muscle relaxant salts into the water as the doctor suggested. The idea is to bring out the bruising but also to warm up your joints and muscles and make you feel a little more comfortable for a while," he explained.

"Okay, you go and get on with something then while I get in then," I said, but he made no effort to move and when I glanced at him he appeared uncomfortable with that idea.

"The problem is you can't be left in the bath on your own in case you pass out in the water," he explained.

"Okay...but I'm not comfortable stripping off in front of you so we'll have to find another solution won't we?" I paused as I pondered the situation. "How about if I get undressed and into the bath while you sit outside and we'll keep the door open."

"Works for me, but you'll have to keep talking while you're in there – if you stop I'll be in to check on you. Give me a shout if you can't get out of any of your clothing," and he turned to leave the room.

I managed to undress myself although it was extremely painful and got into the bath, which was deliciously warm, and as I lay there I could feel its magic relaxing my muscles.

"What shall we talk about?" I heard from the landing.

"We could use this enforced time together to find out a bit more about each other," I suggested, feeling a little odd to be talking to an empty room.

There was a slight hesitation before his response. "Yes, we could."

I imagined him sitting, leaning up against the wall outside the bathroom door.

159

"You obviously have the advantage of having had a background check done on me so I'll ask the questions to start with, if that's okay with you?" Another hesitation and I imagined him contemplating whether or not he was willing to risk the inevitable loss of privacy if he concurred before being surprised by his reply.

"That's fine with me, Grayson, fire away."

"Where do you live?" I asked him.

"I have an apartment in the Manor. It has its own entrance from the rear courtyard opposite the kitchens so is essentially a separate property. Quite a few of the staff live on site actually. Forster and Mrs F have a cottage attached to the Manor, similar to my place but larger. Then there are several small flats that the younger ones share in groups of two, three or four, depending on the size of flat. A few live elsewhere, especially if they're married as they generally buy a house off the estate, but no one lives very far away."

"Have you always lived there alone?"

"Yes," and he hesitated. I thought for a moment I'd asked something too personal, but then he continued, "I moved onto the estate after my marriage broke up and since then I've been on my own."

"How long have you lived there?"

"About five years."

"That's a long time for you to have been on your own." I was suddenly only too aware of how similar our situations were.

"Yes, it is – and you should know." The hypocrisy had not been lost on him either then. I was going to ignore his remark but then couldn't help myself.

"But, we're not talking about me are we?"

"Indeed we are not. Consider me duly reprimanded, my apologies for interrupting your flow." I couldn't see him but I sensed him smiling and I couldn't help but wind him up a little more given the opportunity.

160

"Well…you're not that bad looking," I mused, smiling to myself, considering the understatement I'd just made.

"You're too kind – but that's a statement, not a question, and I believe you're laughing at me again, Grayson," he chuckled.

"I wouldn't dream of it!" I replied, feigning innocence. "It begs the question though doesn't it? Why no one else? In that length of time, makes you wonder what's wrong with you."

"I hadn't considered the possibility before now that there was anything wrong with me, but thank you for bringing it to my attention."

"You're welcome."

Then surprisingly he continued, "It's simply that no one has come along who's sparked my interest – at least no one who has been enough of a challenge, which is what attracts me."

Oh, I thought. The silence following this statement was deafening and I had nothing to fill it. I grasped around in my mind for something to ask as the silence stretched out. "What was your wife's name?" There we go, safer territory, back on the past, a bit personal, but safer than the present, definitely.

"Zoe."

"Do you still see her?" Stop sounding like you're fishing for information, I warned myself.

"No."

That was definite. Time for a complete change in direction, I thought, in the hope of catching him off guard. "What work do you do with Cavendish off the estate?"

He hesitated before answering. "I think you've asked enough questions for one evening and it's time you got out before you shrivel up like a prune. I'm just popping downstairs to grab the towel I've left warming for you on the range and then I'll be back. Do not drown in the meantime," he warned as I heard him run downstairs, effectively distracting me and ducking the question – again. He was back a moment later, coming towards the bath with the towel unfolded and held up so he could not see me.

"Right, stand up and wrap this round you – be careful not to slip getting out." He left me to get dry and although being in the water had made my body feel much better I was now exhausted. The pain intensified in my head, accompanied by an unpleasant spinning sensation when I bent down to pull on my soft, comfortable, cuddly set of pyjamas – the ones I wore when I felt a bit sorry for myself – before shuffling through to the shower room to clean my teeth. Trent dosed me up with painkillers and I climbed into bed, practically falling asleep before my head hit the pillow.

I woke once during the night, the pain of turning over causing me to wake, and when I did I looked up briefly to see Trent sitting in the armchair in the corner of my room, his head resting on his hand as he watched me, but I was asleep again before I could say anything.

Chapter 14

I woke the next morning to see sunlight streaming through my window. As I lay there I assessed my injuries. I hurt all over, and needed to dose up with painkillers, but when I went to move my limbs complained more than they had the previous day. The shock of the impact now resonated throughout my body, my joints feeling like they'd been shaken loose and were now bruised, complaining with every move; my muscles were stiff and sore, every movement seeming to be a mammoth effort.

I needed the bathroom so I managed to get myself into a sitting position and off the bed. I shuffled to the bathroom as if I were ancient to do my business, before returning to bed and sinking gratefully back into it, welcoming the softness on my battered limbs. A few minutes later Trent appeared, looking sickeningly bright-eyed and bushy-tailed and carrying a tray.

"Morning. How're you feeling?"

"Sore and grumpy," I replied, trying to get into a comfortable sitting position, but as I was not succeeding he put the tray down and came over to arrange my pillows behind me.

"Pills first," he said, and handed me the pills and a glass of orange juice before announcing, "I've made you breakfast in bed." I smiled at him.

"How do you know what I like for breakfast?"

"Let's see how I've done, shall we," he said, smiling, gleefully putting the tray on my lap, then standing back to await my verdict. I looked down: a mug of tea, builder's strength with very little milk.

"No sugar?"

"No sugar." Two pieces of toast with marmalade – perfect.

"Well done, good guesswork."

"Good detective work you mean. Can I sit down?"

"Of course," I mumbled through my first bite of toast, and he came round to the other side of the bed and sat on it with one leg folded under the other, facing me. I'd been expecting him to sit in the armchair so was somewhat surprised and suddenly acutely conscious of him on my bed. He was wearing a white tee shirt and soft brushed cotton bottoms in a large checked pattern of varying shades of red and white. He appeared comfortable and relaxed, and as if sitting on my bed in his pyjamas was not at all weird.

"How did you sleep?" he asked.

"Okay, although I woke once to find you watching me. What was that about?"

He grinned boyishly at me before replying, "When the snoring stopped so I thought I'd better come in and check you were still alive."

I glared at him in horror before saying indignantly, "I do not snore!"

Trent laughed at my horrified expression before responding, "Good to see you focus on the important part of what I just said."

I finished my piece of toast but my appetite had disappeared and I couldn't eat the other one so I offered it to Trent who took it happily, wolfing it down as I sat drinking my tea and watching him eat.

"What plans do you have for the day?"

"None, other than to look after you."

"I'm going to get in the shower as I need to wash my hair. I presume you don't need to watch me do that as the likelihood of drowning is minimal."

"Your sarcasm is not lost on me, Grayson. That'll be fine though, but don't lock the door will you, just in case?

Also you're likely to be stiffer than yesterday so if you need help in dressing you'll have to call me. I'm going to leap in your shower first though if that's okay?" He moved to get off the bed and wandered off to his room to get his towel.

I sat in bed finishing my tea as he showered and once I heard the shower stop I started in my efforts to get off the bed so that fortunately I was facing away from him when he walked out saying, "It's all yours." Which was just as well, as when I looked round he was leaving my room and the sight of his strongly muscled shoulders and well-defined back with the towel slung across his narrow hips was a distraction as it was and hardly fair on someone in my weakened condition.

I didn't have too much difficulty getting out of my pyjamas as they were loose-fitting and it felt good to get in the shower once I got it hot enough again, as Trent had adjusted the settings. I managed to wash my hair, though doing so caused stabbing pains down my neck, but I persevered as I couldn't face the thought of having to ask Trent to do it. When I'd finished I towel dried it gently as my head was still feeling fragile, then dried myself and left the bathroom with the towel wrapped around me. Managing to get my pants and tracksuit bottoms on, I dug out a tee shirt which I got over my head, but was grimacing as I tried to get my arm up through the arm hole, groaning aloud with the pain.

"I told you to call me if you needed help. Ouch…that looks painful," commented Trent, who'd appeared in the doorway, making me jump. Looking over at him angrily, I covered my chest.

"Why are you looking at me?" I snapped, questioning more softly, "What looks painful?"

"I was only looking at the bruising on your back, nothing else. Don't worry, your modesty is intact," he said, and coming towards me he offered to help me dress.

"I can't turn my head round enough to look at it in the mirror. How bad is it?"

He was standing behind me as he answered, "I'll show you...excuse me a moment," as gently he eased my tracksuit bottoms down a little so the band of them sat just below my hips. I felt my breath catch with surprise.

"There's a particularly blackish band as wide as this," he said, and he opened up the gap between his thumb and first finger to about four or five inches to show me, bringing his hand round in front of me so I could see it. A distracting whisper of breath caressed my neck as he did so.

"Stretching from here," and he put his fingers gently on my shoulder and then ran them down and across my back to my opposite hip, "to here," he finished, letting his fingers rest on my hip for a moment. I sensed him still behind me, silent for a moment, then clearing his throat he carried on quietly, "The bruising extends out from that line through various changes of colour from purple to a yellowy-green – very attractive. Then there's another bruise extending up from your other hip from where you hit the ground." As he said this his fingers trailed across my lower back to the other hip, where again he paused and I sensed, rather than heard, his breathing deepen. I'd been completely absorbed by the feel of his fingers on my skin and as they settled on my hip a shiver went through me.

"Are you okay?" he murmured.

"Yes, sorry...just ticklish," I explained, trying to find an excuse, feeling flustered as I turned towards him. He gazed at me for a moment."Let's finish getting you dressed then. Promise to close my eyes," he teased. It was certainly easier with his help and considerably less painful. He finished by putting on my socks then excused himself, disappearing downstairs while I finished drying my hair with the hairdryer.

My thoughts and feelings towards him were all over the place. I sat on the bed trying to get my mind straight, wondering if it was only a physical reaction I was experiencing or was it, as I was imagining, something deeper – and that thought frightened me. I'd closed down all those possibilities in my mind when Alex left me – I didn't want to have that feeling again, that connection, that vulnerability to someone else's influence. I don't want this, I told myself firmly. It was just as well he'd be leaving the next day.

Going downstairs slowly I greeted Susie, telling her to go and eat the breakfast Trent had made her. I looked out of the kitchen window to check on the activity in the yard. Carlton was there on Regan, and about to lead Monty out for exercise. Going through to the sitting room I found Trent reading the papers which someone had kindly dropped off for us. Taking a section, I curled up on the other settee to read and we spent some time having healthy, and in some cases rather robust, discussions on topics that caught our eye, which I found stimulating. It was, I thought, an unusual experience for both of us, to have someone to do this with.

We'd just finished lunch when I heard a message come in on Trent's phone. He took it out of his pocket and reading it he frowned, and I thought turned a little pale before looking up at me.

"I need to make a call, I'll go outside. Go and rest next door, I'll clear up when I come in then watch a film with you. I won't be long." He walked out the back door and I stood watching him for a moment as he paced up and down near his truck, listening, and then speaking animatedly into the phone. Normally he was so confident, calm and in control, but this was all gone as he now ran his free hand through his hair as he talked, seeming less self-assured, and instead filled with concern and worry. I'd never seen him like that, and feeling as if I was intruding I went and sat in the sitting room, not wanting him to catch me watching, not wanting to be involved but feeling for him in his obvious discomfort anyway.

I heard him come in a short while later, moving around the kitchen as he put the lunch things away, and I got the second film in the trilogy ready for him to watch. When he came to join me I asked if everything was all right but he shrugged it off, replying that it was. He sat down, saying he was ready, but I was concerned for him. He seemed distracted, troubled even, and sat deep in thought throughout the film.

I walked painfully slowly over to the yard when the film had finished, checking in with Carlton. When I looked back at the cottage I could see Trent on the phone again and wondered who to. Carlton was on good form, however, and soon distracted me from this train of thought. The horses were all fine so I left him to it and returned to the cottage in need of more painkillers.

About half an hour later Cavendish arrived, bringing our dinner with him. I would have thought he would have been too busy to be delivering meals himself and I got the distinct impression that something was up. I didn't miss the concerned looks that passed between him and Trent on arrival but Cavendish quickly focused his full enthusiastic attention onto me and could not apologise enough for what his horse had done to me. I reassured him it had been nothing whatsoever to do with Regan and went on to explain to him what had happened. He questioned me at some length about the woman, not that I could tell him much, particularly as I was doubting my own recollection of her anyway, and had even started to question her existence, so faded was she in my memory. However, I was pleased that he seemed to take my account considerably more seriously than Trent had. He had all but dismissed it initially, but now I couldn't help wondering if something had happened that was making Trent see more credence in it and that was why Cavendish had got involved. Maybe Trent had brought him in to deal with whatever it was. Or maybe that was just my overactive imagination at work.

When we'd finished I saw a look pass again between the two of them. Cavendish said he'd send the boys out to see if there was any evidence that might shed some light on who this mystery woman was and he'd let me know if there was any news. He left soon after, insisting I was not to go back to work until at least the following week and only then if the doctor had signed me off. We said our goodbyes and then Trent and I were alone again.

Trent's thoughts appeared to be elsewhere as he told me to go and rest and he turned his attention to our dinner, which was ready about half an hour later.

"Are you up to coming and eating at the table or would you like dinner in there?" Trent called from the kitchen.

"The table will be fine – would you like me to come and set it?"

"No, that's fine, I'll sort it out, be about five minutes."

When I got up a couple of minutes later and went through to the kitchen the table was set and there was a candle alight in the middle of it. I smiled as I told Trent how nice it was and looking pleased with his efforts, he seemed more relaxed than he'd appeared earlier. As I sat down Trent put a plate in front of me of beef and ale pie with mashed potatoes and vegetables then held up a bottle.

"I know you can't drink at the moment but I asked them to put in this bottle of non-alcoholic wine I thought you might like. Do you want to try some? We can pretend it's the real thing."

"Yes please, although I do have red wine if you want to help yourself. There's no reason you shouldn't have a drink."

"I thought I'd join you...show support for the invalid," he smiled. The wine tasted good and the food, delicious. As we ate we chatted and I asked Trent if he had any family locally.

"I don't have any family left at all actually," he replied. "I was a late surprise for my parents, an only child, and they both died a few years ago so now it's just me."

"That's a shame."

"Yes it is, but I had my parents' love and support until I was more than grown up. Losing your parents at the age you lost yours is what's really hard...Sorry...that was a bit tactless," he finished, a little uncomfortably as he realised what he had said.

"It's fine, it's not something I think about that often."

He was quiet, contemplating me for a moment before continuing. "As it's my turn to ask the questions this evening, I'll carry on with this line, if you don't mind?"

"I don't mind, ask whatever you like. I'll soon tell you if you've gone too far."

"Okay then...do you know how your parents died?" Nothing like getting right to the heart of a subject, I thought.

"Yes, I was told they died in a car accident. I've assumed as I'm still here and have no memory of the accident I wasn't in the car with them."

"Do you have many memories of your parents?" This was something I'd always found difficult.

"None actually," I replied. "I can't remember anything about them at all. Unfortunately, I don't have any photos either. My first memories are of one of the foster families I lived with."

"What was that like?"

"It was fine; it was all I knew so I had to get on with it. Mind you, I said foster families but I never actually lived in a family, I had a series of foster parents with no other children around."

170

"Isn't that a little odd? I'd thought of fostering as something people with families did."

"Like I said, I knew nothing else, so it was the norm for me. It was only at my last school that I came across someone else in my position for the first time. One of the girls there was fostered with a family in a nearby town and I only realised then how different our experiences were. It sounded to me like she had a poorer upbringing but a more stable one with a proper family around her. I'd never had any other children to live with and never stayed anywhere long enough to feel settled anyway, moving on every two or three years."

"Why was that?" He seemed genuinely interested, which made me want to give him the unvarnished version.

"I'm not sure, but I'd become very close to my first foster parents, as you can probably imagine. I found myself alone and I remember being frightened but I was moved on within a couple of years which I found very hard. I wasn't expecting it and wasn't prepared for it at all so from then on I didn't get close to any of them, not wanting to feel like that again. I realised they only had me because they were paid to, so I became independent very young, and I was also quite stubborn so I've always assumed it was because I was a bit of a difficult child."

His face lit up at this. "Surely not! You...difficult...I find that hard to believe."

"Very funny." I couldn't help smiling back at his obvious delight in being able to latch onto this early description of my familiar behaviour. "I guess you'll be pleased to know that you're not the only person in my life I've been difficult with. As it turns out you're nothing special." Ouch...that was a bit harsh.

"Thanks for the reminder," he replied soberly, his eyes never leaving mine, before continuing with his questions. "Did you ever look at being adopted? I don't know how the system works but presumably someone has to instigate the process."

"I do remember asking a couple of times and was told I was on the adoption register but nothing ever came of it. I assumed it was because I was an older child – most people want to adopt a baby so older children are harder to place and it never happened for me."

"What did you do after the foster care ended?"

"Before I had to leave care I was already with Alex so we got married at eighteen and I went straight from one to the other. We were able to buy a house because I'd been left an inheritance from my parents' estate."

"That was very young to get married."

"Yes, and as it turns out quite foolish," I replied sadly, then smiling weakly at him, I thought I'd turn his question back onto him: "When did you and Zoe marry?"

"Early twenties, quite foolish too," he replied, and hesitating he looked away for a moment before looking back at me, adding, "He hurt you badly, didn't he?"

"Yes, he did," I muttered, before adding in a falsely bright tone, "but now you *have* gone too far. I suggest we agree not to talk about our failed marriages or before long we'll be wallowing in our mutual misery."

"Okay, agreed." He filled up our glasses and moved onto safer territory, teasing me about my rather singular film tastes.

"Actually, I have a confession to make – I do have a drawer full of other films, old black and whites, love stories and yes, romcoms, but as I haven't been in the mood for watching anything like that for some considerable time I tend to stick to the ones you see on the shelf. However, if you do prefer something soppy, as you're my guest, and as I'm always happy to oblige as you know, you can choose from the wider selection should you so desire."

"Hmm...I'm not sure I want you thinking I'm soppy," he teased. "Think we'll finish the trilogy we started." He got up to clear away dinner and I watched him wash up while I dried, enjoying being near him, able to observe him while he was otherwise occupied, and when he'd finished he went to set up the film for us.

Afterwards he ran a bath for me and we went through the same routine as the previous evening. Except the difference being that I was finding it harder and harder to be in his presence. I kept telling myself I didn't want this but could almost feel the charge between us crackling, and while I felt all mixed up inside, he appeared completely unaware of it, and was his usual calm and composed self.

I decided when I eventually got to bed and he'd gone to his room that it would all be fine once he left the next day; things could go back to normal and I wouldn't be so affected once his constant presence was removed from my home. However, I had that night to get through and although I was tired I couldn't get to sleep for ages, and once sleep came it was restless, my dreams confused, vivid and overwhelming; dreams of him.

Chapter 15

I woke up already tired and feeling fractious the next morning. Trent appeared with breakfast, got me comfortable, put the tray down then sat on the bed again, so close.

"You look a little tired this morning," he commented.

"I didn't sleep well."

"Perhaps you can have a nap later on to catch up."

"Yeah, maybe," I said, and I started on breakfast, though already horribly aware of his presence had difficulty managing even one piece of toast.

"Sorry, I don't know what's happened to my appetite," and I handed him the other piece, which he dispatched without any problems. I shooed him out of my room so I could get showered and dressed and have some time to pull myself together.

Trent was watching the news when I went down and was going to shower so I walked over to the yard for a short while. Carlton also commented on my tired appearance, which didn't help my mood. Everything was calm at the stables so I went back in and made coffee. When I walked into the sitting room, however, I was greeted by the sight of Trent lying prone on the floor in front of the wood burning stove with his chin resting on his hands. Immediately in front of him was Susie, practically nose to nose with him, as she lay with her nose resting on her front paws.

"What're you doing?" I asked.

"I'm trying to make friends with your dog. I have the feeling she doesn't trust me because we got off to a bad start," he replied, not taking his eyes off Susie. He started blowing gently at her, trying to get her to play, but she was having none of it – once she'd had enough she growled at him in warning, then got up and walked off, giving a couple of huffs as she made her way back to her bed before slumping down into it.

"That's a work in progress," he informed me, rolling onto his back and stretching before getting up and joining me for coffee.

"Will you be okay if I pop out for a bit? I've got an errand to run," Trent asked a little later, having got me comfortable on the settee where I was reading a book.

"Of course, I'll see you later."

Grabbing his keys from the table he left.

After an hour or so I heard his truck pull into the yard and he came through the back door humming. Humming? Poking his head in through the doorway to say hello he asked if I wanted a cup of tea. I didn't so he then entered the room and I could see he was carrying a large, sturdy brown bag, swinging it casually from his hand. He stopped in front of me and I closed my book, putting it to one side. I thought I'd bite as he clearly wanted me to.

"What's that?" I asked, keeping my voice light.

"Ah, this is the errand I mentioned – it's a little present for you." There was something in the tone of his voice that made me look at him suspiciously, my eyes narrowing. He sat down, perching on the other end of the settee, and handed me the bag.

"Open it," he said, raising both eyebrows at me and grinning.

I sat up a little and reaching into the bag, lifted out a large box. It was the sort of box you see in films, solidly made with a close-fitting lid. In the films the lady would lift the lid to reveal some gloriously luxurious dress interleaved with tissue paper. Somehow, I felt this was not going to be the same sort of thing.

He sat back observing me, keenly, I thought. I took off the lid and inside was a bulky red and black object that, when I lifted it out, resembled something you would see the police wearing during a riot. I knew exactly what it was.

"What is it?" Sounding sweet, I inclined my head to one side and looked straight at him. He appeared highly delighted to be given the opportunity to launch into an explanation.

"Well now, Grayson, I'm glad you asked. This is the Point Two Pro Air Jacket, and it has transformed safety in the equestrian world. It offers protection to riders as the air jacket is inflated by a canister of CO_2 stored on the front of the jacket. You see, when a rider is unseated or thrown from a horse, the canister is activated by the release of a lanyard that is clipped from the jacket onto an attachment on the saddle. The jacket will then inflate within one-tenth of a second to absorb shock, distribute pressure and support a rider's spinal column. It also protects the collar of the neck, ribs, coccyx and vital organs within the body. It will then hold the rider tight for fifteen to twenty seconds and slowly deflate over two to three minutes." He stopped spouting the sales brochure and looked at me expectantly, trying to gauge what my reaction would be.

"I see," I said. "And you're expecting me to wear this?" The tone of my voice rose slightly; there was an edge to it and I could feel him stiffen next to me.

"Absolutely...in fact I insist on it," he said, then added as if to challenge me, "You could almost say it's an order."

"I don't have to accept orders, I'm not in the forces," I snapped.

"No, they would never have you, you're far too defiant," he retorted, and I could feel my blood pressure rising as I took a deep breath.

"Whether you insist on this or not, I don't want to wear it. I've never liked these body protectors, I find them too

176

constricting. And I wouldn't have fallen off in the first place if it hadn't been for that wretched woman coming at me out of the undergrowth." I saw him flinch at that.

"We've found no evidence that that is what happened," he replied, looking a little moody. "Grayson, I'm tired of having this argument. I feel very protective of you...That's just the way I am and I'm doing what I need to do." I could see he was exasperated with me, yet again, and this was clearly important to him.

I thought for a moment. Strangely I could feel myself starting to relent, almost wanting to for him, because I knew it would make him happy. But, true to form, I couldn't quite bring myself to do it – why make life easy for either of us?

"How would you feel about a compromise?"

"You want to negotiate?" He deliberated on this for a moment. "Hmm...what are you offering?" It was now his turn to look suspicious.

"How about...I agree to wear this whenever I ride out of the yard. So...I needn't wear it when I'm schooling in the arena or the paddocks."

He thought about this for a moment. "Okay, I think we can work with that, although...if you're jumping anything in the arena or paddocks, say, over three feet in height, I want you to wear it." Looking at me steadily he then smiled as I exhaled with frustration; clearly he wasn't going to give up and I was going to lose this round.

"Okay," I agreed, sighing wearily but reconciled to my fate. He smiled briefly, looking relieved until I continued, "And it's red because...?" and I left the question hanging.

"I reined back on getting the hi-vis one as I didn't think I'd get you to go for that, probably a step too far, so I got the next most violent colour available, to make you stand out."

"Well, of course you did," I replied in resignation.

At this he gave me his broadest smile which I couldn't help but respond to, but he then announced he was going to go and pack up his things and my heart sank. Before he left the room I said, "Thank you, Trent, for staying here with me. It was kind of you to give up your time."

"I know being helped is something you abhor but I've enjoyed looking after you." And as I acknowledged how terribly formal and polite we both were he hesitated for a moment, gazing at me as if he were about to say something else, but then obviously he thought better of it because he left to go and pack.

I didn't know what to do. I didn't want this – that I did know; that was what my head was telling me but my heart was no longer listening and there was nothing I could do about it. I still couldn't be sure how he felt about me. I had such difficulty reading him. At times I thought there was something there, something between us; he'd been so attentive to me, it made me think he was interested but I also knew that it was part of his job to look after everyone on the estate so how was I to know how he really felt? He hadn't said anything obvious, made any obvious move, and right now that was what I needed: something obvious, to be sure – to be sure I wasn't going to look like a complete idiot. I wanted to say something, I wanted to tell him how I felt but I was too afraid of looking like a fool, too afraid he would reject me, and the thought of that alone made me feel sick. As he came down to leave I got up and met him in the kitchen.

"I hope you have a good trip," I said as I started to busy myself as a distraction, looking in the fridge to see what to have for lunch.

"And I hope you continue to improve as the week progresses." He glanced out of the window towards the yard, adding with a grimace, "No doubt once I'm gone you'll have the oh-so-attentive Carlton hovering around you, attending to your every whim," and with that he turned to the door.

"What is it, Trent, you don't want me but you don't want anyone else to want me either?" The words were out of my mouth before my brain had had a chance to vet what I was about to say. I stood there horrified; it was meant to be in jest but it didn't come out that way.

These words caused Trent to stop and he took a deep breath before turning back to me, his tone soft but the words so definite: "Who said I didn't want you, Emma? Just so there's no misunderstanding, I want you very much, but not until you're ready for me."

My stomach clenched, and as he continued to look at me I knew I'd find no peace now, not after this declaration. The strong front of assurance I wore like a mask, the one that I presented to the world, and in particular to this man, was crumbling. I felt panic as the unpleasant sensation of losing my grip on things, on myself, washed over me and I was overwhelmed with anxiety as I had no ability to regain control of myself or my emotions. He must have sensed my discomposure but I watched him close his eyes and shake his head sadly as he started to turn once more to the door. *Say something, anything!* I could hear myself screaming from within.

Then as if from nowhere I heard myself say quietly, "I am ready for you." It sounded pathetic to my ears but he stopped. My heart was beating so hard I could feel it physically pounding in my chest. My breathing was shallow, waiting for his response, even now anticipating his rejection, and I knew my anxiety was reflected in my face as he looked back at me, his eyes warm, his face lit with a hopeful smile. Before I'd even caught my breath in relief he'd turned, crossed the kitchen and I was wrapped in his arms. I closed my eyes as my arms went around him, feeling safer than I had felt in years.

"Oh God, I can't tell you how long I've been waiting for some indication, any indication that you feel about me even a fraction of what I feel for you," he murmured in my ear, loosening his arms slightly as he brought his face up to look at mine. I could feel joyful tears gathering as I gazed at him and as they overflowed he brought his hands up to each side of my face, wiping them away with his thumbs. Dropping one hand back to my waist he held me close as he continued to run his other thumb down my cheek and then gently across my lips, causing my breath to catch.

"Do you think this is wise? Getting involved with someone as messed up as me?"

He kissed my cheek gently. "I have no choice. I don't have the strength to keep away from you any longer, even if I wanted to...and anyway...there are things about me which are just as screwed up, you just don't know about them yet." He hesitated then, and frowned before continuing, "Actually, I hadn't thought about that before now...but you're probably taking the bigger risk here, which might not be good for you. You should think about that and decide if this is the wisest thing for you to do."

"I have no choice. I don't have the strength to keep away from you any longer, even if I wanted to," I echoed back at him, smiling, and as his face broke into a grin, he kissed my cheek again, releasing me, sighing as he did so.

"I can't believe I have to say this but I really do have to go now," his voice full of regret and I nodded, smiling back.

"I know...go on," and he left, promising to be back as soon as he could. Watching him from the back door I waved as he drove off, leaving me to turn back to my now-too-empty home.

Elated by this most unexpected, although surprisingly welcome, turn of events I replayed what had just happened. After all my denials, and all my years of self-sufficiency, I found I'd relished the feeling that had swept over me when I was in Trent's arms. I didn't realise how much I'd missed the affection and how I now welcomed it, however undeserving I felt I was to receive it.

Chapter 16

I knew the time until I next saw Trent was going to drag as I was off work. I caught up on all my household tasks and popped out frequently to see how Carlton was getting on with the yard duties, reasoning that I needed to keep an eye on the horses but probably irritating him no end with my constant checking. Every day my head was feeling a little better and my body less stiff. I could see my bruises now, gradually fading, becoming a rainbow of fainter colours spreading across my back. I'd started doing some stretching exercises to try and loosen up and help the healing process along.

At the end of the week I received a call from the local surgery wanting me to come in for a check-up. I made an appointment for that afternoon then arranged for Carlton to take me as I didn't feel I should drive until I'd been given the all-clear.

I'd already decided that while at the doctors I would discuss another matter that was occupying my mind. Fortunately, the doctor was pleased with my recovery and happy with me driving again and going back to work the following week as long as I didn't overdo things. She dealt with the questions I had as well as giving me the prescription I needed, plus a few more days of painkillers.

On the way back from the surgery Carlton casually asked if I was going to the May Ball being held the following weekend at the Manor. I knew it was taking place, Trent had mentioned it at the hospital, but I'd assumed it was being held as a charity fundraiser and hadn't given it any more thought than that. Carlton explained everyone on the estate was invited, with probably a couple of hundred other people attending. The estate staff would be working at the event, the idea being that if everyone mucked in it kept the costs down for the charity, helped everything to run smoothly, and everyone would get to have some part of the evening off. I said I wouldn't mind going, but as it was black tie I didn't have anything suitable to wear. It was at that point that I realised I'd been set up, as quite conveniently Greene and a couple of the others were going shopping the next day and had room in the car for me to go along – you'd almost think it'd been planned.

Trent managed to call me the next evening for a short while and during our conversation I told him I'd bought a dress for the ball, asking if he was likely to make it back for that evening. He told me Cavendish was already in Grace's bad books for being away for the run-up to the event, and even though they were going to try to get back it wasn't certain they were going to make it. Again, I wondered what sort of business it was that took them away like this. The last time I'd asked Trent he'd avoided answering, only adding to the mystery, and I decided that as soon as we had some time together I'd bring it up again. All too soon he had to go and I spent the evening preparing everything, ready for my return to work the next day.

It was good to be back in the yard and I think Carlton was happy to be relieved of his duties as well. I didn't ride the first day, it being a rest day anyway, which was just as well as I found the yard routine to be tiring enough. I fitted in a trip to the saddlery in the afternoon to buy a new riding hat to replace the one that had been destroyed.

I made sure my first ride out on Regan was back along the same track I'd had my accident on. It had previously been one of my favourite rides and I wanted to get it out of the way so there was no build-up of apprehension in going down there again. As it was, I could see no evidence of my fall, and riding past the same spot in fact helped to banish the lingering, now almost ghostly, memory of the woman. It also helped that I was distracted by the beauty of the woodland surrounding me, which was now carpeted in blue, the heady scent of bluebells filling the air.

On the day of the Ball the stables were quiet, with me sticking to my usual routine while the area around the Manor was a hive of activity. It was exciting when I rode past a couple of times, watching all the comings and goings. Later, I finished evening stables then went to get ready, even putting on make-up after Greene had made the effort to show me what to do earlier in the week.

Carlton had offered to pick me up at seven to save me from walking but when I heard his truck drive into the yard I was still upstairs so I yelled for him to come in when he knocked on the back door. I was putting Trent's jewellery on as the finishing touch, then I walked downstairs feeling self-conscious and awkward. My dress was of the richest, deepest burgundy; it had small capped sleeves, the neckline low enough to be sculpted flatteringly across my chest then fitted into my waist, skimming my hips before dropping elegantly to the floor. Up one side there was a slit ending around mid-thigh level which I found a little alarming but which Greene had assured me was quite discreet. Carlton's look when he turned to see me enter the kitchen could only be described as one of carnal appreciation as he mouthed, "Wow."

I brushed it off: "This is nothing, you wait until you see Greene. Anyway, you're looking pretty good yourself, Carlton." And he was, all handsomely spruced up in black tie.

He held out his hand, indicated towards the door and said, "Your carriage awaits." I made sure the cat flap was locked, and said goodbye to Susie, who was already curled up in her bed for the evening.

We parked round the back of the Manor, noticing there was a steady stream of cars currently arriving at the front, and entered through the kitchens, which were bustling with people. Mrs F was in charge overall but an additional catering company had been brought in for the occasion so she had her hands more than full. I was going to be helping out during the early part of the evening, circulating with canapés and refilling drinks, and I was busy from the start, keeping the guests happy.

I saw Grace early on and asked if Cavendish had managed to make it back but she shook her head sadly. My heart sank a little bit, but determined to enjoy the evening I kept myself occupied, offering help wherever needed. The activity in the kitchen eventually settled down once everyone had been fed and I managed to get myself a drink at last.

Carlton arrived in the kitchen soon after, having been relieved from his bar duty, and after announcing the dancing was starting he whisked several of us off towards the ballroom where there was a band playing. I danced to the best of my limited ability with everyone who asked, and enjoyed it all, having never been to anything like it before.

It was getting late and needing a break from the dance floor I went out to the bar area, managing to find a free bar stool to sit on to give my feet a break. I had no idea how Greene was managing it – she was wearing six-inch heels and had not left the dance floor once. Her feet must have been in agony, unless they were numbed with alcohol, which was the only explanation I could come up with. She looked sensational in the shimmering tawny-gold dress she'd bought and I was pleased to see the effect it was having on Carlton; they'd already danced together several times and I had high hopes in that direction. I asked Stanton, who was now on duty, for a glass of wine and sat deep in thought, enjoying a moment's peace.

"Would you dance with me?" The familiar voice behind me made me start and I turned to see Trent smiling softly at me. He held out his hand and I took it, now welcoming the charge that came whenever I touched him. I'd been anxious when preparing for this evening, nervous in case he was here, concerned that as time had passed my imagination had exaggerated his feelings for me, but as soon as I saw him I was reassured.

"So acquiescent," he murmured. "That makes a nice change." He was looking deliciously handsome and I could see the curls of his hair were still damp from the shower.

"You scrub up well," I smiled at him.

"Not as well as you do...positively edible." As he looked me up and down appreciatively and exhaled softly, I felt my insides do a backflip. "Love the jewellery on you."

"It seemed like the right time and place..." I replied, grinning at him, then looking across the room I could see Cavendish had also arrived and was being greeted enthusiastically by Grace. Trent led me to the dance floor and as he pulled me closer I muttered, "I can't dance."

"Neither can I – I'm only using this as an excuse to hold you close to me. As no doubt all the other men in this room have this evening," and he gazed at me, raising one eyebrow in question. I looked away guiltily, a little embarrassed, as that was exactly what had happened.

"Hmm...I thought as much." Letting go of my hand he brought his up and around my waist until it came to rest in the small of my back, pulling me towards him. I brought my arm up and across his shoulder, my hand stilling, fingers on the collar at the back of his neck. Every now and then I felt his hair lightly touch my hand and had to resist the urge to run my fingers through it. He took my other hand, my fingers curling around his thumb, his fingers closing round the outside of mine as he brought it up to his chest, and we moved slowly to the music.

Looking at each other we spoke quietly for a while, catching up on what the other had been up to over the last few days, but gradually the conversation became more halting as the intensity grew between us. I could feel myself getting warmer, his breathing becoming deeper, and I couldn't meet his eyes any more, seeing only my desire for him reflected back at me when I did. He leaned in closer to my ear, his breath soft across my cheek, and whispered, "I don't want to rush this but I really don't think I'm going to be able to keep my hands off you for much longer." Closing my eyes I reminded myself to keep breathing, and when I opened them again he was still watching me. I could feel myself blush under the scrutiny and looked away, trying to escape his intensity, finding his lips instead to focus on, only to start imagining their kiss, their touch on my skin, and when I looked back up I knew he was enjoying the effect he was having on me, his eyes twinkling with amusement at my discomfort. We danced, savouring each other's company, oblivious to anyone else for as long as the music played, which was not long enough, the evening eventually coming to an end.

I'd been planning on walking home and Trent came with me, holding my hand, untying his bow tie and opening the first couple of buttons of his shirt which was more than a little distracting. Fortunately, he seemed happy to walk in silence as I started to feel nervous and with everything going on in my head I couldn't have coped with holding a conversation as well. I was wondering if I should invite him in, if he was expecting to be invited in. I had no idea what you should do in such a situation – was it too forward to just invite someone in? Should I invite him in for coffee? Or was that too much of a cliché? Should I not invite him in at all and play hard to get? Had there not already been enough of that? My body was telling me there'd definitely been enough of that.

When it eventually came to it, however, the decision was taken out of my hands. As we got to the back door Trent turned to me, saying, "Here you go, safely home. I'm sorry but I'm going to have to leave you now as Cavendish and I have to go straight back to work." And with that he took my face in his hands, kissed me lightly on the forehead, and left. On the forehead! I managed to mumble a goodbye, though I was more than a little taken aback. I must have looked a picture at that point, standing there, my mouth open in incredulity.

I unlocked the door and as Susie came to greet me I kicked off my shoes grumpily, pulled on my wellies and hitched my dress up a little by bunching it up and tucking it into my pants (always so ladylike). I marched over to the stables, accompanied by Susie, and did the watering before heading off to bed. Needless to say it took me ages to get to sleep.

I woke to the sound of a text arriving on my phone the next morning which read:

'Morning Grayson, I trust you slept better than I did. Buoyed by your acquiescent mood last night I was wondering if you might consider coming out with me later in the week on an actual date if that term doesn't offend you too much? Tx'

'I didn't sleep particularly well since you ask so not feeling quite so acquiescent this morning. I like your x or would that one be on the forehead too? Despite that I'd like to accept your invitation to go on a date. When should I get myself ready for you? Gx'

'Friday 8 Tx (this one is definitely not on your forehead!)'

I could see I had another long week ahead of me.

Chapter 17

I woke with a start to Susie's barking downstairs. Looking over at the clock which read 2am, I'd barely registered the fact that it was unusual for Susie to bark in the night when she alarmed me further by leaping up the stairs and coming into my room, agitated and barking directly at me. I leapt out of bed, thinking it must be something serious for her to behave like this. I was wearing lounge pants and a vest top so I grabbed my cotton dressing gown and pulled that on as I ran down the stairs. Pushing bare feet into wellies I unlocked the back door and as soon as it was open I knew what the problem was – smoke, the air was thick with it. Turning back to the kitchen, I hit the panic button then went out, shutting the door behind me and leaving Susie safely in the boot room.

Heading towards the stables I found to my immense relief that after running through the cloud of smoke it was not coming from there, and while the horses were agitated they were not in any immediate danger. I was already calling 999 and as I talked to the emergency services operator I looked back at the cottage and saw the source of the smoke was the garage. Giving the relevant details, the operator confirmed a fire engine was on the way and I ended the call.

Grabbing the fire extinguishers which were mounted on hooks on the walls, I carried them in the direction of the garage. Wrapping my dressing gown sleeve round my hand I pulled one of the garage doors open. It appeared that the garage itself was not on fire, at least not yet, but my car was, and as I tried to edge in closer under the clouds of smoke billowing out, I pointed the fire extinguisher hose in that direction, released the pin and pulled the lever. Foam squirted in the right direction though I couldn't see if it was having any effect on the flames or not. My eyes streamed and, coughing, I struggled for breath. Once the first cylinder was empty I grabbed the second one and starting that, I was trying to edge in closer, when I felt someone next to me; looking up, I saw it was Wade. He took the fire extinguisher from my hands while a pair of strong arms wrapped themselves around me, lifted me clear of the smoke, and carried me across the yard where the air was clearer. I noticed the gates were open and at that moment, much to my relief, a fire engine pulled into the yard, the fire crew leaping out and into action. Carlton put me down, and bending over double I coughed and gasped for air.

An ambulance pulled in a minute or so later, the paramedics putting me on oxygen to help my breathing. I sat on the back step of the ambulance, the oxygen mask on my face, as I watched the fire crew at work. It didn't seem to take too long before the fire was under control, although it was a lot longer before it was out and they were happy it was not going to reignite.

Carlton had been overseeing the activity and after making him go and check on the horses he reported back that they were all quite settled, apart from Monty who was a little overexcited, and as you would imagine they were all taking great interest in the unusual night-time activity.

My breathing was feeling more or less back to normal and I was trying to get the paramedics to let me come off the oxygen when I looked across the yard to see Cavendish and Trent enter it. Cavendish went to talk to the fire crew who were now sifting through the debris and Trent ran across to me, relief replacing the look of anxiety he had been wearing. I raised my eyebrows in surprise above my oxygen mask, silently questioning how he'd got there so quickly, and for that matter, how he knew in the first place. He muttered, "Panic button, helicopter," as he squeezed onto the step next to me, hugging me to him. He didn't say anything else but I could feel his tension and despite all the drama I found myself relishing these few moments of unanticipated closeness.

A short while later Cavendish came over, and after checking on me he asked to have a word with Trent. They wandered off a little way but before they'd gone too far I heard Cavendish say to Trent that the fire crew thought it was arson. Strangely, Trent's head went down at this and Cavendish brought his hand up, putting it on Trent's upper arm in a brotherly, supportive gesture I found curiously touching. They continued walking and talking for a couple of minutes before returning to me.

Cavendish sat next to me and with no preamble asked if I had any enemies, or if I was aware of anyone who might have a grudge against me. I thought for a moment, then rather reluctantly suggested Gary as possibly someone who might feel a little antagonistic towards me, but I really didn't think it was likely he was behind this and it was clear from their reaction that neither Trent nor Cavendish thought so either. Cavendish said he couldn't see a link between this and my fall from Regan if it was Gary, as I'd thought it had been a woman who'd frightened Regan, which was a good point. Although it wasn't until he brought this up that I'd even thought of the previous incident and considered the fact that there might be a link between the two. Trent surprised me then, saying he'd already had Gary checked out after the last incident and had drawn a blank. I couldn't think of anyone else and said so to Cavendish. He asked a couple of further questions as to whether I'd seen anyone hanging around or anything out of the ordinary over the last few days, but again I had to answer in the negative. Trent watched silently throughout this exchange.

Cavendish said goodbye, adding his sympathies for the loss of my car, and indicated to Trent that he wanted to have a word before leaving. They wandered off a little way and although I tried I couldn't catch much of what they were saying, other than I thought I heard Cavendish say something about keeping on searching, to which Trent nodded in response, but he looked worried, glancing over at me a couple of times anxiously during the discussion. Cavendish ended the conversation looking like he was trying to reassure Trent, who appeared to nod reluctantly in agreement; then Cavendish left, lifting his hand briefly at me as he did so. I lifted mine in response, my thoughts on edge, knowing something was amiss but feeling unsettled with not knowing what.

Trent came back and although I asked him what was going on he just reassured me that it was nothing for me to worry about, they'd be doing all they could to find out who was behind this.

The fire crew were packing up and the paramedics took me off the oxygen, advising me I might be coughing for a few days.

Wade was left clearing up some of the debris in the yard while Trent, Carlton and I headed into the kitchen, which fortunately had remained more or less clear of smoke. Susie went back to her bed even though it was getting towards her breakfast time and as I sat down at the table Carlton and Trent remained standing. Trent started speaking firmly and decisively, although I thought I could detect an anxious note to his voice.

"I'm not sure what's going on, or whether the two incidents are linked, but after what appears to be an arson attack we're going to have to put in place some additional security measures. Grayson, once you've finished evening stables and been to the gym I want you in here with the doors locked. Carlton will take over doing the late watering. I do not want you out of this house at night unless one of us is with you, do you understand?" He stared at me sternly as he said this, not continuing until I confirmed that I did indeed understand.

"Carlton, I want two on guard here in the yard overnight, every night. You can arrange a rota between you while I'm away, then I can help out once I'm back. Is that clear?" Carlton nodded his agreement.

"If you're really worried about me perhaps Carlton should move in twenty-four-seven so he could guard me at all times," I suggested, innocently looking up at Trent and smiling sweetly as I did so. Carlton beamed at this as Trent glanced anxiously between the two of us.

"It's bad enough that I'm having to leave the fox guarding the hen house, so to speak – I have no wish to open the door and usher him into it as well. I think we'll leave things as they are," he finished guardedly. And with this he came round the table, bending to growl, "Behave yourself," in my ear, as I smiled at his reaction to my teasing, before saying his goodbyes and heading off.

Carlton gazed at me, then shook his head and smiled. "You certainly know how to wind him up." Then looking at his watch he took charge: "Right, look at the state of you – go and get cleaned up and join me in the yard, I'll get going on the feeding." I hadn't realised it was that time already, and looking down at myself I saw I was covered in sooty patches, looked decidedly shabby and stank of smoke, not that he looked, or probably smelt, much better. I went off to get showered and dressed before tackling the day, which was going to have to include contacting my insurers to get that ball rolling.

Before I went in for lunch I walked over to the garage to have a look at the damage caused by the fire and stared sadly at the burnt-out skeletal remains. I was sorry to have lost my beloved car and thoughts kept going round and round in my head as I wondered who I could have offended so much that they would want to do this to me, as well as there being the possibility that they may have been responsible for my fall from Regan.

I hadn't been concerned after my fall, thinking it was an accident, but now I was starting to feel differently. It didn't seem real at all that this could be happening and I was starting to feel quite jumpy at the thought that there was someone out there wanting to cause me harm. A couple of times during the morning I'd caught myself looking up into the trees that surrounded the stables thinking I'd seen someone there, only to find it was nothing. My eyes as well as my mind were playing tricks on me. I was pleased Susie was around and made sure I kept her close to me, which gave me some comfort.

Trent called that evening to see how I was, to check I was locked in for the night and that my guards were out in the yard. I assured him I'd seen Hayes and Turner arrive and I was perfectly safe. I didn't add how pleased I'd been to see them or that I'd immediately felt better knowing they were there as I didn't want him to know how nervous I was starting to feel, and how much I wanted him to be there with me. There wasn't any point in telling him that when there was nothing he could do about it. I went to bed, trying to get rid of my anxiety by looking forward to the fact I would be seeing him the next day, and fortunately, as I'd been up most of the night before, it wasn't long before I was asleep.

Trent was a little early picking me up and we left the estate in his truck, driving to a pub in a nearby village. Ordering our drinks we studied the menus at a quiet table. I chose quickly and looking up, I took the opportunity to watch Trent while he was still deciding. He looked tired and strained. I mentioned this to him but he shrugged it off as being the result of the long days they'd been working.

"Should be coming to an end soon though and I'll have some recovery time. More importantly, how've you been? You seem tense."

I assured him everything was fine but I wasn't sure he believed me, though before he could ask more the waiter came to take our order.

I updated Trent on the fallout from the fire, and that the insurers would be coming out to look at the damage to the garage and the car before the clean-up could begin, and I started filling him in on any news I had about the estate. Talking about anything other than how I was feeling.

Our food arrived, and as he ate his ravenously I picked at mine, my nerves taking the edge off my hunger.

"Why are you not eating?" he said, frowning at me, to which I replied rather unconvincingly that I just wasn't hungry. I knew from his look he didn't believe me but I chose to ignore it, changing the subject, deflecting his attention onto the blossoming romance between Carlton and Greene.

"That should cool his ardour towards you anyway," he muttered gruffly, though he appeared a lot more relaxed once he'd eaten and obviously felt better too, as we chatted whilst waiting for the bill. I asked if there was any news about who was responsible for the fire but he said there wasn't, it was early days. I felt he was holding back, keeping something from me, as he didn't want to talk any further on the subject.

We left soon after and although I could feel the tension growing between us, as soon as we were in the truck heading home I knew what was coming, and as he walked me to my door I stated a little forlornly, "You're not coming in are you?"

"I can't...I'm sorry...duty calls," he answered apologetically, as I sighed loudly.

"If I'd known you were going to be here for such a short time I'd have taken you to bed the moment you arrived," I sounded as exasperated as I felt.

Trent's eyebrows shot up in sympathy with his rather shocked expression though he then chuckled before saying somewhat wistfully, "While that is certainly an enchanting prospect, it would hardly have been appropriate behaviour for our first date now, would it?" He was trying to be serious, pretending to tell me off, but the small smile at the corner of his mouth betrayed him.

"Oh God, what is happening to me?" I put my hands to my head, running my fingers through my hair in frustration. At this he stepped towards me, reaching for me, but I held my hands up like a barrier to stop him. "Oh no, you stay where you are. No touching, not if you're going to leave me again."

Stopping just in front of me he put his hands in his pockets, exhaling softly in frustration as he gazed at me. "Night, Grayson," and he leaned forward, kissing me softly on the corner of my mouth – it was beautifully sweet and my eyes closed briefly at his touch.

"Trent," I whispered almost painfully.

"I know, baby," he murmured. "Couple of days, I promise," and he was gone.

I went inside, and locking the door behind me I leaned up against it for a moment deep in thought. I'd surprised myself as well as Trent with my rather forward comment and was now embarrassed by it. It made me sound considerably more confident about where our relationship was going than I felt. The truth was that I was nervous about Trent's return and what he might be expecting and that hadn't exactly been made obvious by my behaviour this evening. The truth was I'd had little experience of men and it had been a long time since I'd taken anyone into my bed, however brazen I might have sounded about it. I went upstairs now, my mind full of these concerns but secure in the knowledge Carlton would soon be there to do the watering, and then I'd have my guards reassuringly in place for the night.

Chapter 18

After a restless night I was an unbearable ball of frustration by the next morning, and decided to work flat out to try and ease the tension. I went out to the yard to start the daily routine, waving to Wade and Hayes who were just leaving. Working all of the horses hard, I made both them and myself sweat; I then washed all four of them, rinsing them thoroughly before removing as much water from their coats as possible. As it was a warm, sunny day I turned them out for a few hours.

While the stables were empty I cleaned all the tack, got the boxes ready for the evening and tidied the yard, sweeping it from end to end. Getting each horse in I groomed them until they gleamed before finishing evening stables. Following this with a workout at the gym, I came back for a shower and something to eat.

I'd kept myself busy all day, aiming to block out my concerns of last night as well as any thoughts of somebody out there wanting to do me harm, but I was relieved when I saw Carlton and Turner arrive in the yard and as I went upstairs later I slept better purely because I'd exhausted myself.

The weather was fine and warm the next day and I put myself through the same level of punishing routine. Once I'd finished evening stables, given my still-fractious state of mind I went to the gym and after my standard workout decided to kick the shit out of the punch bag for a while. After half an hour every part of my body was aching; sweat ran down my face and I was bent over, my hands on my knees, breathing heavily when Carlton arrived, his face creasing with concern when he saw me.

"Are you okay? It looks like you might be overdoing it."

"Fine, just ridding myself of some tension," I replied with what I hoped was a grin but probably looked more like a grimace. Making a feeble waving gesture with my hand I encouraged him to go and get on with his workout.

"I know of an excellent way to get rid of tension," he smirked, as I shook my head at him. I had to give the boy his due, he never gave up.

"You're a bad man, Carlton. What do you think Greene would do to you?" He winced at the picture this conjured up for him.

"Yeah…you're right, that wouldn't be pretty," he said, and grinning he wandered off to start his workout at the other end of the gym.

I definitely felt less tense now, probably because my body was too exhausted to be anything other than relaxed, so I went home for a shower. Once dry I pulled on some shorts and a short-sleeved linen top, and took a beer out into the garden.

I sat there, Susie under the table, winding down and enjoying the evening. It was quiet and I could hear the gentle noises of the horses in their stables, listening to them moving around through the straw, munching on their hay, contented.

I heard a car approaching, it slowing down, stopping outside the cottage. Susie's low warning growl started, my personal protector, alerting me along with a prickling on the back of my neck. Hearing the gate open and close I peered anxiously towards the corner of the cottage; not knowing who to expect, my nerves on edge in anticipation.

Trent appeared and I breathed a sigh of relief, noticing his pace slow momentarily as he saw I was there, then he continued to stride purposefully towards me. Wearing a dark suit and white shirt, the collar of which was undone, he looked delicious. Even at this distance I could feel the

200

tension radiating off him. I stood, my heart racing, and as he reached me we took a moment drinking in the sight of each other. He was breathing deeply, then spoke quietly, "The longest two days of my life." Bringing one hand up to the side of my face, his fingers in my hair, he brought his lips softly to my other cheek. I could feel his breath and as he grazed my earlobe with his teeth I inhaled sharply. His other hand was at my waist, pulling me closer to him.

"Mmm...me too," I murmured softly as my fingers found their way into his hair, my concerns from the last time I'd seen him dispelled the moment he touched me. I felt his lips tracing the line of my jaw, a tingle running through me every time they touched my skin. He pulled back a little, looking down at me, his eyes dark and intense, his lips at last touching mine so tenderly I melted inside, moaning softly as our lips parted, his tongue gently finding mine and when it did our mutual passion igniting, our kisses becoming harder, demanding. He pulled back, releasing his hold on me, breathing deeply, and for one awful moment I thought he was going to leave me again. Instead he shrugged out of his jacket and holding that in one hand he took my hand in his and without a word led me into the house.

Throwing his jacket over the back of a chair he kept moving until we were upstairs in my bedroom. He stopped then turned to me, seeking affirmation that this was okay, that he hadn't overstepped the mark. Moving towards him and without losing eye contact I silently removed each of his cufflinks. Kicking off his shoes he removed his socks as I reached to undo the buttons on his shirt, torn in my desires – it was all I could do not to just rip his clothes off but at the same time I wanted to savour every moment. Sliding his shirt off his shoulders and down his arms I let it drop to the floor. I gazed at him, admiring his well-muscled body, I noticed a scar at the top of his chest towards his shoulder, and had to remind myself to breathe; he was looking so intensely at me when I met his eyes I could feel myself blushing. Embarrassingly, I think I might have actually whimpered out loud at the sight of him, and he looked at me as if I amused him. Cool, Emma, really cool.

Passing my fingers through the light covering of dark hair over his chest and down across his stomach where the hair tapered before it disappeared into his waistband his stomach muscles flexed, contracting under my touch. I heard him inhale sharply when I reached to undo his belt, his hands coming up to stop mine as, holding them still, he spoke: "Not so fast – my turn. Arms up." As I obeyed he reached for the bottom of my shirt, swiftly pulling it up over my head and off my arms, it landing on the floor next to his. Taking a breath he looked at me, then reached round to undo my bra, taking it off before putting one arm round my waist to pull me closer. His other hand caressed my breast, my nipple stiffening at his touch. Reaching into his pocket he pulled out a condom, threw it onto the bed, and nervously I glanced up at him.

"We don't need to use that, I've already taken care of it." I hesitated, watching him carefully, wondering what his response would be.

"Have you now…" he frowned down at me. "That was forward thinking of you."

"I'm an all or nothing kind of girl," I murmured. "And I didn't want there to be anything between us."

These words were his undoing. His lips came down on mine harder as I dropped one hand to the front of his trousers, hearing him groan as I touched him. His whole body trembling, as I ran my hands up and over his chest, pushing my fingers through his hair. His hand dropped to my shorts and as they fell to my feet he reached into my pants and I felt his breath hitch when he realised how ready I was for him. Barely containing myself, I moaned as he caressed me, my legs weakening.

"I like that," he whispered against my lips, "I like that a lot." Bereft as he withdrew his hand and feeling a desperate need for his touch again instead he pulled down my pants, and moving backwards, I lay down. He stared at me as he undid his belt and trousers and taking those and his pants off in one smooth motion he stood upright again, gloriously naked. My eyes drifted at that point from his beautiful face, my thoughts clearly showing on mine, as when I glanced up at his again the amused smile was back and he cocked an eyebrow at me. Flashing my eyes I grinned in return, breathless as he approached the bed and bent to reach for me.

Gasping, I arched my back, feeling the lightest of touches from his lips on my lower abdomen; he crawled across the bed, over me, leaving a trail of kisses up my body and across my breasts before reaching my mouth and kissing me hungrily.

Ready to combust as his knee came up to push my legs further apart, I yearned for him, my body aching as he teased me. Then, unable to hold back any longer, I gloried in the feeling of him inside me, filling me as he thrust forward, his eyes finding and holding mine. I wrapped my legs around his ribs as he started to move strongly, urgently claiming more and more of me, building with each thrust. I clung to him, wanting every inch, sensation growing within until it peaked then came crashing through me like an explosion at my very core. Waves of pleasure rocked my body as gasping his name I came around him, my body shuddering in its release as he came too, groaning as he thrust deep into me. Clinging tightly to each other, not wanting to let go, we gradually came round, our ragged breaths easing.

He gently pulled out of me, and rolling onto his side looked at me a little anxiously.

Emotionally overwhelmed, tears had formed, and though I tried to blink them away a couple leaked out, running down my temples. He noticed, and speaking softly but with a voice full of concern he asked: "Hey, what's wrong?" I shook my head, suddenly unable to speak. "I'm sorry, was that not okay? I'm sure I can do better, it was a little rushed." I couldn't bear the look on his face; I'd ruined this for him and I hadn't meant to. All of a sudden he didn't seem his usual confident self at all, but more vulnerable, uncertain. "I'm sorry but I've been desperate for you since I last left here – you've been all I've been able to think about."

"It wasn't only you that found it a long two days," I reassured him, finding my voice. "And that was..." I hesitated. "That was..." Incapable of thinking of the appropriate words, I saw his brow crease in concern. "That was...more than okay." It was inadequate for how I was feeling but all I could come up with.

"More than," he repeated, his face relaxing as he suddenly appeared inordinately pleased with himself.

"Yes...I'm sorry about my reaction, it was unexpected. I know it's been a long time but I don't remember it being quite that intense."

"That must be the whole delayed gratification thing."

"Maybe we should leave it another year before trying it again then," I teased.

He replied dryly, "Yeah, I don't think that will be happening."

We lay there for a while, relaxed, and enjoying being with each other.

"Why didn't you tell me earlier?" I asked.

"Tell you what?"

"How you felt about me."

"I couldn't risk you running from me."

I stared at him, puzzled, as he explained further.

"When should I have told you, Em – at Christmas, your birthday, that night in the gym or on one of the many other times we've been together? Be honest with yourself, your mind has been so set against having a relationship, if I'd made a move, you would have run. I'd heard what you'd done to the others who'd asked you out and didn't want to get blown out like that."

I thought about this for a moment then nodded in agreement. "Yeah, I would have run."

"It had to come from you, like I said, you had to be ready. It's been my job to be patient...well, that and to keep Carlton off you."

I grimaced at this uncomfortable reminder before responding, "I wasn't sure how you felt at all, I couldn't read you – you were always so calm, controlled, and you seemed unaffected by me. I even gave you an opportunity." I was specifically thinking of our picnic on Eva's birthday.

"I know. I nearly did take that...you have no idea," he said, grinning at me, his eyes twinkling with amusement. "But...I decided to play hard to get instead." We both burst out laughing at that, and once we'd lapsed back into silence he carried on, his tone more serious now.

"I was definitely not unaffected by you, believe me. I've been trying to give you the time you needed, that's all," and he kissed my cheek softly before briskly announcing, "Anyway...changing the subject, I'm sorry to have to bring this to an end but we've been invited up to the Manor for a barbecue this evening. I actually only came over to invite you to it but then you seduced me and it went clean out of my head." He started laughing at the feigned look of outrage on my face.

"I've worked up quite an appetite as it happens so a barbecue is a great idea," I said, getting up. "I'll just go and have a shower, then I'll be ready."

Trent leapt out of bed eagerly. "I'll join you."

We arrived at the Manor half an hour later. Trent got out of the truck and came round to open my door for me. Climbing out he took my hand, then leaning towards me he asked somewhat shyly, "May I stay the night with you?"

I liked that, his formality, the natural air of authority he exuded still there but taking nothing for granted, which I appreciated. As I replied simply, "Yes," his slightly anxious expression changed to one of elation. Holding my hand as we walked from the car he dropped it as we passed through the gateway into the walled garden.

Grace looked up and, spotting us arriving, came straight across the lawn, hugging Trent and saying, "Welcome back."

"Thanks, Grace," he responded. "It's been quite a homecoming." Grinning, he winked at me over the top of Grace's shoulder, and as she pulled away from him I saw a look of curiosity on her face as she glanced fleetingly at me, a small smile forming on her lips. I started to blush and looked away, realising it had not gone unnoticed that we both had wet hair.

Trent went to his apartment to get changed into jeans and a tee shirt but was back quickly as separately we mingled, drinking, chatting and eating, but throughout the evening I was acutely conscious of his presence, several times finding myself looking for him, and each time I found his face his eyes would come to meet mine and he'd smile softly, reassuringly in my direction. Later I helped by carrying some dishes into the kitchen and as I walked back out Trent was coming in; as we passed our hands brushed fleetingly, inconspicuously, his hand briefly enclosing mine, giving it the slightest squeeze, a touch so deliciously intimate I could feel it tingling throughout my body.

It was looking like the gathering was going to go on for a while but at around ten I found Trent at my elbow announcing it was about time he got me back to do the late watering to give Carlton a break. We said our goodbyes and walked quickly out to the truck. When we got back to the yard I set off towards the stables but Trent quickly caught up with me, grabbing my hand and pulling me hard up against his body.

"I do actually have to do the watering you know, seeing as how you've cancelled Carlton."

"I know and I'll give you a hand with it. But come here first, I can't keep my hands off you a moment longer." Kissing me deeply he then added, "I've also cancelled your bodyguards – I told them I'd do the stint instead."

"Oh...So I have my own personal bodyguard for the night...now that's very appealing."

We got the watering done at record-breaking speed and as we headed for the cottage Trent made a short detour to his truck and came back carrying a small bag.

"What's in there, your pyjamas?" I teased.

He grinned across at me. "Damn it, I knew I forgot something...I'm not really used to the whole sleepover thing."

"We'll just have to see if we can manage without them then, won't we?"

The next morning I woke to hear Trent moving around downstairs. My body was feeling relaxed though a little achy and I was tired, having not had much sleep. Pulling on my lounge pants and a vest top I went downstairs, greeting Susie when I entered the kitchen. Looking over at Trent I suddenly felt inexplicably shy. He was making breakfast and looked gorgeous with his hair all messed up; turning round he grinned at me.

"Morning, I have good news...I've made a breakthrough with Susie. She's eaten the breakfast I made for her." He was triumphant and it pleased me that it was so important to him. Coming across the kitchen he wrapped me up in his arms before he kissed me.

"Being invited into your bed last night has melted even her icy heart towards me. I was just going to bring you up some tea. How're you feeling?" he asked.

"Well used," I replied, smiling softly up at him. A look of concern clouded his face.

"I didn't hurt you, did I?"

"No," I reassured him. "I think I gave as good as I got... You were quite right though."

He looked at me questioningly. "Right about what?"

"I can definitely remember you the next morning. In fact, every part of my body can remember everywhere you've been, every time it moves." He glanced at me sheepishly; in fact, I thought I even detected him blushing a little. "And," I added mischievously, "I'm damn glad I don't have to get on a horse today." He chuckled. "I'd better go and get showered, dressed and out to work or there will be complaints from the yard about feeding being late," I explained before kissing him, extricating myself from his arms and heading back upstairs. He soon joined me, hopping in the shower as I left it.

I'd finished feeding when he appeared by the feed room door.

"I'm going off to work. I'll be busy over lunch but can I see you this evening?"

"I'd love that. I'm not going to go to the gym tonight so do you want to come round once you're done? We could eat together," I suggested.

"Excellent, see you later." He kissed me longingly. "Something to keep me going," he sighed before walking off to his truck.

I went in for breakfast and sat there dreamily, finding myself smiling as I thought about the night before. I turned the horses out into the paddock then started on the stables, singing to myself as I did so, only interrupted once by Stanton and Peters who arrived to do some work in the garden. I prepared everything for evening stables then turned my attention to tidying the yard.

I had some shopping to do so I went first to the saddlery for some fly repellent as both Monty and Zodiac were being bothered, and then the supermarket, thinking that if Trent was going to be staying over I'd better get in some supplies of food and drink. I was back by lunchtime and as I set about making myself a sandwich I noticed I'd received a food parcel from the Manor, including a small bunch of sweet peas in a vase on the table which must have come from the gardens.

After I'd eaten I had a nap, waking a couple of hours later feeling a lot better. I went to get the horses in and by six was back at the cottage and looking forward to seeing Trent, although aware it would probably be another hour or so by the time he'd hit the gym. As it was he arrived ten minutes later.

"I didn't expect to see you yet," I said, greeting him at the door, as he kissed me.

"I was eager to see you so thought I'd skip the gym," he responded, smiling at me.

"That's good to hear. I'd decided, before last night that is, that you were quite ambivalent in your feelings towards me."

"What on earth would make you think that?" he replied, obviously surprised.

"Well the previous couple of times I've seen you, you more or less did a runner at the end of the evening, leaving me with a kiss on the forehead and another on the cheek. The signals you were giving out were quite confusing."

"Sorry about that." Putting his arms around me he continued, "You weren't to know but I shouldn't actually have been here at all. I had to snatch the brief trips home because I wanted to see you. However, it meant it was always a rushed visit and I couldn't trust myself to kiss you the way I wanted to, knowing if I did I'd be lost in you and it would've been impossible for me to go back to work." He looked down at me and I smiled gently.

"Show me," I whispered and he brought his lips down to mine, his touch gentle, unexpectedly hesitant, and I knew what he meant when my body melted with desire.

He pulled back a little to look at me, his voice taut with need: "Bed?"

Taking his hand I led the way.

Sometime later, as we lay together, I asked quietly, "Can I ask you a question?"

"Anything."

"How did you get your scars?" I'd noticed a second one, just above his hip, and I traced the line of it now with my finger.

"That one was from having my appendix out and the other one on my shoulder was the result of falling from a great height out of a tree and being impaled on a branch."

"Ouch." I was quiet for a moment, and then went off on a tangent. "I know I haven't had that much experience of you yet but you do seem to have quite a voracious appetite for sex." He chuckled. "So how have you managed all these months that I've known you without getting any?" I realised just as I said this that I'd made an assumption he hadn't been getting any. For all I knew he'd been working his way through the estate, and this thought suddenly concerned me.

"I run every morning, work hard every day and work out harder in the gym every evening. All of that kind of takes the edge off." He paused, before adding, "Plus I take cold showers," and he closed his eyes as he reiterated, ¹ots and lots of cold showers. At least I'm not going to ⌐ to endure one of those for a while."

"Ah, that explains the setting changes to my shower when you stayed here." I remembered the water being freezing when I got in after him.

"Yes, that was a particularly difficult time, being that close to you – quite unbearable actually. Thank God that's over." Leaping out of bed he announced he was famished and was going to cook us some dinner.

"You cook? Brilliant, I'll follow you down in a moment."

Taking a quick shower I dressed in my lounge pants and a tee shirt before joining him in the kitchen. He had some new potatoes on to boil, a pan heating up and a bowl of salad made up and on the table.

"I see Mrs F has been busy," he commented.

"Yes, I came back from shopping to find I'd received some treats in my absence. Isn't she wonderful."

"Absolutely," he agreed as I walked up behind him, wrapping my arms around his waist in a hug before moving round to his side to see what he was cooking. He was dropping a steak into the pan and as I watched my eyes widened in surprise.

"Hey, wait a minute, what's going on?" I questioned, gesticulating towards the pan.

"With what? I'm cooking the steaks how I'd normally do them – why, what would you usually do with them?"

"No, not that, the cooking is fine. It's just there are two, two steaks. Don't you see? If I get a food parcel I get one steak because there is one of me, not two. Why are there two steaks?" Hesitating, I stared at him, waiting for him to answer but he didn't, he looked bemused, so I continued, explaining, "There are two steaks because they know you're here, they know we're together. How would they know that?" I asked in bewilderment. Trent had gone very still, didn't answer and was concentrating hard, I thought, too hard on the steaks. "Trent? Have you told anyone?" I asked, although to be fair to him we hadn't discussed keeping it from everyone else. It was just that I thought it was something private only the two of us were sharing for the moment.

"I haven't told anyone..." he said slowly, still focusing on the steaks.

"But? Come on...I'm sensing hesitation," I probed.

"I was whistling," he admitted, his voice quiet.

"Whistling?" I repeated, not knowing what that had to do with anything.

"Yes, you know whistling, it's a sign of happiness. I was doing it at work today...it was commented upon. Apparently I don't normally sound happy.

"You must have been aware that some people have been watching us, Em, I think hoping we were going to get it together eventually and that is all it would have taken – me sounding happy. Plus the fact I cancelled Carlton doing the watering again, and the overnight guards, so I guess that confirmed it for them."

"Ah."

"Are you angry?" He winced theatrically, as if waiting for the blow to strike.

"No," I laughed at his reaction as I said this. "I guess it was expecting a bit too much to keep anything secret around here and it's probably a blessed relief for our friends. Anyway, I can hardly have a go at you when I could be accused of similar behaviour." I made a face at him, looking a little guilty.

"Ah, now we're getting it. What gave you away?"

"Singing...I was singing in the yard," and I glanced up at him a little embarrassed.

"Oh, I would've loved to have heard that...What is it like, your singing?"

"Tuneless...but enthusiastic!"

212

"Brilliant," he chuckled. "Right, dinner is ready. There's a bottle of red over there I've opened for us as well."

While we were eating I complimented him on his steak-cooking ability to which he replied, "Don't get too excited about the fact you think I can cook, my range is basic."

"I'm just delighted you know where the cooker is. How did you learn to cook?"

"By necessity rather than anything else. I've been on my own a long time so I had to do something to keep myself alive. But in fairness I've had a lot of support from Mrs F and a couple of others who've provided me with food, so like I said, my skills are fairly limited." There was silence for a few moments while we concentrated on the food, then I couldn't hold back any longer.

"A couple of others?" I questioned, looking at him expectantly. He gazed back at me with a puzzled expression on his face, feigning his lack of understanding.

"You said 'Mrs F and a couple of others'," I clarified.

"Ah…hoped I might have gotten away with that."

"Not a chance," I said, and he sighed.

"A couple of the girls have tried to…how would you put it…make advances on me over the years by trying 'the way to a man's heart is via his stomach' route."

"And did that work?" I questioned, trying to sound nonchalant.

"No, it didn't. I'm not good at being pursued, and just so you know, Em, I've not had a relationship with anyone on the estate. I've actually not wanted to be in a relationship since Zoe and although I've tried the casual sex thing it doesn't do it for me. I enjoy the chase, and let's face it, no one has ever had to chase a girl for as long as I have had to chase you." I felt some relief as this certainly allayed my earlier concerns.

213

"I'm surprised you wanted to, especially after I gave you such a hard time when I was first here."

"I think that's what interested me – you were a challenge, and who doesn't like a challenge?" and he flashed his eyes at me, smiling as he said this.

"When did you decide then?"

"You caught my attention during our first conversation, before we'd even met. But my interest was inexplicably raised the first time I saw you in those ridiculous overalls, then when you went for me over the dog that sealed it. Anyone who showed that much passion on behalf of their dog was definitely the one for me...it just took a long time to make you realise you felt the same way."

"It certainly did. Particularly after one of our early meetings when you came across as a misogynist," I recalled, still baffled by the behaviour he'd displayed.

"Yeah, I wanted to wind you up but realised I'd taken it too far that day," he grimaced uncomfortably.

"Why did you want to wind me up?" I frowned, confused by his desire for a reaction generally best avoided.

He looked away, deliberating on his explanation before looking back at me a little sheepishly. "I'd been surprised by the strength of my attraction to you when you defended Susie, seeing your passion rise, colour coming to your cheeks, anger lighting your eyes, your breathing..." he swallowed, "...and I imagined for a moment that passion in you rising for me. I couldn't stop thinking about it...wondering if I'd exaggerated it in my mind, so when the opportunity came along to get that reaction out of you again I took it."

"And did it meet your expectations?"

"More than..." he grinned.

I smiled at his explanation, thinking how deeply depressed my mind and body must have been at that time. "I didn't actually realise you were chasing at all, I thought

214

you were just trying to irritate the hell out of me," and I smiled at him as I said this.

"Very funny – and to think I wasted my best flirtation techniques on you!"

"Oh boy, are you in trouble if that's the best you had – no wonder you've been on your own for so long!" I was enjoying teasing him.

"I didn't want to scare you off by unleashing my full powers on you, that's why I reverted to playing hard to get," he said, laughing as he turned his attention back to his food. A little while later he said casually, "While we're on the subject, what about you?"

"What...my history? Not much to tell, only Alex actually."

He went quiet at this, thoughtful for a moment, and then added, "I know it's ridiculous at our ages, and incredibly possessive of me to feel like this, but I wish there hadn't even been him. I wish you were all mine," he added wistfully. I understood his possessiveness; I'd felt a pang of jealousy when he'd told me of his past, yet how could I be jealous of relationships that had happened long before I'd even met him? It was completely irrational but I realised I didn't like the fact that he'd been with anyone else before me either; I, too, wanted him to be all mine. However, that was what Alex and I had had and he hadn't appreciated how special that was at all, – clearly it wasn't all it was cracked up to be – and I pushed my possessive thoughts to the back of my mind thinking that they wouldn't lead to a healthy relationship at all.

I woke early the next morning to find Trent still asleep beside me. He looked relaxed and I enjoyed having this time to watch him. He was truly beautiful, his dark, full eyelashes swept down towards his high cheekbones, his full lips relaxed, his skin darkening towards and across his jawbone where he needed to shave. I realised in our short

215

time together I'd fallen for him completely, though the reality was I'd been falling for him since the first time we met; his patience in waiting and desire to understand me had drawn us inexorably towards this point where we were wrapped up in each other as close as it was possible for us to be.

I'd felt considerably safer since he'd been back, realising after fighting against it for so long that I appreciated his protectiveness, so much so I'd all but forgotten the fact that somebody out there might want to hurt me, especially as there had been no further incidents. My thoughts were interrupted as Trent stirred, opening his eyes and smiling when he saw me watching him.

"Morning," he said sleepily.

"Morning," I responded, as leaning over I gave him a quick kiss and made a move to get up, only to find myself suddenly pinned on the bed, Trent looking down at me.

"I think we can do a little better than that can't we," his lips finding mine.

The rest of the week passed quickly. The insurance assessors came out, together with some structural engineers who confirmed the garage was still sound. The insurers gave the all-clear for my car to be taken away then Cavendish arranged for the boys to clear out the rest of the garage, and scrub the walls and ceiling to remove as much soot as possible. A local carpenter came to measure up for new doors, which he then went away to make. There was no rush for these as I had no plans to replace my car anytime soon.

There had been one awkward moment with Carlton when they were cleaning up the garage. He'd come over to the stables to chat to me while I was grooming Regan. I knew I was going to have to deal with this at some point but hadn't yet worked out how to handle it, so I took the easy option and left him to ask.

216

"Am I right in thinking you won't need us to pick you up on Friday evening?"

I looked up at him, frowning a little. "I hadn't thought that far ahead actually but I guess not." He hesitated for a moment.

"So the rumours are true then…you and Trent."

"Yes, they're true." A long silence followed, during which he continued to look at me as I tried to think of something to say to lift the moment, ending up gabbling much too perkily.

"I hear you and Greene are getting on well. I've always thought you two suited each other."

"Yeah, we're having a good time together." He paused, before adding, "I hope you didn't mind me asking, Em, only I wanted to hear it from you. I hadn't realised that was where your feelings lay."

"I hadn't realised either, Carlton. But I'll still see you here and at the pub on Fridays – that's not going to change." He smiled at this, a little ruefully, then nodded before disappearing back to the garage. I exhaled with relief that that was over before returning my attention to Regan.

Chapter 19

On the following Friday evening there was quite a crowd from the estate at the pub. We'd pulled an extra table in towards the one in the booth and everyone squeezed together to fit round. Trent and I were squashed in next to each other and the evening was getting fairly raucous. I felt, rather than saw, the door open, but something made me look up and there stood Alex. My mouth actually dropped open. What the hell was he doing here? Hastily pulling myself together I let go of Trent's hand from under the table and stood, putting my hand on his shoulder. Alex had spotted me from the door and walked over to our table.

"Hello, Emma."

"Hi," I replied quietly, increasing the pressure through my hand into Trent's shoulder, discouraging him from standing up. I hesitated but then turned to the others, who had all gone quiet, all looking at the newcomer.

"Um, everyone this is Alex, my ex. Alex, this is everyone," and with that I pointed to a table in the corner that was empty, indicating that Alex should go to it, wanting to get him away from the others as quickly as possible. I followed him, taking my drink with me and glancing back at Trent, smiling reassuringly before sitting down with my back to him and the others.

"Can I get you a drink, Em?"

"I already have a drink," I replied quietly as he went to the bar and came back with a pint for himself and another glass of wine for me.

"I got you a glass of red, Cabernet Sauvignon, Em, I assume that's still your favourite?"

"I said I had a drink. How did you find me?" I sounded cold.

Alex appeared to be a little embarrassed as he mumbled, "Letting agent." I'd left strict instructions with the agent that my address was not to be given out, so I knew he had to have used some subterfuge to have obtained it. I sat there for a moment watching him, and as he leant forward to reach for his drink he looked up from his glass to me through his eyelashes and that was all it took for the reminder of Eva to hit me. Nothing had changed in that respect, despite our time apart.

I looked away as I muttered, "What do you want?"

"I wanted to see how you are."

"Now you've seen when are you going?" I was curt and I could see he was irritated by my abruptness but trying hard not to show it. He took a deep breath.

"I also wanted to update you on the court case."

I was silent. This had nothing to do with me. Alex had decided to sue the hospital that had treated Eva. I was not involved. He carried on regardless: "We won the case, Em. The hospital has admitted liability, admitted their negligence and we've received a payout."

"You've won the case, Alex, you've received a payout. It was your crusade, not mine. I already know who was responsible for her death." I was trying to keep my voice low so as not to attract attention but my anger at him being here talking like this was growing, and I was finding it difficult to control myself. He snapped right back at me.

"It was not your fault – how many times do you have to be told, Emma? You have to allow yourself to recover from this, get over it and move on." That did it.

"I have moved on, this is me moving on, and just because you've managed to find someone to use as a scapegoat, someone to take the blame, do not deem to tell me to 'get over it' – and I will repeat, what do you want?" My teeth were clenched as I said this, my voice still low as

219

I suppressed my anger. He tried to pacify me, opening his arms wide and resting them on the table between us, his hands relaxed, palms upturned. A gesture of calm, meant as much for him as for me.

"Sorry, Em, bad choice of words. I know neither of us are ever going to get over it but please….just stop for a moment and listen." Presumably taking my silence for agreement he pressed on. "There was no scapegoat, Em, the investigation was thorough, right from the doctor who shouldn't have fobbed you off by sending you home, to those who didn't take your fears seriously at the hospital…the whole system was found to be at fault. An inadequate triage system, too few doctors covering too many patients, the list goes on. But the good that has come out of it is that all this has now been investigated and systems have been put in place so no one else should ever have to go through that again."

My eyes were fixed on my hands in my lap. I became aware he'd stopped and was now sat watching me. I didn't know what to say, what to do with this information at that moment. I looked up at him and could feel his empathy as he continued, his voice subdued, "I feel guilty as well, Em, because I, like them, thought you were being too cautious, thought you were an overly anxious mother when all of us should have listened to you. I should have trusted you, supported you better. I don't know why I didn't and I can't tell you how much I regret not doing so." This was quite an admission and a lot to take in, certainly too much for me to deal with at that moment.

"Thanks for coming and telling me all of that, Alex, it's given me a lot to think about." I sat in quiet contemplation. He shifted uncomfortably on his chair and I knew he wasn't done.

"You look good, Em." His voice was soft and looking up at him I raised one eyebrow – surely not, I thought, but I knew him too well.

"What do you want, Alex?" I had a sneaking suspicion that I knew what was coming.

"You, Em...I want you." Crap.

"Oh dear, trouble in paradise?" I queried, although I couldn't have cared less.

"We tried to give it a go but I guess the way it started it was never destined to last. I realised what I'd lost and thought I'd come and see if we could give it another go. We were great together, Em, you know that. We could go back, start again...What happened...what I did...it doesn't mean it has to be the end." He gazed at me pleadingly.

Taking a deep breath, I knew that at last I had the strength to say what I needed to say and when the words came they came in a torrent, words I should have spoken to him years before but was too frozen by my grief to articulate them.

"I can't be with you, Alex, it's difficult for me to even look at you. When I do it breaks my heart all over again. I see Eva in you, all the time. I remember the first time we held her together and the last, and all of our lives in between. I loved you so much and I thought you loved me but you destroyed my trust in you by adding to my suffering when we lost her, choosing to betray me when you knew how alone I'd been all my life. You knew I had no one else to help me, yet that still wasn't enough to stop you from fucking her." I was shaking, the tears that came a mixture of sadness and fury. Alex looked shocked – I had never been so open with him.

"I had no idea of the depth of pain I caused you – I'm so sorry, Em, please forgive me. You always seemed to handle everything so well, and were so tough. Why couldn't you talk to me like this before?"

"Because by the time I was capable of talking, capable of finding my way back to you, Alex, it was too late, you'd already left me." I saw the tears come to his eyes as they fixed on mine.

221

His voice broke as he started speaking, barely above a whisper. "I thought you blamed me."

I didn't understand – blamed him for what? I waited patiently for more. Confusion must have shown in my face as he cleared his throat. "When you couldn't even look at me I thought it was because you blamed me for taking her away from you." We were still and I knew we were both reliving the moment: the moment of him prising my arms open to take her body from me – I could feel it as clearly, and as painfully, as if it were happening right at that moment. I closed my eyes, reaching across the table to take his hand, which I clasped tightly, feeling his hand tighten on mine in response.

I shook my head at him. "I never blamed you. Better you than someone else and I knew what it cost you. What have we done to each other, Alex? We have both been so damaged."

"I know...that's why I think we could make things better by being together. Please think about coming back to me." His voice was tight with emotion, his face a mask of misery.

Throughout this conversation I'd felt Trent's stare searing into my back and I thought I probably didn't have too much time in which to make my point and to end this now. I stared at Alex steadily and spoke calmly and firmly, knowing my words would hurt but knowing I had to say them anyway.

"The moment you chose to screw her, Alex, was the moment it ended and you lost me...forever. There is no going back – you ruined any chance of that ever happening." I didn't think I could make myself any clearer and yet he sounded astonished when he replied, still unable to believe my words and let it go.

"Please, Em, I promise you we could make things right between us again if we spent some time together. I'll wait for however long it takes."

I hesitated only a moment before saying, "Don't," then watched his face fall, as letting go of his hand Trent slid onto the bench next to me and I wondered how much he'd heard. I was shaken, my emotions scattered, which Trent picked up on immediately.

"You okay?" he asked, concern showing on his face, not looking away until I nodded and he was satisfied.

He introduced himself to Alex: "Hi, I'm the boyfriend, Trent," and he held out his hand. They shook briefly then Trent brought his arm back and around me, running his hand up my back until I could feel his fingers lightly caress the back of my neck, soothing me, and that's where he let them rest.

It was clearly a proprietorial move but Alex chose to ignore it, responding, "That's strange, I thought you were just introduced as part of 'everybody'." I could hear the challenge in his tone and was sure it was not lost on Trent.

"Well, you know Emma, she likes to keep things on a strictly need-to-know basis and she obviously didn't feel you needed to know. I, however, feel differently." He was staring impassively at Alex, a small smile on his face.

Alex looked back at me, ignoring Trent, and said, "Please think about what I've said, Em. I'm serious. You know where I am and you know my number if you want to talk." With that he got up to leave and I watched silently as the door closed behind him. Trent was quiet and still for a moment, deep in thought, and then he glanced across at me.

"Home?" he said, inclining his head to one side and looking serious. We said a brief goodbye to the others and left. The journey was silent. Trent was tense but I couldn't tell what he was annoyed about. Should we talk about it? I didn't really want to bring it all up again but I didn't know what to do. I didn't know him well enough to know how best to deal with this.

We checked the horses then went to the cottage. Trent had been staying with me every night; it wasn't something we'd discussed it was just what happened, neither of us wanting to be away from the other, but as we headed off to bed that evening I thought it was unlikely we'd be able to sleep, the tension being almost palpable.

"Is there anything you want to talk to me about, Em?" His voice was quiet in the dark as I climbed into bed.

"No." I wasn't ready to talk to him about what I needed to yet. I had to find the time to process all that Alex had told me. To try to work out in my own mind how I felt about the result of the court case and whether it changed anything for me. I heard his sigh.

"Then I have something. Why didn't you introduce me to Alex as your boyfriend? Are you ashamed of me?" Ah, I thought, his ego was hurt. This I could deal with.

"Of course I'm not, I just didn't want to let Alex know who you are or what you are to me. It might have complicated the situation."

"How would it have complicated the situation?"

"It's nothing to do with him who you are, that's all."

Trent was silent for a moment, then turning towards me he propped himself up on his elbow. "He came back for you, didn't he?"

"Yes." My answer was as blunt as his question but there seemed no need to add anything more to it.

"If he'd known I existed, he'd have backed off. As it was it made it look like I was someone you're not that serious about." He hesitated for a moment, continuing softly, questioning, "Perhaps that's because you're not serious about me?" I sat up, annoyed, looking down at him; my response had a steely edge of anger to it.

"Firstly, no, he wouldn't have backed off – I know him and you don't. He came to say something and he wouldn't have left until it had been said. You have to remember that he knows me well and he will know that if I don't call there will be no point in him trying again. My mind will not be changed.

"Secondly, it is irrelevant what he thinks about you or what he thinks about how I feel for you. It has nothing to do with him and I do not want him knowing about or getting involved in my new life.

"Lastly, you can't believe I'm not serious about you. You know something of what I've been through and how difficult I've found it to form any sort of relationship and yet I've given myself to you completely and I couldn't have done that if I wasn't serious. You're behaving like an idiot." I ended my rant, glaring at him, his eyes softening as he reached across. Taking my hand in his he brought it to his lips, kissing my palm gently before looking back up at me, a little shamefaced.

"I'm sorry, I shouldn't have said that, I didn't mean it." He couldn't, however, just leave it there. "If he hadn't backed off though, I could have sorted him out."

"How, Trent? By picking a fight with him? Because that's what would've happened if you'd got into it with him."

He sounded a little sulky as he responded, "I would have won." Oh, good grief.

"This is a ridiculous conversation to be having. I don't want you and my ex fighting, for any reason, and that's the end of it." My response had been spiky and his retort was incisive.

"It's important to me that my rivals know where they stand. In order for that to happen you need to make it clear to them what I am to you. I wouldn't hesitate in introducing you as my girlfriend."

"What do you mean by 'rivals'?"

"Emma, you're so naive, you have no idea how many men are waiting for their chance to get into your pants. Alex is a prime example." I started to reply that it wasn't like that but I knew that that was exactly what it was like with Alex.

"Alex is an exception."

"He's not an exception. There's obviously Carlton, plus some of the other boys, and don't even get me started on the farm staff...I've waited too long for you and I'm not about to let you go, at least not easily, and not unless that's what you want." He was getting wound up, and realising this he stopped for a moment, closing his eyes as he took a deep breath, letting it out slowly.

"I'm not going anywhere, Trent," I murmured, hoping to reassure him.

"Emma, you have to realise that in this world, men chase and women choose," and with that he wrapped his arm around my waist, pulling me down towards him before adding, "I need to show you why you should choose me," and he brought his lips down hard, effectively silencing the words on mine.

"I've already chosen."

My mind was racing as we lay in bed later and once Trent was asleep I slipped from beneath the covers and went downstairs. Susie curled up beside me on the settee, no doubt sensing my troubled mind. I stroked her as I thought about what Alex had told me. I tried to think it through rationally; from what he'd said it had been brought up in court that I should have been taken more seriously from the start, that the doctor had made a mistake in sending us away. I'd believed him, believed in his superior knowledge and authority, even when my instincts told me differently. I thought back to our arrival at the hospital: the initial assessment of Eva and her condition being put down to dehydration. I remembered pleading with them to do something, to run some tests, but I was ignored. Orders were only given for her to be rehydrated before being reassessed. No one listened to me despite my pleading; I remembered my humiliation at being written off as a hysterical mother.

I felt now, after this passage of time, that I could see clearer, and that while I still thought I was to blame, I was not the only one. The burden I'd shouldered lifted slightly as I thought about all those who now carried it with me.

"Are you ready to talk to me yet?" I looked up to see Trent's frame in the doorway, his face gentle.

"Yeah, I think I can now." He came to fold himself around me, holding me as I told him everything that had passed between me and Alex that evening.

Trent listened attentively, then when I'd finished he spoke: "That's good, isn't it? Doesn't it ease your guilt, make you feel better?" I knew he wouldn't understand what I was about to say.

"I don't want to feel better, Trent. I want to feel raw inside, I want to hurt, it reminds me. I'm afraid if I lose that feeling I'll lose her, and everything she was to me." I hung my head, imagining his disappointment that this wasn't going to be the easy fix he probably wanted.

"I don't think you'll ever lose her, Em, but maybe you can help to heal the rawness so that it becomes easier to live with by being more open about her...making her a more natural part of your life."

"What do you mean?" I questioned.

"Well...you never talk about her. I'm not suggesting you start telling everyone but talk to me, I'd love to hear about her."

"You would?"

He nodded. "She's part of you, Em, and that makes me want to know everything." I smiled softly at him and we kissed; then, held tightly in his arms, I started talking.

Chapter 20

Over the following week the weather became hot and sunny and I received a call to say a hay delivery was coming but it was early evening by the time Porter arrived with the lorry. Just behind him Trent drove into the yard, followed by the pickup containing Hayes and Turner. It was hot and dusty work so I was pleased to have so many hands to help. Once the lorry was clear Porter was keen to get off, as were Hayes and Turner, even spurning my offer of a beer, and as I quickly swept up the debris around the stack I could feel Trent watching me. I turned to look at him.

"What?"

"You're looking deliciously fuckable." He grinned at me salaciously.

"Oh, you've got to be kidding…time and place, Trent," I replied. "I feel disgustingly filthy and sweaty." He moved closer to me, his voice rough.

"Yes indeed. You're quite right, really filthy," and grabbing my hand he led me out of the barn and towards the cottage. "Come on, time for a shower I think." Looking back at me he grinned wolfishly and irresistibly.

Later that evening once we'd showered and eaten we lay curled around each other on one of the settees and I thought that this was maybe the time to find out the answers to a few of my questions.

"Can I ask you something?"

"Anything." This was Trent's standard response to this question, but he then continued with, "You know I'm sure you do this on purpose."

"Do what?"

"You weaken my defences by sedating me with sex and then start probing me with your questions. You could be very useful when interrogating people, you know, it's quite a technique you have."

"Let's see shall we, seeing as how you usually duck this line of questioning. I'm interested to know what sort of work it is you do with Cavendish, off the estate."

"Ah, I thought that might come up. What do you think you know already?"

"I think it must be something important and secretive because otherwise why would we have to sign non-disclosure agreements before working here? It's a bit of a strange thing to have to sign for this type of job."

Trent chuckled a little at this before saying, "Cavendish told me how you quizzed him at the interview as to whether or not he was up to anything nefarious. He thought that was hilarious."

"Yes, so I gathered at the time, but a girl has got to protect herself."

"He told me that was the moment that he thought you'd be perfect for me."

"Did he indeed? I don't know what made him think that."

"It was because you were not afraid to speak out. He thought you'd be quite capable of putting me in my place, and how right he was." At this Trent brought his lips across to my ear, gently grazing my earlobe with his teeth before kissing my neck, making me lose focus on my line of questioning for a moment.

"Don't try to distract me," I said, moving a little away from him. "So," I continued, getting back to the matter in hand, "I think it's something to do with the military, particularly because of the helicopter, but none of you dress in uniform so it can't be standard forces stuff and it's also a bit odd that you come from different branches of the military," I mused.

"How do you know that?" His expression told me that this knowledge surprised him.

"Carlton told me when I confronted him about why he was so happy to leave me when you turned up, on the night I'd had a little bit too much to drink. He tried to tell me it was because you were his boss but eventually admitted you were his Commanding Officer and that all the boys were from the forces, but different branches."

"Did he indeed? I'd better make a mental note that Carlton is never going to stand up to any form of torture." I smiled at this.

"Tell me," I asked gently, and he gazed at me for a moment before deciding.

"Okay, I guess you should know what I get up to. You're right about the military connection. The helicopter is an Apache, although not currently armed. To put it briefly, we work with the Secret Intelligence Service, SIS, which you would know as MI6, offering them an external independent team to call on when needed to protect the country against threats from overseas." Even though I'd been expecting something like this it was still a surprise to hear what I'd thought had been my rather fanciful ideas being confirmed.

"Oh...so you're what...secret agents?" I said, my voice becoming a high-pitched whisper. He chuckled as he confirmed I was correct.

"Like James Bond?" I clarified, still squeaky, and he nodded, smiling mischievously.

"Yes, it's just like James Bond, but unfortunately the job generally involves a bit less sex." I frowned at him, my eyes narrowing. "Obviously any that does occur is purely for Queen and Country, and as Cavendish is married I obviously have to shoulder that burden on his behalf...It's not like I like it," he teased, as I punched him playfully on the arm and then squealed as he wrapped his hands round my waist, tickling me. Suddenly I gasped, both hands coming up to cover my mouth.

"Oh my God." He stopped immediately, looking concerned.

"What?"

"I've become a Bond girl!" I said, horrified, to which he threw his head back with laughter, looking as young and carefree as I wished he would all the time.

Once he'd stopped laughing we lay quietly for a few minutes while I thought this over.

"So," I started.

"Uh oh," I heard him mutter. "I was hoping the interrogation was over."

"What's with the hair?" I asked.

"What do you mean?"

"Well all the others, even if they're not technically in the standard military, still wear their hair in that style of cut, very short and neat, and you don't."

"You don't like my hair?"

"I do like your hair, I like it a lot. I like it being longer, a little curly, unruly and tousled, it's very, very sexy." He started nuzzling my neck again, not needing much encouragement. "But it's maverick, it doesn't fit in with the others."

"That's because I'm not like the others, Em," he murmured into my neck, but then stopped, sighed deeply and pulled away to look at me as he explained.

"Carlton was being loyal when he told you I'm his Commanding Officer. He and the others treat me as if I am – they are loyal out of respect for me as they think I was mistreated but the truth is I was discharged from the RAF a few years ago." He was watching me carefully as he told me this.

"Why, what happened?" I asked, puzzled.

Trent sat up, suddenly tense. I sat up too, sensing his discomfort with this line of questioning. This seemed to have become awfully serious awfully quickly. Turning towards me he ran his hands through his hair, then down over his face, clearly concerned over what he was about to say, sitting for a moment, collecting his thoughts, before looking at me, composed and ready. I tried to prepare myself for what was about to come at me with no idea as to what it could be.

"Sorry if my behaviour is concerning you, Em. But something happened, several years ago now, that I need to tell you. However, I've never had to say this out loud before, at least not to anyone I've cared about, and it's difficult for me. It may well make you think very differently about me," he finished, a note of caution in his voice. I was feeling nervous now, concerned over what was coming. Taking a deep breath, he started.

"We were all based on an RAF station in the north of the country. Cavendish and Grace had not long been married. Cavendish was away on an officers training course one weekend. I was on station, going home from work late one night, having stopped off for a drink on the way. I became aware of a commotion behind one of the staff buildings so I went to investigate, and found a woman being attacked by a man who was trying to rape her. I dragged him off her, only then realising it was Grace. Unfortunately, he didn't take my intervention well and rather than running or backing off he took me on and we got into a fight..." He paused, closing his eyes for a moment. I put my hands on his, hoping to offer some sort of support as he was obviously struggling. He continued, his voice quiet, "He died, Em. I killed him. He wouldn't stop coming at me and it was going to be either him or me." I was silent for a moment, absorbing what he'd said. Meeting my eyes, his clouded with uncertainty, he waited for my reaction.

"Who was he?" I asked quietly.

232

"He was a civilian, temporarily staying on the station with a company that was carrying out repairs to the runway. He'd been out drinking and it was a senseless, random attack. Grace happened to be in the wrong place at the wrong time."

I paused, but only for a moment. I knew what to say.

"You don't have to justify anything to me – I know you're a good man and you wouldn't have done that if there had been an alternative. You saved Grace, Trent, you did a good thing." I thought I saw a flicker of relief in his face.

"It doesn't bother you that I've killed someone?"

"As I'd already thought you were in the forces I'd reconciled myself to the fact that that might be the case. That is your line of work – it kind of comes with the territory."

"I guess it does, although it's not quite the same. However, I'm glad you can see it that way. Unfortunately the RAF didn't. They didn't appreciate me killing a civilian, whatever the circumstances were, and I had to face a court martial. Despite Cavendish's considerable influence I was found guilty of bringing the Service into disrepute and had to resign my commission, losing my job and the career I'd worked so hard for.

"So you're right, I don't fit the mould and I guess the hair is a conscious choice, a point of rebellion. No doubt it drives the powers that be mad that I don't toe the line but I don't worry about upsetting them anymore. I'm there for Cavendish and him alone, to do whatever he needs me to do, to protect him, and that's it."

"You said the boys thought you were mistreated? Some of them couldn't have even been around when you were going through this."

"Well the RAF rather threw the book at me and it backfired on them. The civilian police had dropped all charges as they regarded it as self-defence but the RAF wouldn't let it go. It was the opinion at the time that I was made an example of, and that they'd used this incident as a reason to get rid of me. That didn't go down too well in the ranks, so the whole sorry tale has become a rather well-remembered and frequently retold piece of history, with me, rather embarrassingly, becoming the unwitting, and unwilling, hero. It's one of the reasons people like to come and work here."

"But why would the RAF want to get rid of you in the first place?"

"I didn't realise why at the time, I was too young, but looking back on it now I had a problem then accepting discipline and admittedly was a little hot-headed, struggling with authority, getting into a few fights, same as at school really. But I caused the RAF some headaches which they could have done without and they took their opportunity when an excuse conveniently presented itself." I hesitated, taking in the description that had just been painted for me of a Trent I didn't recognise. I felt very protective towards him, angry at how he'd been treated.

"I'm struggling to accept you as some sort of bad boy, it's not the view I had of you at all."

"That's because I'm all grown up now, Em. I learnt to control myself eventually, though that part of me is never far away." He managed to smile weakly at his explanation.

"I'm shocked you were dismissed by them like that. I understand now what she meant when Grace told me they owed you everything." He smiled softly, though his eyes remained sad.

"Did she? That's rather exaggerating it, although as they'd just found out Grace was pregnant they were doubly thankful and they've been very supportive to me ever since, over Zoe and everything with the setup here." He looked so despondent my heart went out to him.

"Thank you for telling me, I could see that was difficult for you...you haven't ever told anyone that before?"

He looked at me and smiled, remembering a similar conversation in reversed roles. "No."

"Then I'm honoured that you told me," and I kissed him softly. "And I understand now where your sadness comes from."

He nodded, and clearly relieved that it was over, visibly brightened. "I'm going to get a glass of wine, do you want one?"

Confirming I did he went out to the kitchen, returning a couple of minutes later, handing a glass to me before he sat back down.

"So, tell me what happened then with the setup here?" I continued.

"After all of that was over Cavendish decided he wanted to change things. He'd just inherited the estate and took me on to manage it. As I said, he carries considerable influence and he put forward a proposal to set up an independent force to carry out the sort of missions that we do now. SIS were keen, though less so with me being involved, but Cavendish insisted and here we are. We've been putting together an elite force for a few years now. Nearly everyone employed here has some sort of forces background, specialist skills, etcetera."

"Apart from me."

"Yes...you are the anomaly," and he grinned as he said this. "As you know I was keen on employing another candidate we had for your position. He was ex-Household Cavalry and would have been perfect."

"But you got me instead...how very disappointing for you." I frowned grumpily at him.

"Well, you were on our shortlist of applicants. You made it onto that purely because Cavendish was keen on the kickboxing. You wouldn't have got a look-in without that but, as it happened, the other applicant then withdrew his application so the decision was made for us, although in hindsight, I don't suppose I would have had as much fun with him as I've had with you." He laughed at the look on my face as he said this.

"Anyway, to continue, Cavendish, myself and the boys are the ones who currently work away; the others are here as backup and as a protection force for the family and the estate. We've worked hard to provide an environment where we can get the right people together and where they're happy and want to work in the way we want them to. Cavendish's philosophy is that he wants people to work with him rather than for him, and that seems to attract people to want to come here.

"We've had a couple over the years that didn't fit in and wanted to leave – obviously it doesn't always suit – but everyone here now is committed and keen to provide the support we need. To date it's been quiet in terms of action on the estate but as you know we've been working away quite a bit recently and there are some things brewing abroad that could have an impact here. Though with all the setup work Cavendish and I have put into place we should be well prepared to face any eventuality. Anyway, enough questions...come here," and pulling me onto his lap he kissed me hungrily and we were soon lost in each other again.

The weather was still hot after the weekend and as I was putting Zodiac's head collar on to take him out to the paddock I was startled, suddenly feeling someone close behind me, his arms wrapping around my body, his breath hot on my neck as it was nuzzled and kissed, sending shivers through me. I smiled to myself as I said, "Carlton, you know how mad Trent is going to be if he catches you."

At this Trent growled a fierce "Don't" into my neck as he then spun me round and I looked at him, grinning innocently.

"Oh, it's you! Did you just growl at me?" He was glaring at me warningly.

236

"Yes I did, don't wind me up. I've still not got over the night when you almost took him into your bed. I couldn't bear the thought of him touching you then and I can bear it even less now."

"Well you shouldn't creep up on me then, especially now I've lost my early warning system." I stared accusingly at Susie who was lying flat out, dozing in the sun. She glanced up at me, giving me a look which clearly told me I only had myself to blame, before stretching back out.

"I'm sorry, I won't do it again," I said, trying to mollify him, though couldn't help smiling at his discomfort. Then I kissed him deeply, deeply enough to distract him sufficiently so that he'd moved on by the time the kiss ended.

"I came back to ask if you had any plans for the day?"

"Not particularly," I replied, wondering what he was up to.

"I thought we might go to the beach once you finish here."

"That sounds great. I should be ready in an hour or so."

"Okay, well I'll go and sort out lunch for us and be back in a while," and with that he kissed me again and left.

I eagerly set about leading the ponies out to the paddock and then getting all the stables set up for the evening. Once I'd finished I went to change into shorts and a tee shirt and by then Trent had arrived to pick me up. Locking Susie in the cottage I went out to meet him.

We drove to the beach, parking at the far end then wading round the point to get to the private bay. I'd brought a couple of towels and Trent was carrying a picnic, which he put down in the shade. I lay the towels out on the sand next to each other but before I had a chance to sit down Trent grabbed hold of me.

"It seems to me that you have too many clothes on, Em...let's see what we can do about that."

237

Later we lay together soaking up the sun, then ate a delicious lunch of poached salmon, salad and pasta, followed by fresh strawberries and pineapple, washed down with chilled white wine.

As Trent lay dozing I sat up, bringing my knees up and wrapping my arms around them as I looked out to sea. I was deep in thought when I felt his hand lightly caressing my back.

"What're you thinking about?"

"I was just thinking that I was feeling contented."

"That's good, isn't it?"

"Mmm…" He was silent for a moment, then I realised he was sitting up next to me.

"What's the matter?" he asked, a trace of concern in his voice.

"It's going to take some time for me to realise that it's okay to feel this…settled…and that I shouldn't have to feel guilty for feeling this way."

He paused before answering, "You keep working on it because I intend on making you contented and settled for a long time to come. Eventually I'm even going to aim for making you happy." He raised his eyebrows at me in exaggerated surprise at this lofty ambition before moving to sit behind me, stretching his legs out to each side of mine; hugging his arms around me he pulled me close to his chest, and silently we watched the sea until it was time to leave.

Chapter 21

The next day as Trent left for work I told him I was going to the gym that evening so I'd either see him there or later if he wanted to come round.

"I'll probably go to the gym too so see you there," he said, and he headed off.

I worked through my day, feeling good after my day off, and once I'd finished evening stables I got changed into my gym clothes and walked to the Manor. I was surprised to find Trent already there with the boys, by the weights. He looked up when I walked in, then jogged over, kissing me on the cheek when he reached me.

"Hi, I finished early so I came straight over. Thought I'd put in some extra time seeing as how I've missed a few sessions recently," and he grinned, raising his eyebrows as he flashed his eyes at me. I liked seeing him like this, relaxed; it pleased me to see the effect only a couple of weeks of us being together had wrought in him – him feeling good made me feel the same.

"Okay, I'll get on and catch up with you later," I said, as he returned to the others and I started on my routine.

The gym was reasonably busy and I steadily worked through each of my pieces of equipment, although not necessarily in the order I preferred, having to finish on the one for my abdominals. I glanced across the gym to see that the boys appeared to have finished, and at that moment Trent met my gaze and started to stride towards me. There was a grin on his face and I could see he'd been working out hard from the sweat soaking his tee shirt. As he got nearer he put one hand under his shirt, bringing the bottom of it up to wipe his face, ruffling his hair at the same time; I was treated to the full view of his clearly outlined abdominal muscles rippling as he walked, which was more than a little distracting. He was watching me closely as he approached and I knew he knew exactly what he was doing. I tried to appear calm and composed – I'd like to think nonchalant but that might have been pushing it – as he stopped next to me.

"I'm done now, are you nearly finished?"

"Not yet."

"Do you fancy cutting your workout short?"

"You're being a bad influence on me, Trent!"

"What makes you think that?" he asked, feigning innocence.

"You're trying to lead me astray; usually you're only too keen for me to increase the number of reps I do, not cut them."

"Yeah, well I'm bored now and need something else to entertain me," he said, grinning, clearly in a playful mood, and then added enticingly, "and I thought I'd take you over to show you my apartment."

"Oh, yes please!" I yelped, as finishing the crunch I was doing I leapt off the seat, bouncing up next to him. I could resist anything now it seemed, apart from temptation.

He grabbed hold of my hand and giving me a wink headed off out of the gym with me in tow. We quickly crossed the courtyard and entering under an arch, went up three steps to a door. Trent had his key in the lock, the door open and I was whisked in, not getting a chance to see anything as the door closed, and he was immediately on me, slamming me up against the wall, his lips on mine as he peeled me out of my tight clothing. We didn't make it to the bedroom, and a little while later as I was getting my breath back I said, "I thought all that exercise was meant to cool your ardour?"

"That doesn't seem to be the case when you're working out near me and doing all that stretching and stuff in that outfit of yours – it's really not fair on me. What did you think was going to happen?"

I smiled at this before saying, "I'm going to get in the shower now if that's all right."

"Of course, I'll join you and then get us some dinner." And it was then that I had my chance to look around.

We'd only managed to make it into the entrance hall and that went straight into the sitting room. The walls were undecorated stone, the same as on the outside of the house, and the floors were tiled, again in stone. There were large rugs scattered throughout the apartment in rich reds and browns with highlights of copper. Two large settees were gathered around a stone fireplace with a wood-burning stove in it, and these were covered in dark-brown soft leather. Some of the walls were broken up by large hanging tapestries which were something I hadn't seen before but looked impressive. A bedroom led off the sitting room, the furniture made of solid dark wood, but the dominating feature of the room was a huge four-poster bed up against the opposite wall.

"It's a shame we didn't make it to that!" I exclaimed, pointing at the bed.

"I'm sure we'll get to that at some point," Trent said dryly, as without stopping he led me through to the bathroom. This was again stylish: white and chrome against the stone.

We showered and dried each other, then as Trent went off to sort out some food I realised I had nothing to wear. Going to his bedroom I opened some drawers to see what I could find, ending up putting on his red-and-white checked brushed cotton lounge pants, which I turned up a couple of times to fit, and one of his white tee shirts. Then I wandered out to the kitchen which was all black granite and dark wood with under-cupboard lighting. As with the rest of the apartment it was masculine and I liked it a lot. I could hear soft music in the background, a beautifully rich soulful voice coming from discreet speakers.

"Very cute," he said, as he glanced up at me from his cooking.

"Hope you don't mind," I replied.

"Not at all. There's a bundle of your post over there on the worktop." He gestured towards it with his knife. "I picked it up from the Manor today and was planning on bringing it over tonight but you might want to check through it now for anything important while I sort out the dinner." He went back to his chopping.

"This is nice," I said, as I indicated generally to the sound around me. "I didn't know you liked music."

"I play music when I'm in here, and when I run. I have eclectic tastes so have a varied selection if you fancy choosing something different." Alex had been into music and since he left my world had been largely silent. I would not have known what to choose.

"No, this is lovely, soothing."

I took the bundle over to the table, taking the elastic bands off it. A fair amount of it was rubbish though there were a couple of letters from the letting agent regarding my tenants renewing their tenancy which was good news, and a couple of bills, but nothing that needed urgent attention. In the middle of the pile was a cream envelope with my name and address handwritten on it. It only occurred to me as I was opening it that there was no stamp on the envelope, but that immediately went out of my mind when I unfolded the piece of paper it contained:

'If you do not leave my husband alone, I will kill you.'

And that was all it said. Black ink, handwriting I didn't recognise, although why I was thinking about that at all I didn't know. As I took in these words I felt the blood drain from me. Gasping, I struggled to breathe as I whispered, "Trent." He glanced over, dropping his knife as soon as he

242

saw the look on my face, and moved rapidly across the room to me.

"What is it, what's wrong?"

I held out the piece of paper to him, my hand shaking. He read it, turning pale, then stared at me, concern and fear written across his face.

"My husband?" I said, my voice questioning and sounding hoarse. A look of confusion passed over his face as he looked from me back to the piece of paper again. I stood and started to move away from him.

"My husband?" I repeated louder now, anger building in me at the implications of this message.

"No, no, no," he said rapidly as he reacted to the change he could feel in me, "Emma please don't misunderstand this."

"Misunderstand! It seems crystal clear to me."

"Emma, please…no, don't do this, she's mad."

"Of course she's bloody mad!" I was yelling now. "I was mad too when I found a woman, my supposed best friend, in my bed with my husband. What do you expect her to be? I can't believe you've put me in this position. Made me into the sort of woman I despise with every fibre of my being. The sort of woman who steals other women's husbands – how could you? You knew what that woman did – how could you do this to me? I trusted you…How could you make me be that person?" He looked utterly horrified as he listened to this and quickly responded.

"I didn't know that was why your marriage ended, Emma. I had no idea there was anyone else involved in the break-up. I assumed it broke down because of Eva." His ignorance as to the reason for the breakdown of my marriage came as a surprise but I was in no mood to discuss rationally now.

"Well your supposedly comprehensive background search on me wasn't that comprehensive then, was it," I spat back at him. He reached for me, desperation in his face. "Don't touch me," I hissed, as I backed out of the room and away from him.

"Please don't leave," he was pleading with me, distraught. "I need to explain."

"What is there to explain?" I replied harshly. "Either you are or are not married to this woman. Which is it?"

He hesitated. "It's not as simple as that. Please stay, we need to talk." I was beyond being able to listen to his voice of reason.

"I'm too furious to stay, I can't bear to be near you."

His look was one of devastation as I turned to leave the apartment, picking up my keys from the pile of clothes in the hall. Shaking with fury, I struggled to open the front door in my haste to leave and I'd just got it open a fraction when it was slammed shut again by Trent's weight. He'd come up behind me, his arms outstretched to each side of mine, his body pressed up against my back; I could hear his harsh rasping breath in my ear as he pleaded desperately.

"Don't leave me, Em." Feeling myself unravelling as I struggled to cope with this, I needed to be free from him and yet was desperate for more, as always, when he was near me. I took a deep breath to regain control.

"It's Grayson to you and we're done. Back away from me now, Trent, or you will regret it." My reply was cold and angry and I felt him still behind me, then I was released as he took a backward step. Without looking back I pulled the door open and left, slamming it behind me. I could already feel the pain of my heart starting to break once more.

Walking away quickly across the courtyard to the exit, I had to wipe away tears of fury as I struggled to try and regain some sort of composure. I hadn't even made the exit before I heard a door slam behind me and looking round I saw Hayes and Wade running across to their pickup. I carried on walking but within a minute they'd caught up with me, Wade leaning out of the window offering me a lift.

"No thanks, better off walking," I muttered through gritted teeth, then felt guilty at the hurt look on his face; it wasn't his fault.

"You haven't got any shoes on, Grayson, get in," he remonstrated with me but I ignored him. I could feel the rough ground beneath my feet, the residual heat in the road surface, small bits of gravel stabbing into my soles, but I walked on oblivious to the pain. I wasn't sure where Wade and Hayes were going but rather than pass me they pulled the pickup back a little and followed me at my fast walking pace back to my cottage, even following me into the yard, at which point I realised with annoyance that Trent had sent them after me. Wade leapt out of the cab, catching up with me at my back door, and I stared at the ground miserably as I listened to him.

"Once you're inside, Grayson, lock the back door for the night. I'll be doing the watering later so don't come out again. Call if you need anything...and, Grayson..." I looked up at him as he hesitated; he was looking at me kindly, "...look after yourself, won't you?" I nodded at him, on the verge of crying again.

I went in, bolted the door, and after briefly stroking Susie and opening the cat flap for her, I went upstairs and crawled onto my bed. Lying on my side I stared sightlessly out of the window. Anger coursed through me as I thought through what had happened. I couldn't believe how stupid I'd been, allowing myself to fall in love with someone who'd lied to me. Who'd told me what I wanted to hear to get me into bed like some stupid kid. He'd called me naive, and as it turned out that was exactly what I was, and clearly that was why he'd thought I would fall for his lies. I was shocked he'd behaved the same as Alex, only this time I was a party, however unwittingly, to the betrayal of his wife. Disappointed...I'd thought he was better than that.

I couldn't believe I was going through this again, the tortuous heartbreak of another betrayal. Angry tears came, hot on my cheeks as I curled up in my pain. I should have stuck to my resolution on first coming here of not letting anyone close to me. I should have been more determined to follow that path. But I knew deep inside that this was not an argument – I'd been irresistibly drawn to Trent; resisting him had been useless as nothing could have kept me away from him. Although, as I argued back and forth in my anger, I had some moral fibre and if I'd known he was still married I would have kept my distance and would never have been drawn into this.

Later, hearing movement in the yard, I went downstairs to check it was Wade, back to do the watering. I could see the pickup parked in the same place as it was earlier with Hayes in the driver's seat, and it occurred to me then that they'd not in fact left the yard since I arrived back. Wondering why Carlton wasn't doing the watering, I then remembered he was out with Greene. Susie came in and locking the cat flap I turned out all the lights, and went back to bed, where I lay awake, engulfed in my own misery, going over and over the evening's events in my head.

As the night passed my anger gradually dissipated and as I thought through what had happened I realised I found it difficult to believe Trent was a liar. I thought back over all the conversations we'd had where his divorce had been mentioned, where we'd discussed it, until eventually I had to concede there hadn't been any. He'd never actually told me he was divorced and I'd never asked. I'd assumed but never clarified the situation and only had myself to blame for being in this position. While I could accuse him of withholding the truth of his situation, and in particular showing a lack of sensitivity because of the way my marriage had ended, it had become clear during our row that he'd been unaware of the facts surrounding that, so I supposed the fact that he had only behaved like a pig and not an insensitive pig was something. I couldn't believe how things had turned out. After being so unhappy for such a long time I'd found some level of happiness again and fallen in love with a wonderful man, a man who I'd foolishly believed I could see as my future partner, and yet here I was with everything lying in tatters around me.

The next day started badly. When I let Susie out she limped along the path into the garden. Examining her foot I found it hot and swollen; she'd been licking it and it was now looking sore. I suspected she'd got a grass seed embedded somewhere which had become infected. This had happened before, but in the past I'd always discovered the problem early on, managing to remove the offending grass seed and clean up the wound enough to head off any problems. This time it appeared the infection was well and truly set in and I was ashamed I'd failed to look after her properly. She'd been constantly faithful to me but I'd let her down, neglected her needs, and now she was suffering.

I went out to the yard to feed the horses, noticing Hayes and Wade still sat there in the pickup, raising my hand in greeting which they acknowledged. When I'd finished feeding I put Susie in my pickup and we set off to the vets. Wade and Hayes followed me, which was strange, but I was too exhausted and miserable to ask them what was going on.

Susie was examined, the vet concluding she needed to stay for a small operation to open the wound, drain it, and find the offending grass seed before patching her back up again. As she'd been fed already they wouldn't be able to do that until much later in the day so that meant an overnight stay. I gave her what I hoped was a reassuring hug and left her to be looked after, worrying she wouldn't cope well with the separation, especially as she would have sensed how unhappy I was and would know I needed her. I'd pick her up in the morning, I told myself, and it would all be fine.

I was followed back to the stables, at which point Wade and Hayes resumed their overnight position in the yard again. I shook my head at what I assumed was Trent's latest attempt at controlling me, by having me watched continually, then went over to the stables to start the morning routine, which I was already behind with. I'd not long got going when Carlton and Turner drove into the yard, and after a quick exchange Wade and Hayes drove off, Carlton's pickup taking their place. As soon as the pickup was in position Carlton got out and walked towards me looking concerned.

"Hey…how're you doing?"

"Not so good actually," I mumbled.

"Come here," he said, as opening his arms he wrapped them around me, pulling me into his chest where I promptly started crying again.

"How did you know?" I sobbed.

"I saw Trent this morning."

"How is he?" I asked pathetically.

"He looks like shit, much like you, and miserable, but there was considerably less sobbing from him into my chest," he said in an attempt to be jovial. At that moment a message arrived on his phone and, taking it out of his pocket, he read it while not letting go of me.

Cursing softly he said, "Have you eaten?" I shook my head. He responded to the message and almost immediately another pinged in, which he read before saying abruptly, "Right, come on," and grabbing my hand he led me over to the cottage. Sitting me down at the table he flicked the kettle on, taking two pieces of bread and putting them in the toaster before spreading them with jam and putting them in front of me together with a strong cup of tea.

"How did you know?" I asked, looking at the breakfast in front of me.

"Those were my instructions," he said, holding up the phone and looking at me. He raised his eyebrows.

"Trent?"

He nodded. "Look, Grayson, I don't know what's going on between you but you must be able to work it out?"

"I don't see how that will be possible," I responded weakly, shaking my head.

"Much as it pains me to say it, you two make each other into better people; that's been obvious from the last couple of weeks, so you need to find a way…and eat," he said sternly, indicating towards the toast. I stared at him blankly.

"I'm going to be sick if I eat anything…I'll try the tea." I managed to drink a little though I found even that a struggle to swallow.

Carlton watched me before questioning, "Has he tried to contact you?"

"No…and he won't. I was furious with him. Accused him of lying to me…when it turns out he didn't. If he tries at all, and I doubt he will, it won't be until he can be sure I've calmed down enough to be receptive to him, so I wouldn't hold your breath."

"If you were in the wrong then, falsely accusing him, why don't you contact him and apologise?"

"Because it's not as simple as that. I'm still angry over what he's kept from me and because it won't change the situation in which we find ourselves. One that means we can no longer be together." Pausing for a moment, I wanted to change the subject. "Why am I being followed?" I asked curiously.

"Because of the threat, of course," he answered, sounding a little exasperated. For a moment I was bewildered by this and frowned. What threat? Then remembering the full content of the note I'd received I realised I'd only focused on the revelation it contained, completely ignoring the threat made towards me. It then became clear that when Trent had read it he'd taken the completely opposite view of it to me.

"Ah...I hadn't thought about that."

Carlton shook his head, clearly baffled by my indifference to the situation.

"I think I'll ride out with you this morning, in case of any...er...problems. You haven't eaten so it's probably best you only ride out once anyway. Turner can go home while we do that and come back to watch over you with me for the rest of our shift. West and Burton are coming to clean this morning so they can keep an eye on the place while they're here. Shall we go?" At that we headed back over to the stables to tack up Regan and Monty and got the ponies ready to lead out.

As we rode out of the yard Turner drove out behind us, and a short way up the road I saw West and Burton arriving, raising my hand to them as Carlton and I turned off the road onto one of the paths through the trees. I did manage to ask Carlton about his date with Greene, which had gone very well, but otherwise was content to let Carlton talk, and I responded only when it was absolutely necessary.

We rode along for a while, me listening to Carlton while looking round at the beauty of the estate around us when it dawned on me I wouldn't be able to stay here. It'd be unbearable to have to see and work with Trent after this so I'd have to leave the place where I'd become so settled and go back to my old home, my refuge, to lick my wounds again. Although it then occurred to me that of course I couldn't even do that because the tenants had just renewed their lease.

The thought of leaving this place, this home, this job and this family, for that was how I felt about everyone here now, started the tears again. I couldn't bear it.

We got back from exercise, turning all the horses out for the rest of the day and, as Carlton was going to be on duty 'guarding' me anyway, he gave me a hand to get the stables mucked out and ready for the evening. We cleaned the tack before he called for Turner to return to the yard and when he arrived I thanked Carlton for his company. Giving me a rueful smile he told me to take care before joining Turner in the pickup.

I went back to the cottage, curling up on the settee for a couple of hours staring at nothing. I wondered how long Trent would leave it before he contacted me, or perhaps he was waiting for me to contact him. I didn't know what to say to him if we did speak, it was all such a mess. These thoughts kept turning over in my mind as I went to do evening stables.

Chapter 22

Coming in from work I locked the back door as per the instructions received from Carlton, then called the vets, who confirmed that Susie had come through her operation without any problems and was now in recovery. I was relieved by this piece of good news, having missed her presence all day. It would be fine for me to pick her up in the morning and feeling that at least something had gone well that day I went upstairs to shower.

I was definitely not going to the gym, thinking it would be best for me to keep out of the way for as long as possible, or at least until I'd worked out what I was going to do. I knew I'd have to see and speak to Trent at some point but I needed to decide how I was going to deal with that.

I couldn't eat or settle to anything so after not sleeping the night before I decided to go to bed, knowing, because of the latest restrictions placed on me, Carlton was doing the late watering and would check all was locked up and secure for the night. So after double-checking the back door was locked I turned out the lights.

I started to go upstairs, vaguely aware as I did so of a strangely sweet metallic smell in the air. Getting to the top of the stairs, from where I could see into my bedroom, I noticed clumps of white fluffy feathers on the carpet. What on earth...? As I went into my room my mouth dropped open, aghast, as I stared at the mess. I didn't need to turn the light on to see that my pillows had been slashed open, feathers gaping out of the wounds, cascading across the bed and onto the floor. But that only held my attention briefly because daubed across the white cover in vivid red were the words 'He is mine'. My first thought was that it must be paint but I immediately corrected that – that was why there was such a strange smell in the air.

Where did the blood come from? My stomach turned over with revulsion, my thoughts crashing to another conclusion, and as they did so my legs weakened as a coldness swept across me, the hairs on the back of my neck standing up. The back door had been locked all evening; whoever had done this had already been in the house when I'd come in from work, whoever had done this had done it since I showered – whoever had done this was still here.

Feeling panicky, nausea clenched my stomach, and in that moment a slight movement made me start, drawing my attention to the shadows in the corner of the room. A woman rose into a standing position from behind the armchair and I recognised her immediately as the woman who'd leapt out in front of Regan; every detail I hadn't been able to recall before suddenly flooded back with this realisation. She was a little shorter than me, with shoulder-length straight brown hair, straggly and unwashed. Her face was pale, gaunt-looking, and her dark eyes had darker shadows under them, making her appear tired. Her gaze was fixed on me but I found I couldn't take in too many other details as when she lifted up her arm all my attention was drawn to the fact that she was holding a gun, and it was pointed straight at me.

Adrenaline spiked through me as I felt my breathing constrict; the cold rush of fear slithered down my back, weakening my knees, which made my legs feel they could collapse under me at any moment. I took a deep breath to try and control the panic welling up inside, finding I was struggling to swallow.

"Zoe?" I asked, my voice tight. She didn't respond, but instead frowned at me and seemed confused. "I'm Emma," I said, not sure why in my panic I was introducing myself.

253

"I know who you are, Emma." She spat the words out venomously at me, as moving out from behind the chair she took one step towards me, coming further into the light that shone through the doorway from the landing. She looked perfectly calm holding the gun, which I found alarming as I thought she might be just as much at ease using it. "You're the one who's been screwing my husband." I had to agree with her, she did know who I was.

Trying to overcome my panic I forced myself to think – how the hell was I going to get myself out of this? It was ironic that the one time I actually wanted help was the one time there was no one around to give it. I thought of the boys in the yard, wondering how I could attract their attention. A gunshot would do it, but it'd probably be too late by then, at least for me, and once I'd fixed on this thought I couldn't come up with anything else.

I jumped as noise erupted from my pocket, my phone bursting into life – with Trent's ringtone. I looked sharply at Zoe, who'd also been startled, though fortunately this had only caused her to bring her other hand up to join the first holding the gun.

"That's Trent. If I don't answer, he'll know something's wrong." The gun continued to be levelled at me.

"Answer it…but don't tell him I'm here or he'll get to listen to you die." That concentrated my mind considerably, and as I reached for my phone I came up with a plan, answering in as chirpy a voice as I could muster, "Hi, Trent." Admittedly it didn't come out as chirpy as I'd hoped for but under the circumstances that was perhaps not all that unexpected. His response was one of surprise, probably because he was expecting it to go to voicemail but also because of my apparent chirpiness when he must have known I'd still be pissed at him. Hell, he'd been keeping his distance all day, no doubt hoping I would calm down before he had to approach me.

"Oh! Hello, Grayson," he replied cautiously, his voice sounding bleakly flat. I could imagine his lovely eyes narrowing, crinkling at the corners as he contemplated my strangely enthusiastic greeting.

"How can I help?" I spoke quickly, perkily.

"Um...I'm sorry to call and interrupt your evening but I needed to tell you I'll send a couple of the boys round in the morning to help with the feed delivery."

"Oh, that would be great actually, really, really helpful although I could probably do with all four of them if you can spare them, and anyone else who's available," I gushed, and continued, not allowing him to respond, "Anyway, many thanks for calling, Trent, I really appreciate it. See you soon, bye." I ended the call abruptly.

I could only imagine how confused he'd now be by our rather one-sided conversation, but I really didn't want there to be the slightest chance he would hear my brains being splattered across the room by Annie Oakley over there.

Looking down at the phone I suddenly realised in horror what I'd done. I'd thought I was being clever by alerting Trent to the possibility that something was wrong, knowing that if he put two and two together he and the boys would come to find me, but now because I hadn't thought this through I'd selfishly put all of them in danger, rather than just me, and I didn't want that on my conscience. You stupid, stupid woman, I thought. I was going to have to get myself out of this mess before he had a chance to get here and that thought galvanised my mind.

Looking up again at Zoe I found her eerie calmness unsettling and then remembered the words Trent had used during our row: 'She's mad.' Suddenly recognising I'd misunderstood his meaning, I was in fact now dealing with something I knew nothing about and that was the most chilling realisation so far. I had no idea how I should approach this. Swallowing, I tried to get a grip on myself, taking a deep breath before speaking to Zoe in as calm a voice as I could find.

"I'm so sorry, Zoe, I didn't know he was married. I wouldn't have gone near him if I'd known." I held up my hands in what I hoped was a placating manner, adjusting my stance and bringing myself up so my weight moved onto the balls of my feet, looking and waiting for my opportunity. She moved a little closer, peering at me, shuffling forward slightly, as if to get a better look, and I noticed a tremor in her hands. Was it caused by the weight of the gun or by the fact that she wasn't as confident as she first appeared? I wasn't sure and it didn't matter anyway, she wasn't close enough for me yet.

"I saw you with him on the beach," she muttered pitifully. Seeing her absolute desperation, my heart bled for her, feeling her pain only too vividly. I felt shame at what she must have witnessed and not to have just suspected her husband's infidelity but to have actually been exposed to his betrayal I empathised with her with every part of my being. Having more in common with her than she could possibly know, this thought made my stomach churn.

As she'd moved closer, coming into the light, I'd been able to see her face more clearly and Trent's words echoed in my mind again: 'She's mad.' Realising his meaning more clearly now, there was a wildness in her eyes as they glittered, and while they never looked away from me, they were at the same time unfocused, distracted, and this scared me. I didn't know how unbalanced she was.

"I can only say I'm sorry," I croaked hoarsely, my apology sounding feeble. How do you apologise for doing something like that to someone? She clearly wasn't impressed with my apology either and it tipped her over, her face curling into something approaching a snarl as she leapt forward. I had no idea why she moved towards me when she did but it was all the opportunity I needed and I was ready for her, launching into a roundhouse kick, aiming for her head with the front of my foot and connecting, hard. At that precise moment there was a deafening explosion as the gun went off and I felt a viciously hard thump in my shoulder, the power of which threw me violently backwards until I was stopped abruptly by the door frame, and I crumpled into a heap on the floor.

The gun had flown out of her hands as my kick connected, skidding across the floor into the shower room. I took a deep breath as pain burned through my shoulder, bringing tears to my eyes. My kick had thrown Zoe against the wall, which she'd hit hard, but not hard enough; she was not unconscious as I'd hoped and was already attempting to get up.

My hearing had been affected by the gun blast, everything dulled and muted, but I could still hear her snarling in anger at me, realisation hitting that I needed to get to the gun first – to get to it before she could use it on Trent or the others. I tried to rise, crying out with the shock of the pain this movement caused, blood soaking through my clothes, my left arm useless, the pain already starting to overwhelm me as I struggled to get up. Dizziness and nausea swamped me, along with the feeling of everything moving in slow motion as I scrabbled along the floor, trying to get to the gun.

I knew Zoe was up: I could hear her harsh breathing as she saw where I was moving to, saw what I was planning to do, and she started to shriek chillingly as she came for me. Sobbing in pain, in desperation, trying to get across the floor, all I could hear was Zoe closing in on me. Then it hit me, a sudden vision of the slashed pillows spewing feathers, and I realised she must have a knife. Oh dear God, I wasn't going to survive this, I thought, at the same time recognising that that didn't matter anymore, as long as I stopped her first. Feeling I was going to pass out from the pain and in a last-ditch effort before I did I lunged forward, closing my hand around the butt of the gun, twisting onto my back as pain seared through my shoulder once again. Finding the gun to be surprisingly heavy I brought it quickly up in front of me as when I turned to face her Zoe was already lunging towards me, the knife held between her hands. Trying to move, I couldn't get out of the way fast enough and the knife sliced down through my sleeve, slashing into my right arm.

I fired. She was close, too close, the gun bucking in my hand, the manic expression on her face freezing as she fell, landing across me.

I collapsed back, gasping, trying to take a deep breath, feeling faint from the pain and the loss of blood which I could smell and feel running out of me. As the world became hazy I wondered vaguely if that meant I was dying. I felt peaceful so it didn't matter. Before recent events this would have been a win-win situation for me. If I lived I'd get to be with Trent, if I died Eva would be waiting for me. As things were now I welcomed the sweet oblivion, the mist descending over my senses, disappearing into unconsciousness, at the last moment dimly hearing the sound of a door being kicked open, footsteps leaping up the stairs.

Chapter 23

Slowly becoming aware of my surroundings, groggily waking up, my eyes opened to see Cavendish sitting on a chair next to me. I tried to look round the room, another hospital room, trying to find Trent, but he wasn't there. Of course he wasn't there, I thought, as the memories came flooding back. Of course he wasn't there, I repeated to myself, I'd killed his wife – he obviously wouldn't be there for me now. This thought brought tears to my eyes as Cavendish reached out to take my hand, trying to comfort me.

"Trent has had to go and sort a few things out, Grayson. He asked me to be here in case you woke up. Grace is here too."

"What time is it?" I asked, wondering how long I'd been out.

"It's late afternoon."

"Susie? I need to pick her up." My voice sounded croaky.

"Grace picked her up this morning. She's fine and is staying with us for the moment," he tried to reassure me.

At that moment the door opened and I glanced up expectantly but it was Grace who entered, coming across the room quickly when she saw I was awake, trying to comfort me, but I was beyond help. I couldn't stop the tears coming now in my anguish as I felt the familiar pain of the old wounds in my heart tearing open afresh. By my latest act I'd managed to ensure that if there'd ever been even a glimmer of hope for my future with Trent that had now been quashed and there was now no chance of a recovery for our relationship. The realisation of this brought further waves of unending pain that I didn't think I could endure again.

Cavendish called for help from the door as Grace tried to calm me down, and as she did she pleaded, "Please don't give up on him, Emma." Before long the nurse was there injecting something into whatever contraption they'd inserted into my arm and I was drifting into a haze where the pain muted and nothing seemed to matter anymore.

The next time I woke Trent was there, sitting in an armchair in the corner. His head rested on his clenched fist as he stared at me, his eyes dark and brooding. He looked dreadful: tired, pale and drawn, a shadow across his face where he hadn't shaved, his beautiful mouth a harsh line. Even from across the room I could feel the anger simmering within.

I didn't know how long I'd been there but the pale light coming in at the window suggested early morning – another night had passed. I was uncomfortable but guessed the painkillers were taking care of most of the pain. Looking down I could see my right upper arm was bandaged. The top part of my left arm was strapped to my side and the lower part was held in place across my chest by a sling. There was heavy strapping to my shoulder, across onto my chest.

Trent walked over and looking up at him, a little fearfully, I wondered how furious he was going to be with me. I wasn't sure I could take too much from him at the moment. Bringing his hand up to touch my face, his fingers were in my hair as he caressed my cheek softly with his thumb; the gentleness of his touch was almost unbearable but beyond that I could feel his fury boiling, the tension radiating off him, and tears pricked the back of my eyes again. Taking his hand away I felt the loss acutely as he continued to gaze down at me.

"I'm sorry," I whispered, having to clear my throat as my voice was so croaky.

"Don't...just don't..." his response brief and I could see him clenching his jaw as he spoke, his eyes closing. "We need to talk but now is not the time or place. I'll get you something to eat and try to sort out getting you home." He turned, leaving the room.

A little later he brought me tea and toast, propping me up in the bed, though I was too nauseous and miserable to eat so I feebly sipped at the tea. While I did, a little awkwardly as both of my arms were constricted to some degree, he went and stood, looking out of the window. Trent had suggested I would be going home but I didn't see how I'd be able to do that. I needed to know what was going to happen to me and although saying this was going to make the awkwardness between us even worse, I still needed to know.

My anxiety was expressed as I spoke. "I can't go home – the cottage is...well...it's not going to be possible."

Without looking at me he said bleakly, "That's already been taken care of by Cavendish. The police have done what they needed to and as long as you feel you can go back there it's ready for you." That gave me some relief, though his mention of the police raised another issue.

"What about the police?"

"I've made arrangements for them to interview you tomorrow. You were still sedated when they arrived here." His manner perfunctory, I felt as if I was trying to swallow something jagged at this news, worry gnawing at me.

He left the room while a doctor and a couple of nurses came in. The doctor explained I'd had an operation where they'd removed a bullet from my shoulder, repairing the damage it had caused, which fortunately had not been too extensive. Similarly they'd repaired the damage caused by the knife and stitched me up. My dressings were changed and I was given strict instructions on my recovery which initially meant daily trips to my local surgery for wound checks and dressing changes. As long as I adhered to their instructions they were happy for me to be discharged.

When they'd gone Trent reappeared with the paperwork for me to sign, helping me to get dressed. Greene had sorted out and sent in my tracksuit again, only this time she'd included a jacket top rather than the sweatshirt. I could only put this on over my right arm, carefully, with Trent's help, and he then pulled it round me, enclosing my left arm in it before doing up the zip. It wasn't like the last time. During all this he was cold, detached and unable to look me in the eye. I knew from his behaviour that what we'd had was over. I couldn't actually understand why he was here with me at all when it was obviously painful for him. Surely one of the others could have come and done this, but I didn't dare ask. It was too awful watching him this unhappy.

We were eventually ready to go and there was silence on the journey home. We'd barely spoken since I'd woken up and now the atmosphere between us was filled with misery and tension. Once we'd driven onto the estate I said quietly, "You can just drop me off at the cottage, Trent. I understand that you won't want anything more to do with me so please don't feel you need to come in to help or anything. I'll be able to sort myself out." As I said this I could feel sadness flooding through me again, the tears welling up. He responded coldly.

"You can't be left on your own as you've had a general anaesthetic. Also, it was you who finished with me, not the other way around, if you remember. We need to talk and you will listen to me this time. If you would then rather someone else was here with you, I will arrange it." He said all this without once looking at me, staring through the windscreen as silence was resumed along with my nausea.

There was no activity in the yard when we drove in as it was by then late morning and all the horses were out in the paddock. Trent helped me out of the truck but when I got to the back door I stopped, suddenly feeling nervous about entering, looking at Trent anxiously.

"It'll be fine, I'm here with you," he reassured me, before opening the door and ushering me in. I went straight through to the sitting room and sat perched on the edge of one of the settees. Trent followed and started trying to get me comfortable, asking if I wanted a drink, some lunch, until I snapped at him.

"I don't want to be made comfortable, Trent, and I don't want anything to eat or drink. I just need to get this over with so you can go." I hesitated, looking at him as he sat on the other end of the settee facing me, before continuing in a more measured tone: "Let me speak first. I know this sounds feeble and inadequate but I don't know what else to say other than I'm so sorry for killing her." I saw him flinch uncomfortably as I said this. "It was self-defence, I promise you. I thought I was going to die." My voice sounded hoarse as it shook with emotion. This was at least partly the truth – there had been a natural instinct in me to defend myself but I didn't think he would understand or appreciate that in me that instinct was not very strong and I'd been more concerned about ensuring his survival and that of the others. I'd always have Eva waiting for me. Trent started to put his hand out towards me but then stopped, withdrawing it again as I took a breath to steady myself.

"I'm sorry for the row, the way I reacted, the things I said. I realised afterwards that I'd misunderstood," I continued. "I thought you'd divorced Zoe, but I realised during the night that followed that you'd never actually told me that, it was just an assumption I'd stupidly made. I'm the one responsible for putting myself in that position and I shouldn't have taken it out on you, because you didn't lie to me. If I'd checked the facts in the first place I wouldn't have become involved with you, and all of this would never have happened. I'm so sorry…" I'd run out of anything to say and sat there anxiously waiting for him to let go of his fury on me. I could feel it simmering, but when he spoke it was in a far calmer voice than I'd been expecting.

"I know you're sorry, Grayson, and while I appreciate you saying that, you shouldn't have to be sorry for what you did because I also know it was self-defence. You did well to survive at all…I understood, eventually, why you reacted as you did when the note arrived and that you're sorry for that too but there was a lot you didn't know because I thought it was too early in our relationship to tell you. In hindsight, if you'd known all the facts I think you'd have reacted differently and we wouldn't now be in this situation…What I'm trying to say is…that it's me who should be apologising, not you." He hesitated for a moment before continuing, "I need to tell you everything so you have the full story and can make your decision on what you want for us. Okay?"

"Okay," I whispered in agreement, a little surprised he hadn't already made that decision, feeling the first tiny spark of hope.

"You're right about one thing. I didn't divorce Zoe but there is much more to it than that and you need to give me the chance to explain." I nodded at him mutely but tears were already coming to my eyes and spilling over as he'd just confirmed my worst fear. One which I'd been desperately hoping I was wrong about. He looked at me in despair, running his hands through his hair.

"I'm not explaining this very well…Please don't cry. Look, I didn't divorce Zoe, I desperately didn't want to separate from her but she chose to divorce me." I stared at him now in horror – this was even worse than I'd imagined.

"You didn't want to separate? You were still in love with her?" I hadn't anticipated this, and felt hurt at the revelation.

"It's true I didn't want to separate but I'll explain that as it's complicated, and no, I'm not still in love with her. I was, and it took me a long time to get over it but that's all very firmly in my past. Just hold on." He leapt up, disappeared into the kitchen and came back with a box of tissues which he put down next to me.

"It looks like you're going to need these…Let me start at the beginning, no interruptions," and looking at me for agreement I nodded, wiping my eyes again. He took a deep breath, exhaling slowly before starting.

"Okay, Zoe and I got married in our early twenties and, to borrow a phrase from you, I'm an all or nothing kind of guy, and when I make commitments, such as the vows I made to her, my intention is to stick to them. Unfortunately, fairly early on in our marriage Zoe showed signs of becoming mentally unstable. To be fair there had been signs of that before we got married – manic behaviour, that sort of thing – but I just put it down to her personality. However, as time passed it became worse. It was as if I was living with two different people – one my loving Zoe and the other a jealous, vindictive woman who I didn't recognise and who on a couple of occasions actually attacked me. I'd never know who was going to be waiting for me when I came home from work.

"Things really escalated when I got into the fight, killing the man who attacked Grace. Zoe seemed to feel threatened, jealous even, because I'd protected Grace, and her behaviour became worse, irrational and, at times, frighteningly vicious.

"I tried to cover for her for a while but after the second attack I ended up in hospital and it all came out. Cavendish and Grace made me take her to a doctor and she entered a mental institution for a while for assessment. She was diagnosed with schizophrenia and paranoia which was what led to these psychotic episodes. She was put on medication and eventually came home but as you can imagine it was a difficult time for both of us." I could feel the sadness in him as he recalled these events.

"I'm deeply ashamed that the other night I told you she was mad, that was such a crass thing to call her mental illness, but I was desperate and blurted it out, hoping it would stop you. Instead it only inflamed your misunderstanding." I nodded.

"I didn't realise until I met her."

"I know, that can't have been easy." As I shook my head he was quiet for a moment, collecting his thoughts before continuing.

"As far as I was concerned, following her diagnosis, we were muddling along all right but Zoe was deeply unhappy with me staying with her. She, sadly, did not feel about our vows the way I did and started straight away saying she wanted a divorce, so that I could apparently 'go and live my life and not be weighed down by her' as she put it. I wouldn't listen to her, and fought her all the way every time she brought it up. However, eventually during one of her settled periods she managed to get a court to support her application and she got her divorce. It destroyed me."

"Why didn't you tell me that earlier?" Full of regret, my eyes closed against the pain this omission had caused. I'd meant this to be rhetorical, more an observation, but he answered anyway.

"I don't know…it didn't come up…I thought…I hoped you saw me as a man who wouldn't have moved on without being in a position to do so. In my arrogance I felt it unnecessary to have to explain myself." I realised this was indeed the reason I hadn't ever asked the question; I'd believed he was a good man, a man of principle, and I was relieved, even after everything, that my judgement and trust had not been misplaced after all.

"I did…That's why I was so shocked…and angry," I explained, as he nodded in understanding – and relief, I thought, that he hadn't been completely misjudged.

Then he continued: "To make it worse, she refused to let me continue to be involved with her in any way. She made sure none of the doctors or specialists were allowed to speak to me and she completely cut me out of her life or, as she saw it, she freed me.

"So…ever since I've been trying to move on, and I thought I had with you. I'm sorry I didn't believe you when you said Regan was spooked by a woman. I dismissed it as something to do with the head trauma. I didn't imagine for one moment that my past was going to have any impact on our present or I would've told you all of this from the start.

"However, if you remember when I was staying here after that accident I received a message on my phone. It was from a doctor who was treating Zoe. He wanted to contact me to let me know that Zoe had disappeared from under his care and he knew her prescription hadn't been filled. He was concerned that off the medication she would revert to her altered self and come looking for me.

"He shouldn't have called me, of course, but he'd always been sympathetic to my situation and was particularly concerned for my safety, as he knew what she was capable of. Alarm bells started ringing and it was then that I spoke to Cavendish and brought him up to speed with what was going on. He was more convinced than me that your story of the woman causing the accident was true. I still couldn't, or wouldn't, believe Zoe would do that. I honestly thought if she attacked anyone it would be me and I'm so sorry that I put you in that danger." He paused for a moment, shaking his head in disbelief that this could really have happened.

I'd been listening intently, shocked by what I'd heard, what he'd been through, and now I smiled weakly at him, encouraged by the fact that his previous anger seemed to have disappeared as he carried on talking.

"We alerted the authorities looking for her but they could find no trace of her. We also had parties out searching for her from the estate but again no luck. We've tried to piece together what probably happened and we think that Zoe saw us either when we went out for the first drink or more likely the night you had too much to drink and I stayed over. She must have mistakenly assumed we were already seeing each other. She then caused the accident for you and Regan, ironically bringing us together. She must have still been watching and saw us again after the Ball, as we believe she was then responsible for the arson attack, hence the extra guards at the stables. I'm not sure at the moment what triggered her final threat and then the attack—"

I interrupted at that point. "She saw us...at the beach; she told me when we met."

Trent's eyes closed and his head went down as he took a deep breath before sighing, "Oh God...poor woman." Looking up at me his pain was etched on his face and I nodded in empathy.

"I know...that was the final straw. I think she'd tried to warn me off with the note, but possibly that had been hanging around for a couple of days before I got it in the pile of post and as she saw no signs of us breaking up she pressed forward with her attack, presumably making the most of the opportunity when she saw Susie was not around to warn me of an intruder." He nodded his agreement with this theory, but I was puzzled.

"I don't understand one thing though – why would she send the note threatening me for being with her husband when she knew you were divorced? That doesn't make sense."

"Well, Zoe knew we were divorced but when she was off her medication her alternative personality believed we

268

were still married. That was why Zoe was so keen to sever all ties with me, as she thought that if I was still in her life, helping her in any way, it could cause a problem if I formed another relationship. This is what I needed to explain to you back at my apartment. It was not as straightforward as just saying I was divorced, Zoe's mental state complicated matters."

"So she was her other personality when I spoke to her then. Is that why she didn't respond to me calling her Zoe?"

"Yes, she doesn't recognise herself as Zoe when she's off her medication, she calls herself Annette." Then he groaned, running his hands through his hair before looking up at me, studying me carefully before continuing.

"I hadn't planned on saying this to you under these conditions, I'd imagined something very different...but I need you to know that I love you more than you can ever imagine, and I can't apologise enough for what I've put you through. The time since our row has been unbearable and when I ran into this cottage and for a minute thought you were dead, it was the worst moment of my life. I hope that someday you can find it within yourself to forgive me." He looked at me, his red-rimmed eyes tense with emotion and brimming with tears.

I reached out my hand, my arm stiff and sore and placed it on his face, my fingers touching his hair. Feeling his stubble, rough on my skin, and running my hand down his cheek, his eyes closed. Bringing his hand up and over mine he brought it round to his mouth before softly kissing my palm. Feeling choked, I whispered, "There's nothing to forgive." His release of tension was palpable as leaning in closer he kissed my lips gently before pulling back, smiling anxiously at me. I felt immense relief, glowing inside at his unexpected, but so welcome, words. However, I was still confused by the anger I'd felt in him earlier but which had not been expressed.

"I thought you were angry with me. Not that I would blame you for that, obviously." He looked surprised.

"I was struggling to control my feelings but my anger was never aimed at you, Em. I'm sorry if you felt it was. I was angry because of what had happened to you, what could have happened; angry at myself for being at fault and for ruining what we had because of my stupidity, and angry because I'd lost you." I couldn't believe he was going to let me get away with what I'd done that easily.

"But what about Zoe, you must be torn up about what happened? What I did? Aren't you angry with me for that?"

He looked downcast at me bringing this up, then pensive, before answering, "No, I've told you, you did what you had to do...I'm obviously very sad that Zoe has died...I know it will take some time to work through and I'm going to have to deal with all that. I wish it hadn't happened and I know that what I'm about to say is going to sound bad but I can't deny it, the alternative outcome would have been a far worse one, as far as I'm concerned." I thought then that we had gone about as far as we could for the moment. He looked at me apprehensively before tentatively asking, "Will you have me back?" I nodded, smiling in response, not trusting myself to speak as a fresh supply of tears threatened to overflow and a wave of relief swept through me.

"What now, Em?" he asked, gently.

"Now we need to do something about getting me comfortable as the pain's getting worse and I'm suddenly hungry – not a good combination!"

Trent leapt up to get my painkillers which he delivered to me with water, then arranged the cushions behind me so I could sit back at last which brought some relief. He went out to the fridge and came back with a tray of assorted sandwiches and fruit left for us by the saintly Mrs F and we sat and ate in silence. For both of us it was the first time we'd eaten in about two days and we soon demolished the tray of food.

Trent looked up at me then and said, "I know we've probably still got a lot to talk about but for now I suggest I run you a bath which will make you feel a bit better and then we try and get some sleep." It seemed like a good plan as I was uncomfortably grubby and needed some help as I wasn't allowed to get my wounds wet. He went to run the bath and I followed him carefully upstairs, a little dubious about going into my bedroom, but when I did everything appeared normal. Other than the fact that the smell of cleaning products and bleach hung in the air you would never have known anything had happened there. He saw me looking round the room.

"Are you okay?"

"Yeah, just a little…you know." He nodded.

He washed my hair and the rest of me carefully and tenderly, then, after shaving, joined me in the bath and we sat, both exhausted, looking at each other.

"I've missed you."

"And I missed you. I don't like being without you."

Weariness swept over me and after washing he got out and dried himself before pulling on his lounge pants and a tee shirt. Then helping me out he dried me, dressing me in the same, though pulling the tee shirt on loosely over the arm that was strapped to my side.

"Time for bed I think," he said, as I smiled sleepily up at him. "Not for what you're thinking, you naughty girl, we both need some sleep." I frowned a little though I was in full agreement with him. I wanted to cuddle up to him in bed to feel safe, but I could only get comfortable lying on my back so making do with that instead we fell asleep holding hands.

Chapter 24

We slept all afternoon, waking to hear activity in the yard. Getting up, me only with Trent's help, we went downstairs to see what was going on. I could see Carlton at the stables and was pleased to see Greene there helping him. When they'd finished they both came over to the cottage, knocking timidly on the door, sounding as if they wanted to see how we were while at the same time not wanting to disturb us.

"Come in," I called.

I was sitting on one of the chairs in the kitchen and smiled at them as they entered. Carlton looked relieved when he saw me, bending to kiss my cheek in welcome. Greene grinned at me, her happiness obvious, and she greeted Trent, although she was then as surprised as I was when Trent approached Carlton and, after holding out his hand to him which he took, then pulled him into a half-hug, slapping him on the back before thanking him. Carlton indicated that it was no problem and they separated, both looking a little self-conscious.

I glanced at Trent, raising my eyebrows at him in question, not that I wasn't highly delighted that they were getting on. He ignored me and, flicking the kettle on, asked if anyone wanted a cup of tea or coffee. We all opted for tea and sat round the table catching up on the news. They were good company and I was pleased to see how relaxed they were with each other. Getting up to leave a little later, as Carlton passed me he bent down, whispering, "Good to see you've made up," before pecking me on the cheek again. I laughed lightly, though I stopped when I saw the look on Trent's face as he watched us.

"I do wish you were not so familiar with her," he warned Carlton, who grinned back at him, winking at me before leaving. Whatever truce they'd briefly had was obviously over.

Trent then received a call to say Cavendish and Grace were on the way to see us and would be bringing our dinner. I also hoped they'd be bringing someone else.

I was not disappointed when they arrived a little later with Susie racing ahead of them. She rushed into the kitchen, crying with delight as I knelt down to hug her. She too had a bandaged leg which didn't seem to be slowing her down at all.

When Cavendish and Grace entered they greeted us both warmly and were all dressed up, Cavendish informing us they were off to a dreary charity dinner to which Grace rolled her eyes. They both appeared so pleased to see me and while I tried to apologise for my behaviour in the hospital, which must have made them uncomfortable, they would hear none of it. Highly delighted we were back together again Grace had tears in her eyes as she gently hugged me goodbye, saying she was so happy for us.

I'd been worried about what was going to happen to the horses in the immediate future but Cavendish informed me that they'd decided they'd be turned out for the next couple of weeks as a holiday for them and then we could see how I was progressing and take it from there. This put my mind at rest as I'd still be capable of doing all that was necessary for them for the time being.

After they'd gone Trent put the dish of carbonara in the oven to warm through and we went to sit more comfortably in the sitting room.

"Why the sudden display of affection to Carlton then?" I asked.

"He was the first person to get to you with me the other night, and he held everything together and took charge when I...struggled...initially on finding you. He helped keep you alive and get you out of there. I owe him one."

"I didn't realise that."

"No, well you know what a shy and retiring bloke he is; I daresay you'll hear all about his gallant efforts in the fullness of time," and we both chuckled at this.

Later when we were eating dinner I said, a little carefully, "I hope you don't mind me talking about her but I was thinking that Zoe must have been quite a woman."

"I guess she was...but what makes you say that?"

"I think she must have loved you a lot to do what she did."

Trent grunted at this. "I don't think so. I've come to the conclusion over the years that she didn't actually care for me at all. Not even at the very start of our relationship." I thought for a moment before continuing.

"I think you're wrong there, Trent. I think she knew what she was doing to you, to your relationship, and she loved you so much she wanted you to go and live your life. That's why she divorced you and cut you out of hers. It must have been incredibly difficult for her to do that at a time when every bone in her body must have been wanting and needing to hang onto you and yet she found enough love for you to give you up." He was silent as he contemplated what I'd said.

"I hadn't thought of it like that before."

I knew I was going to find it difficult to say these next words, to open myself up to him. Declaration had never been my strong point so I took a moment and a breath.

"Trent...I love you." His face lit up, his warm eyes glowing at me. "And I found it unbearable to think I'd lost you. But I'm not sure I'd be strong enough, unselfish enough, to do what she did and set you free. She must have been an amazing woman and I suspect her true

274

feelings for you came out in the jealousy and possessiveness shown by Annette."

He gave a shrug. "You might be right...who knows. Sadly there's nothing that can be done to change anything now anyway."

We were silent for a while as we ate. I thought I might as well press on with the questions.

"What's going to happen about the funeral?"

"I've contacted the hospital to see if I can arrange it but because of the instructions she placed on the files I can't do that so they'll have to organise it. It's going to be a cremation which I can go to and I was wondering...if you would go with me." He was looking at me cautiously as he asked this. My immediate reaction was that it wasn't a good idea.

"Don't you think that will be a bit...weird?"

"I want you with me, if you can manage it, that is. Cavendish and Grace will be there too. Have a think about it, will you?"

"Okay, I will," and I thought for a moment, wondering if I should bring my next idea up. "One thing I do think though...if you're allowed to and obviously if you think it's a good idea, do you think we could put her ashes in the same graveyard as Eva with a stone marking them? I'd like to think of our loved ones being together." He blinked at me, clearly taken aback.

"That...is incredibly generous of you, to think of her that way after what she tried to do to you."

"That wasn't her, Trent. I genuinely feel very sorry for her. She must have been a great person and she was someone who loved you and was loved by you and after what she did for you I can only admire her."

Chapter 25

The next day I was interviewed by the police. I knew this would have to happen and they were good enough to come to the cottage. Trent was with me and Cavendish had asked to attend as well, and so as Trent stood, leaning up against the kitchen worktop, Cavendish and I sat with two police officers going through the events in minute detail. I told them everything that had happened, realising on glancing up at him a couple of times how painful an ordeal this was for Trent. The police were at last satisfied that they had their statement and I asked them what would happen to me now. They confirmed it was unlikely there'd be any charges against me as every piece of evidence they had, including the forensic evidence from the scene, showed I'd acted in self-defence. There'd be an inquest into the death but it was highly likely it would reach the same conclusion. I was very relieved once they'd left.

I also had to go to the doctor, as I would have to every day to have my dressings changed, and Trent went with me. It was the first time I'd seen my wounds, although one of them struck me as being similar to a scar I'd seen before, and while it all looked a bit of a mess to me they seemed happy that I was healing up all right.

When we got back to the cottage later I heard Trent on the phone to the hospital asking about Zoe's funeral arrangements and I took the opportunity to wander over to the yard, Susie following me as always.

Carlton had come over to turn the horses out for their holiday so as he cleaned out the stables I sat and chatted to him. Thanking him, a little awkwardly, for what he'd done for me, he was unusually reticent in accepting the thanks. I thought that like Trent, he'd found the whole thing a bit difficult, and I was glad I'd been unconscious throughout.

When Trent and I were in bed that night I felt I needed to bring something up with him.

"Do you want to talk me through how you got your scars again?"

"Why do you ask?"

"I saw my wound this morning, Trent. It looked familiar, and I haven't been impaled on a tree."

"Oh...I guess you're right. I took a bullet to the shoulder a few years ago. I didn't tell you at the beginning because you didn't know what I did and it would have seemed a bit dramatic."

I was quiet for a moment, then asked, though already suspecting I knew what the answer would be, "And the appendix?"

Trent was still, hesitant in his answer: "Zoe...or rather, Annette."

I concentrated on my recovery for the next couple of weeks. I had to go to the doctor each day and found I needed to rest more. I was on my own some of the time as Trent had to go to work occasionally to keep everything running smoothly on the estate, although I knew everyone was helping him out where they could. Otherwise he was with me, and I was concerned for him. I knew he must be grieving but because of the circumstances I thought he felt he shouldn't show me how much he was hurting. I could understand this, but now knew from experience it was better to have someone to share this with, and I tried to be there for him, knowing only time would help.

The day eventually came when Cavendish and Grace arrived to pick us up and we set out on the journey to attend Zoe's funeral. I was still not convinced I should be going and felt extremely uncomfortable doing so, worrying about who would be there, worrying about who might take offence that the person responsible for Zoe's demise had the audacity to show up. However, Trent had made it very clear he needed me to be there with him and Cavendish and Grace were as supportive as always.

The service was at an unremarkable crematorium and there were only a few others in attendance besides us. Trent had discovered Zoe's parents had both died within only a few months of each other the previous year, and she had no brothers or sisters. It was only this information that had persuaded me to go at all. There was no way I could have attended if any of her family had been there.

We managed to get through it. That's all you can ever really say about a funeral. It was terribly sad, a wasted young life, and I felt particularly awkward being the reason for that. The other people who came were all doctors or nurses who'd treated her. Some Trent knew, others who had cared for her more recently he didn't. The doctor who had texted him spoke to us after the service and was kind to me, feeling the guilt along with me as Zoe had slipped from his care in the first place. We briefly discussed why things had gone wrong for her recently, when apparently she'd previously done very well on her medication, but the only explanation he could come up with was that the most recent change in her life might have been the catalyst, and that was the loss of both of her parents.

The day following the funeral I went to the doctor to have the stitches taken out of the wound on my right arm, pleased that at least I had one arm that didn't need dressing anymore. I was going to be left with a reminder in the form of a four-inch long scar, although whoever had originally stitched me up had made a good job of it, and at least the scar was quite thin. I was already using that arm more or less normally anyway so it would soon be back to its full strength.

My other wound was going to take a lot longer to heal because the damage was more extensive internally. I'd already started some physiotherapy exercises to get the movement back which were excruciating, then I'd need to work on building up the strength again. I was going to be bringing the horses back in soon and hoped that by taking things slowly I'd be able to manage. Trent was not happy with this...so no change there.

Susie had also had her bandage off. Her stitches had dissolved and fur was growing over the wound.

Trent and I were back on track again but since the shooting I thought he was working hard, too hard, on trying to make me happy; it was as though he felt he had to do something to compensate for what had happened. It took time to make him understand and believe that I was fine and all I needed was for him and for us to just be as we were. Slowly he started to relax with me again, his grief and guilt beginning to fade, though I knew only too well how long these things could take.

He got the call we'd both been dreading, telling him he'd have to go away on business for a while, and that night we made love, neither wanting to let the other go but eventually falling asleep curled around each other. I woke to his scent on my skin but my bed empty and I knew this was something I was going to have to get used to.

Trent had left me a present in the form of an iPod on my bedside table which I knew he'd have loaded up with what he considered to be a suitable playlist for me. After my abysmal musical knowledge had revealed itself to him he'd seen it as his duty to start educating me – his words, not mine. Since then I'd teased him about what I considered to be some of his more dubious musical tastes and he reciprocated with my predilection for the maudlin. I placed the iPod on the speaker that morning while getting my breakfast, finding myself soothed by the sound that filled the kitchen.

Grace called to check on me as she, more than anyone, knew how I would be feeling. She suggested I joined everyone that afternoon for tea and cake. In the weeks since the shooting I'd been touched by how many of my friends on the estate had made the time to pop in and see how I was doing and I looked forward to seeing them.

I worked through my jobs steadily, if a little more slowly than before. The hardest thing for me to do was tack up but it felt good to get into my routine and to be back with the horses that had contributed so much to my new-found sense of well-being.

I set off on my first ride out on Regan, Susie following me out of the gate. The day was already hot and I stayed in the woodland, taking advantage of the respite from the sun. I watched Susie snuffling among the undergrowth, realisation dawning as to how relaxed I was now. Susie was as constant as ever but I'd come a long way since arriving here a little over a year ago, never imagining then how much my life would change.

Eva still occupied a large part of my thoughts and Trent encouraged me to talk to him about her, prompting me with questions, and this had made a perceptible change in the way I thought of her, making my memories of her into a more positive experience as she became a natural presence in our life together.

Trent understood my grief but had shown me it was okay to find room in my life for other things as well and we were doing all right. I felt his love surrounding me and I did my best to make him feel the same. We'd been together for such a short time and having already faced such enormous challenges I couldn't imagine for one moment our future together would be anything other than rocky, but as Carlton had so succinctly put it, we made each other into better people and now that seemed to me to be something worth fighting for.

Acknowledgements

I would like to thank Julian Westaway, General Manager of Point Two , for allowing me to reference his company's product together with the managers at Ride-Away magazine for agreeing to me using their descriptive wording.

I thank Kate Haigh of Kateproof who I approached far too early, in ignorance, for proofreading and who set me straight by recommending SilverWood Books to me.

A huge thank you goes to Helen Hart and the team at SilverWood Books for their skills in assisting me with structural and copy edits, proofreading and cover designs as I worked to polish this novel and who have been unfailingly supportive and enthusiastic as this book has come together.

I thank Claire Millington for her expert help with the RAF terminology. Any errors remaining are mine and mine alone!

Last, but of course by no means least, I am truly thankful to all my family and friends who support me and make me who I am but in the writing of my first novel there are a few who deserve a special mention and my thanks.

To my beautiful and talented daughter, Katherine, who I trusted to read this first for her feedback and who had the bravery and honesty to do so.

To Debra Cartledge and Sarah Postins for being my next readers; thank you for your comments and encouragement.

To Dave Holland of Deeho for his knowledge and assistance in helping to get me set up to publish online, for my website and for assistance with my explorations into social media.

To my wonderful son, Patrick, who continues to surprise me every day and who has had to put up with my increasingly erratic behaviour – along with Russell, of course, but he signed up for that and I love him for it!

Contact details

Thank you for reading this far. I'm always interested to hear from readers with any feedback, thoughts or observations they are willing to make. If you'd like to get in touch, or you want to hear about what's coming next you can do so through my website at www.georgiarosebooks.com where you will also have the opportunity to follow my blog. Alternatively you can email me at info@georgiarosebooks.com for a chat or to request to go on my mailing list; follow me on Twitter @GeorgiaRoseBook; find me on Facebook or 'like' The Grayson Trilogy Page on Facebook. I look forward to hearing from you.

Finally, if you have enjoyed reading this, please tell ~~someone~~ *everyone* you know and, whatever you think of it, if you are able to, would you please consider leaving a review? Of whatever rating! You might not think your opinion matters, but I can assure you it does. It helps the book gain visibility and it informs other readers whether or not to purchase it, so if you could take a minute or two to leave a few words on Amazon and/or Goodreads that would be hugely appreciated.

Now, if you're sitting there holding a beautiful paperback in your hand and you're thinking that request doesn't include me... well please think again. It doesn't matter how or where you bought your paperback Amazon and Goodreads will still accept a review from you.

The story continues for Emma in *Before the Dawn*, and concludes in *Thicker than Water*.

Thank you.

Made in the USA
Charleston, SC
15 October 2015